IN CROW'S FIELD

IN CROW'S FIELD

JUDITH THOMPSON

CORMORANT BOOKS

We acknowledge financial support for our publishing activities: the Government of Canada, through the Canada Book Fund and The Canada Council for the Arts; the Government of Ontario, through the Ontario Arts Council, Ontario Creates, and the Ontario Book Publishing Tax Credit.

LIBRARY AND ARCHIVES CANADA CATALOGUING IN PUBLICATION

Title: In Crow's Field : a novel / Judith Thompson.
Names: Thompson, Judith, 1954- author
Identifiers: Canadiana (print) 20250101963 | Canadiana (ebook) 20250101971 | ISBN 9781770867925 (softcover) | ISBN 9781770867932 (EPUB)
Subjects: LCGFT: Novels.
Classification: LCC PS8589.H4883 I53 2026 | DDC C813/.54—dc23

United States Library of Congress Control Number: 2024951792

Cover and interior text design: Marijke Friesen
Manufactured by Friesens in Altona, Manitoba in February, 2026.

MIX
Paper | Supporting responsible forestry
FSC® C016245

Printed using paper from a responsible and sustainable resource, including a mix of virgin fibres and recycled materials.

Printed and bound in Canada.

Easy Access System Europe
Mustamäe tee 50, 10621 Tallinn, Estonia
easproject.com, +372 5696 8939, gpsr.requests@easproject.com

CORMORANT BOOKS INC.
260 ISHPADINAA (SPADINA) AVENUE, SUITE 502,
TKARONTO (TORONTO), ON M5T 2E4

SUITE 110, 7068 PORTAL WAY, FERNDALE, WA 98248, USA
INFO@CORMORANTBOOKS.COM / WWW.CORMORANTBOOKS.COM

For my family

IT'S NOT EVEN dark yet. I'll just lie here for a while longer, in this lush, overgrown farmer's field off a dirt road, about ten miles outside of Kingston, Ontario. It's late August 1971, about eight o'clock, I think, because the sun is beginning to set. The sky is like the inside of a blood orange — which I only ever had once, on a school trip to France. I was surprised and a little disappointed that they tasted just the same as orange oranges. And the nightbirds are singing to each other ridiculously loud, but I love it. I've been dozing, on and off, for hours, I think. I should really get up and go home, but every time I try to move, my body feels like cement. I can't remember exactly why I'm here — maybe we dropped that Windowpane acid Matthieu had. Maybe the others got paranoid and hitched back into town, but I stayed. I stayed because it is just so beautiful here.

I hear the sound of someone on a noisy old bicycle, not too far away. The bicycle stops. I try to open my eyes to see what is happening, but everything is blurry. I can make out that you are a woman, I think an older woman, and you are leaning the bike — a faded red? — against the scrubby pine tree. I have a feeling you are not from around here, just from the way you look around and move with uncertainty. You are standing at the far edge of the field. I don't think you see me. You scan the field, looking for something. I know you see something you like because your eyes widen. You smile. Maybe the mustard flowers? They are so pretty, and they are scattered everywhere across this field, in the dark green grasses; they are bright yellow, and springy. You stride onto the field in a way that makes me nervous. I don't want you to see me; I don't want anyone to see me. I am very happy drifting in and out of sleep. But it isn't me you are after — you bend down and pick the mustard flowers whenever you spot them. I guess you are making a bouquet, maybe to take to a friend. When you are closer, although the setting sun in my eyes is making everything blur and shimmer, I see you are beautiful: older than my mother but not as old as my grandmother, about sixty-five or so. You are wearing bell-bottom jeans, and a violet top which flows with the wind. I love violet, it's maybe my favourite colour, maybe because I used to pick violets for my mother. Your hair is snow white and thick and pulled back in a ponytail. You seem nice.

You get on your hands and knees to pick more of the flowers. You breathe in the scent of the mustard flowers. They smell like vanilla extract, which reminds me of making cakes with my mother. You stand up and you notice the stand of white birches, which the farmer must have planted to mark the border between the field and the woods. You walk through the birches and into the woods — these woods are particularly dark — the thinnest rays of light spray through the trees only occasionally — and almost impassable, thick with black spruce, thorn bushes that scratch your arms and your ankles, Jack pine, and sugar maple, as well as many dead and dying poplar trees. You wonder if anyone has stepped foot in these woods since the farmer left, but then you notice a few disappointing signs of humans: a girl's blue sandal, maybe size five or six. You pick it up, it's alive with some kind of beetle. You throw it down and there you see a half a pack of Export "A" cigarettes. The pack looks quite fresh, with the iconic image of the blond Scottish lass wearing the tam, not discoloured by time. There is also the lurid yellow wrapper of an Oh Henry! bar, and a colourful woven friendship bracelet — the kind traded by middle-school girls. You think about picking it all up and taking it to a garbage bin, but you don't. You keep walking, gingerly, taking care not to trip on a root or a rock and, after ten minutes of struggling through bush, you arrive at a clearing, with the inevitable abandoned campfire site. The blackened logs, the cigarette butts, and a few beer bottles. A chipmunk skitters past, disappears up a tree. You watch. You wait. There must be deer, somewhere in these woods, feeding on bark or berries. There must be more life. You listen, but there is only silence.

You leave the dark woods. Now you are back in the field, just as the sun is setting. You breathe in the cool, clean air. You scan the field once more, and this time you notice that someone has left an old, tattered, green car blanket on the far end of the field. You missed it before. I'm praying you don't come closer. It's a cool evening and I need the blanket. You imagine young, careless hippie picnickers who left hastily, forgetting their blanket. Perhaps they heard thunder and wanted to escape a storm? Or they were stoned and paranoid, convinced a faraway police siren was meant for them. That's what goes through your mind. You think about picking the blanket up, but what would you do with it? Too complicated, too big to carry on your bicycle, could get trapped in the wheel. You decide to leave it. Thank God. You climb back on the bicycle and pedal back down the dusty dirt road. But at the end of the road, you stop. You have a funny feeling. An unsettled feeling. You turn back and when you can see the field, you stop. Without getting off your bike you narrow your eyes to see the blanket more clearly. Is there something underneath it? Perhaps a pile of picnic garbage. But then it seems to move, to heave. Is it racoons, nesting? you ask yourself. Or a coyote? You don't want to come face-to-face with a coyote. And it is getting dark. You only have one bike light, and it's pretty dim. You should really leave.

If I had the energy, I would reassure you: It's only me! Me, feeling the wind across my face, warm, and thick, hearing the rabbits move across the field, and the birds singing goodnight. I don't want to leave this field ever. It feels like home. Because it reminds me of another field. From a long, long time ago. I can see that field, the field behind our old house in Connecticut, in my mind, perfectly. It's like this field in some ways, but not in others. Maybe I can time-travel back there, like that show *The Twilight Zone*. I imagine Rod Serling's voice, "Picture a teenage girl, in a field, sleeping peacefully, when she is suddenly transported to another field, an almost forgotten field, a field where her life changed forever."

I HEAR THE sounds of a party. Kids screaming with happiness, water splashing, grown-ups laughing, telling stories. Where is that party? Sounds like it's not too far. I peek my head out of the green blanket. I don't see the party, but I do see the Easy Tree. Our magnolia tree. I haven't seen that tree since we left Connecticut in 1966. But I am seeing it now. Not in the way of a strikingly realistic dream, but really, truly seeing it. And it isn't sunset anymore; it's bright daylight and it's hot. Am I in the Twilight Zone?

I am nine. Or am I eight? One of those "Don't ask me how I know, but I do." I'm nine years old again and I am on my hands and knees with my best friend since we were two. Frances. She has straight, golden brown hair and she wears glasses already, which are called cat's eye glasses; she got them after she fell out of the Easy Tree one time and went to hospital and came back with a broken arm and glasses. Her party dress is green with a sash and mine, mine is red, red corduroy with little flowers all along the edges and a white blouse underneath with puffy shoulders, and I especially like the sash. I have a sash that my mother tied with a big bow in the back. I have a scab on one knee, and I can feel its nubbiness on the grass. I was chewing on my scab this morning at the breakfast table before my Mom said to stop it and eat my toast and strawberry jam. She said eating your scab was a bad thing to do, so I stopped. But I remember the taste of the scab. I liked it. I liked the taste of the *blood candy,* that's what I told my Mom and she laughed her best laugh, like a whole room full of people laughing.

Just twenty minutes ago, Frances and me had been at the cookout for my brother Paulie's sixth birthday party just a ways down the hill in our backyard. Our backyard is big and green with trees and grass and weeds that my mother hates because they prickle her hands when she pulls them, and our house is a red brick square and we had been having the funnest time ever: There were grown-ups drinking gin and smoking cigarettes and shrieking with laughter, and kids running around chasing each other and swimming and dunking each other in our blue above-ground pool. There were hot dogs and hamburgers and ketchup and mustard and potato chips and paper plates and pickles and strawberry ice cream cones that had to be licked really fast or they would drip all over, and homemade chocolate cake with really thick frosting that Mrs. Risley brought. "That's why Don Risley is so enormously fat!" my mother whispered to me when we saw the cake. And watermelon for everyone.

Frances and me were lining up for our second strawberry ice cream cones and talking about how we would get our bathing suits on after. I was saying how annoyed I was that my mother wouldn't let me get a two-piece, when she gave me a shoulder squeeze from behind.

"Why don't you two beauties run up to Crow's Field and pick some wildflowers? They'll look so nice on the table."

It always tickled when she whispered in my ear, and I wasn't sure if I liked it or not. But I loved picking flowers.

"Yeah! Frances, wanna go?"

"Sure. Why not? I'll get the daisies, I love daisies. I love daisies so much it isn't funny!"

We run up to Crow's Field in our party dresses and bare feet shrieking with excitement all the way. We are on our hands and knees in the long grasses looking for daisies and violets and buttercups to make the best bouquet ever when we feel their shadows behind us.

"Hey. What are you girls doing?"

A crackly man's voice: like he is mad at us.

We both freeze, thinking that we might be in trouble for trespassing, because it was, as my mom would say, "strictly speaking, not our field." I turn around and see that it is not any kind of field policeman, it is Miles Carver and that friend of his, ugly Bernie. They are like storybook giants standing there looking down at us.

Frances knows Miles better than I do because their families see each other all the time. We see them only when we are over at Frances's house and they are there.

"Hey Miles."

"You look nice today, *Franny-Pan.*"

I hate it that he called her that. Her daddy calls her that, so no one else should.

"Ummm, thank you?"

"You are most welcome."

Why is he talking like that? Frances tries to talk like she is older. "What's up, boys?"

"We were wondering the same thing, Frances."

Bernie seems to have a frog in his throat when he asks us what two "pretty little things" were doing on their hands and knees in the grass.

I very quietly say, "We are not things, we are girls."

"Okay, girls," sneered Miles. "What. Are. You. Doing?"

When she answers him, Frances is acting like they are starting a game.

"That's for us to know, and you to find out!"

Her older sister, Lori, used to say that when we asked her anything at all. Her sister, Lori, is scary, even scarier than Frances. She has shiny dark hair down to her waist and she seems to just hate us. She sometimes slaps Frances across the face for no reason. It leaves a big red mark that Frances covers with her hand and her hair until it goes away.

"Oh ho ho ho! Okay, okay, I like that challenge," says ugly Bernie, folding his arms in front of his chest. He peers down at us and asks us if we are playing hide-and-go-seek.

"No," I say, in the sassiest tone possible for me.

"That's for babies!" screams Frances. I don't know why Frances said that, because we play hide-and-go-seek all the time, and she loves it. In fact, she loves it more than anybody.

"Then can we play with you? We love hide-and-go-seek."

Frances hisses, "I said we're not playing hide-and-go-seek. Got something wrong with your hearing?" Frances is being a tough girl. I'm glad.

"You're funny," says Miles, with a strange edge in his voice.

"Sassy. I like that," croaks Bernie. "So, anyways, what are you girlies doing down there? Lookin' for ladybugs?"

"No," we both say at the same time.

We are still on the ground, sitting in the grasses. They stand over us.

"Well, I give up. Whatcha doing?"

I muster up my courage to speak to the big boys. "We're just picking flowers for the party."

"Where?"

Are they just pretending to be stupid? I point down at the party in the backyard, which they had actually been at for a few minutes, till they got bored and left.

"Can we help you pick flowers?" asks Miles, his voice breaking, which sounds like me practising violin, before I gave it up. Frances looks Miles right in the eye.

"If you want."

Why did Frances say "If you want"? I wish she hadn't said that. Now we are stuck with them, in the middle of Crow's Field, where nobody else can see us.

We call it "Crow's Field," because in the late afternoon the blue-black crows as big as Frances's dachshund dogs gather in the magnolia tree and caw at each other, so loud you can hear them all the way up at Frances's, which is at the top of Mansfield Terrace. Sometimes we catch them stealing the pale blue speckled robin's eggs when the mother robin is away plucking earthworms from the ground after it rains; when we see her we shriek "Hurry back, hurry back to your nest, now!" and then we run back to the crows and scream at them "Go away, Mr. Crow. Go away, Mr. Crow" and run towards them flapping our arms wildly. But it doesn't do a thing. They aren't scared of us. Crow's Field is wild with long green and red grasses up to your eyes, but if you crawl around on your hands and knees you see purple violets and yellow buttercups, wild daffodils, and ladybugs and sometimes a long stripey garter snake, which always unnerves me and fascinates me at the same time. If you look up, you see our Easy Tree: a big old magnolia tree that Dad claims is about five hundred years old. Every spring it bursts into bloom with gigantic whitish pink flowers and when Mom said the tree was "laughing in pink," Paulie and I groaned and said, "Mom, you always say that." But really, we like it when she says that. Makes us feel safe. Mom is so beautiful. One of the other moms even called her "slinky." I don't really know what that means when applied to a person. All I know about Slinky is the toy, which Paulie and I love watching go down the stairs. I am pretty sure it was a compliment for my mother — something like silky, which means soft to touch and shiny. I whisper the word to myself when I am alone, because I like saying it. Mom is tall, six foot one, just like her mother, my grandmother, Vera, who was famous for being tall and strict and very religious. My mom said Gramma was a proud teetotaller, which meant she didn't drink a drop of alcohol. Unlike my parents and their friends. I asked Gramma why she didn't drink alcohol, one time when I was feeling brave, and she said that gin ruined families, because the men would spend all their paycheques on gin and their families would not have money for food. I guess that was true in her day.

Now what ruins families is speed. Seeing those speed freaks down on Princess Street — emaciated and wild-eyed — is scary. Especially when it is someone you used to know, someone you went to school with. They're basically ghosts now, not people.

In a strange way, I miss Gramma Vera. I only knew her till she died when I was fourteen or so. She lived a long way away, in Alberta. My mom said she would sing Irish songs to me in the Irish language when I was a baby. I wish I remembered that. My grandpa, Joseph, died before I was born, because he was hit by a red car. We see quite a lot of my other grandparents, though, the ones in Ottawa, who are Dad's mother and father. We call them Nanny and Pop. Every Christmas we drive through snowstorms all the way from Connecticut to Ottawa in our creaky car to spend the holiday with them, even though Daddy and Pop always seem to be arguing about something. In the mornings, Pop would make me a boiled egg and buttered toast with marmalade on it, which was exactly what he and Nanny were having. I only ever had that for breakfast when we were in Ottawa.

At home it is always an orange cut into four pieces and a piece of dry toast. Dad makes us breakfast because Mom sleeps late, till ten or eleven. Definitely not like my friends' mothers, but I think it's cool.

My mom has dark auburn hair past her collarbone. So pretty. In the mornings, it is flowing and wild and reddish brown everywhere, but as soon as she gets dressed, she throws her hair up in a bun with a yellow pencil. When we were little, Paulie and I would sometimes pull out that pencil and hide it so we could brush her hair while she lay on the couch, always after school, before Dad got home. We would take turns. Her hair would shimmer when the sunlight came through the venetian blinds in our front window. It just made me so happy. Mom knows a lot about light because she is a watercolour painter. Sometimes she sits in the grass of Crow's Field on a blue and grey checkered picnic blanket and paints a picture of our magnolia tree with her watercolours. "This, this is a perfect light!" she will say, so softly. When she finishes, she carefully places her pictures along the kitchen window. One had me sitting in the tree, wearing the lightest blue shorts and a *Flintstones* T-shirt. Not sure what happened to it. As a little kid I would pick as many violets as I could while she was painting and then bring them back to the house. She would put them in a glass of water on the kitchen windowsill with the watercolours. Looking up at them when I am at the sink is nice.

After May is over, and all the magnolia flowers have fallen to the ground and turned brown, the tree is easy to climb, so we called it the Easy Tree. Sometimes, after playing sardines or kick the can until dark, we climb into that tree in our bare, dirty feet and talk about nothing, feeling the dark like a magical cloak, till our mothers call us in for dinner. My mom says it is a Connecticut call to prayer.

Everyone eats dinner late because we are "faculty brats, all of you, with your unbrushed hair and raggedy clothes." That's what my mother's friend Johnsia said. I even heard her, but it isn't true. We brush our hair sometimes and our clothes are not rags; they are nice. They just aren't fussy, and a lot of them are hand-me-downs from older sisters or brothers, so sometimes the sleeves and the pants are a bit too long, but we don't care, as long as they are comfortable. None of the mothers work at a paying job, so everybody we know has to be careful about money.

Up in that Easy Tree you can hear the crickets chirping and there are fireflies we sometimes catch and trap in jars with holes in the lid so they can breathe. They keep lighting up even after we take them inside, and my dad unscrews the lid every morning and breathes into the jar because they love the warm, humid air that comes out of a human.

Miles is smiling a smile that shows all of his teeth and makes me think of the wolf in "Red Riding Hood" when it said, "All the better to eat you with."

"Well, that's nice. That's so cute, little girls picking flowers."

Frances's eyes narrow as she lies. "I wasn't going to pick flowers. I don't care about flowers. Flowers just die."

I feel like she punched me in the solar plexus. I can hardly breathe for a moment.

"Frances, you just said how much you love flowers. You told my mom that just now," I say out of the side of my mouth.

"Did not," she says, lying, and I catch her looking at Miles and rolling her eyes, as if to say *Ana is such a baby.*

Sometimes Frances lies. Actually, she lies a lot. Probably every day, about something or other. I mostly always know when she is lying, and she even knows that I know but we pretend. Even stranger than that: She steals dollar bills from her mother's pocketbook! I could not even imagine doing that, but Frances just does it.

She sometimes catches me gaping at her.

"What?"

"Aren't you gonna get in trouble?"

"She won't even notice."

I figure maybe she can lie and steal without it bothering her because she is an atheist. Her whole family is. Atheists don't believe in God or the devil or heaven or hell, so they can sin without feeling any fear at all. I feel sorry for them because they don't realize they will be going to hell.

I am wondering if that is why she said "If you want" to Miles and Bernie.

Frances and me have been best friends since we were two years old, but being with Frances is sometimes like walking through thorny bushes to see what you can see. Lots of scratches, quite a bit of bleeding, but so worth it. She is more intelligent than me, so naturally she is impatient with me sometimes, just like I am with my little brother, Paulie. "Why are you *so* stupid? You are *so dozy*!" Her mother, Cora, overheard her once and scolded, "Frances May that is not a nice word to call your friend."

I said, "I don't mind it, Mrs. Kester." Because at the time I didn't, because it was kind of like a nickname, and you only give nicknames to friends. And anyways, I believed I *was* dozy, and because of that I was pleased that she would be friends with me. So pathetic. When she cuts me with her words, I always forgive her because I believe she doesn't really mean it. Later on, she hugs me and says I am her oldest, best friend in the world. That always makes my eyes and even my ears water.

I'm wondering what Miss Lawrence would think about all this. I wish she were here. If she were here, she would just shoo those boys away and she would take my hand and Frances's hand and bring us right back to the party. Miss Lawrence was my first-grade teacher. She was the best teacher I ever had.

When we were in first grade, me and Moses were Miss Lawrence's favourite kids in the class. She hardly even noticed Frances. I'm not sure why she liked me, but Moses was the sweetest boy ever. On the last day of first grade, he went around the classroom and kissed every girl on the cheek.

"Did Moses kiss you too?"

"Yah!" "Me too!!!" "Me too!" "Me too!"

"I kissed all of you!" he shouted with a laugh in his voice, his eyes shimmering like those little rivulets on the sidewalk when the snow melts.

We all thought he was cute because he was tiny and fast moving and had big dimples when he smiled, which was all the time. We also wanted to show each other and him that we weren't *prejudiced.* Stillman School is a Quaker school and so we don't believe in fighting wars, and we don't believe in people being prejudiced against other people. We learned about how there was this thing called *slavery* right here in America. Miss Lawrence would say, "Can you imagine being pulled away from your parents? Forever? And beaten with a whip?"

Some of us cried when we thought about that; the others weren't really thinking about it, they were just picking their noses or daydreaming. I arranged my face to look sad because I actually could not imagine what she was talking about. Now that I am nine, I think I understand better how terrible it was. Most of us in Miss Lawrence's first-grade class were from fairly nice families so the worst we could imagine was being yelled at or maybe spanked with a hairbrush. Most parents spank their children. They lay the kid in trouble over their knees and pull their underpants down and smack them on the bare bottom with a hand or a hairbrush. I once was there when my friend Cathy was spanked by her dad because he had caught us playing doctor in her closet. I will never forget the sight of her bottom after he smacked it hard with the hairbrush. Bright, bright red and just not nice. I wanted so much to go home but my mother hadn't picked me up yet.

My parents don't spank us like that, but my dad sometimes whacks me on the back of the head for whining or hiding a disgusting lamb chop under my chair.

"We do not spank you. We don't believe in that, darling. We lose our tempers sometimes when you drive us into a state!" Like, if I say I hate liver because it stinks and it makes me sick, my dad thunks me on the back of the head. I don't mind the thunk that much because it doesn't really hurt.

Once, though, when she was mad at him for yelling at her and slamming the door like he always does, my mom told me that when I was about two, he had hit me so hard on my back that there was a red handprint there. I think it happened at least two or three times, so the third time the doctor said, "Joanna, you know that I'm going to have to report this if I see it again." And that meant my dad could go to jail so she must have told my dad and that is why he started hitting me on the head. Because it doesn't show.

My dad is not slinky like my mom; he is more like the Tin Man in *The Wizard of Oz* because of his arthritis. He walks like the Tin Man before Dorothy gave him the oil from the oil can. He always has a cigarette between his fingers or dangling from his mouth, usually Marlboros. His fingers are dark yellow because of the cigarettes. He has midnight black hair, which he slicks back every morning with Brylcreem, a giant nose, and eyes that someone once said were blindingly blue. It is true he is hard to look at in the eyes because they are so blue that you can't even register what he is saying sometimes. My mom says my dad is "black Irish," because his hair is honestly black as the night sky when there are no stars and you are in the countryside, and his eyes are tropical blue and that is a combination that people say is uncommon everywhere but in Ireland.

I sometimes wonder if all those thunks on the back of the head are why I'm epileptic. And why I can see the Virgin Mary with that almost blinding light around her when I feel like I might have a fit.

And why I'm a coward. If I had any guts, I would just get up right now and walk down the hill and back to Paulie's birthday party.

I'm trying to think about Ruby Bridges just walking into William Franz Elementary School even though all those monster people were yelling at her. My mom called those yellers "white trash, bottom-of-the-barrel harridans, and Neanderthals." Thing is, they may have frightened Ruby deep in her stomach and in her knees, but they didn't stop her. They did not stop her from walking into that school in her pretty dress with the petticoat fluffing it out.

After Miss Lawrence made us watch the newsreel on Ruby Bridges, my friends and I talked about if we would have been scared away. I admitted that I would have just run home to my mom and dad, but Frances said that just like Ruby Bridges, she would have walked right into the school, not scared at all by the screaming white trash people. And she probably would have. One time, she walked right up to a group of boys who were holding a long black snake and teasing us. "Come on, girlies, you're not scared of a black mamba, are ya? What if we throw it at ya?" She walked right up to them, and she reached out her hand and she held the snake, but it wriggled, and Frances laughed and threw it hard, and it slithered so fast under the broken green fence. Even though I was scared of the snake and I hated it, I kind of felt sorry for it. Because I noticed that it had eyes, like us.

Miss Lawrence was the reason for some of the best days of my life, but also the reason for one of the worst. It was the first day of second grade. I walked into the school after a long, hot, and boring summer except for the one fun week at Bearmac camp where I got the Miss Graciousness award and the visit to Canada to see my Nanny and Pop in Ottawa. There was Miss Lawrence! I was so excited to see her and show her my new violet dress with a real petticoat under and hug her and smell her perfume that was like pink roses and tell her all about my summer. I knew she would want to know everything, every single detail.

I ran as fast as I could towards her: "Hi, Miss Lawrence!" She glanced at me with a polite smile. "Hello Ana, nice to see you." Then she turned away. She was fussing over a round little girl with very short bangs who had come all the way from England and had a prissy English accent. Her name was Clare. Miss Lawrence seemed to be hypnotized by her. I knew at that moment that the special feeling she had for me was not there any longer. It was all for Clare.

MILES IS CROUCHING down, right beside Frances.

"You little girls wanna play with us for a while?"

Frances stands up for the first time since they started bothering us.

"That depends."

"On?" Bernie's voice is different than Miles's — more from the nose.

Frances answers without even looking at him. "If we're gonna do something fun."

I look right at Frances and say, "Nope, sorry, we have to pick flowers and take them back to the party. My mom is waiting for us."

"We have something really special in mind."

Frances looks over at Miles, even though it was Bernard who spoke.

"I'm waiting." Frances sounds like her dad. She looks right at Miles.

Why is she playing along?

Miles looks like a movie star, and his mom, Roberta, who everyone calls Robbie, is one of Frances's mom's best friends. According to my mother, Robbie also looks like a famous movie star, and her name is Katharine Hepburn. "Just like Kate Hepburn, darling. Always wears pants, has an opinion about everything, hair swirled up in a bun like Kate's, and a voice like a box of crackerjack. They could be sisters!" His dad, Warren Carver, is one of the most famous painters in America. My mom showed me articles in *Time* magazine that were all about him and his paintings and he was even on the cover of *Life* magazine as The Greatest American Painter. My dad said the paintings were loony, and that people were suckers to pay so much for them. He said they looked like a bunch of three-year-olds just poured paint on a canvas and then rolled around on it. I liked all the colours in them. They look like the feeling I have inside when Mom and Dad fight.

"We could go up to your clubhouse — the attic over Ana's garage — and play a real game. A game that we teenagers play." I don't like that he called it a *clubhouse.*

"It's not a clubhouse." I hope I sound as annoyed as I feel.

Frances did not want to disappoint Miles, so she argued with me.

"Ana! Yes, it is. Remember, the Daredevil Club? We met up there a few times. You, me, and Francine Pinel and Cathy Rister!"

Bernie licks his skinny lips. "The Daredevil Club? Well then, if you two girls are daredevils you aren't gonna have a problem with our party games, are you?"

I think both of us feel uncomfortable with Bernie saying "party games" like that, with his lopsided smile.

Then it is quiet for a long time. The buzzing of the telephone wires is loud like June bugs but then like a siren. I look over at

Frances to see what she is thinking. Frances looks like a big wave has just gone over her; but then, a minute later, she looks ready to dive back in. I have seen her do this. At Hammonasset Beach, into the Atlantic Ocean. She is the bravest person I know, although this time being brave is going back to the party, not going along with Miles and Bernie. That would be that word that means not brave but crazy, like when kids cross the street without looking. *Reckless?* I start picking every violet I see. The violets could give me a good excuse to run back to the party.

Miles stands on one foot, like a big, ugly, pink flamingo bird.

"Okay, girls, is it yes, or no? We don't have all day. If you want to miss out on the best game ever — is it yes or is it no?" He smiles that smile that makes a taste in my mouth like how cough medicine tastes.

Frances looks at Miles and Bernie, and she looks at me and says, really loudly, "Yes. Sure. Why not? Anything is better than this boring day."

Boring? How can a cookout and a birthday party be boring? I know she is lying. She's just trying to show off that she is brave.

"No!" I croak out. I'm upset that she said our family cookout was boring. I know that she hadn't been bored, she had been laughing and singing and playing just like the other kids.

I have a soft but a gravelly voice, just like the gravel on our driveway. That's what my mom always says. Babysitters say, "Oh, I love her voice! It's adorable!" My mom says, "Like broken glass on maple syrup."

"No, I don't want to go to the attic." My heart is racing. I said it. Frances gives me the stink eye. "What's wrong, Ana Roonie? You scared?"

I hate it when she calls me "Ana Roonie." That's what her father, Mr. Kester, calls me and it makes me feel sick. His bow ties make me sick too.

"You scared, little mousey?"

Meow. Bernie tries to meow like a cat. It sounds weird because his voice breaks and goes high.

Meowww. Miles does it too. And then they look at each other and laugh a laugh like the joke isn't really funny.

Then Frances leans in close to me — so close her eyes are only an inchworm away from my eyes. I can smell orange Life Savers on her breath.

"*Meowwwwwwwwww.* Little mouse, if you don't come, I'm gonna eat you!"

I look right into her eyes and tell her I was not and never had been a mouse. I feel my face go very red because this is the first time I have ever stood up to Frances. Other times, when I even sort of stood up to her, she would punch me in the stomach so I couldn't breathe. My dad told me it was my *solar plexus*, a place where you breathe, and that's why it hurt so much, and why I gave up the fight every time. I always wondered who taught her that, to punch in the solar plexus. Maybe her nasty dad, who always wears an ugly, polka-dot bow tie.

I wonder if she called me a mouse because of my hair, because my mom cut it so short, like a mouse's hair is short, because Frances had spit her Juicy Fruit in my long hair and we couldn't get it out.

"That little demon was clearly jealous of your hair."

"It was a joke, Mom."

"Her hair is lifeless, darling, and yours is luxuriant. That's why she did it."

I did not believe her, even though I kind of believed her. So, she plonked a blue plastic mixing bowl on my head — the one she made Betty Crocker cake mix cakes with — and with a Pall Mall cigarette in one hand and her scissors in the other, she cut all around the bowl, even though I was crying. "Please, mommy, please no, please don't cut my hair." She was good at ignoring my crying. It's like she didn't even hear it. Her nails were long and bright red, just like movie stars like Bette Davis, and her hands were cool, like the way the inside of a cucumber feels.

All the time she was cutting it she was saying, "It's going to look gorgeous, darling, it's the fashion. Don't you want to be in fashion?" I said no, I didn't want to be in fashion, I wanted to be pretty, I wanted to keep my long hair. I liked it. I liked wearing two braids that went halfway down my back, with blue ribbons tied around them. I liked to have a ponytail, and I liked to wear pink and yellow barrettes that looked like butterflies. I didn't care about what was fashionable. Short hair wasn't pretty, and everyone knew it.

"No other girl at school has short hair except Patty Wissy's little sister, Loreen, and that's because she has lice."

"Well, you will not be scratching so they will all know that you do not have lice. And who is Patty Wissy again?" She kept snipping, this way, that way, fast.

Patty is the girl in our class from the welfare family of eight kids and two retarded parents. It's what everybody says. Just because her dad wears grease-stained white T-shirts and dusty pants from his work and doesn't talk at all and their mother is no taller than a child and has greasy black hair and broken glasses and only talks in a whisper or a shriek. "Hello, Miss Opal, good day" was the whisper and "Get over here now, Leland, now or you're gonna get it" is the shriek. They live in a condemned house at the edge of town with peeling yellow paint and broken front steps.

Patty Wissy is my secret best friend.

Yes, a closer, realer friend than Frances because she doesn't call me dozy or punch me in the stomach and she plays Superman and Invisible Girl with me, and never says it's babyish. We have so much fun playing Superman and Invisible Girl. We are the most beautiful, pretty, cool superhero girls in the universe. We can fly from earth to Venus and save people from evil Martians. We can swim around the rings of Saturn and lie around in the stars eating popsicles. Playing that game, I feel a kind of happiness that I never feel with Frances.

I wish I were playing it now.

She is secret, because I never tell Frances when Patty and I play together. If she asks, I say I'm going to the dentist. I don't want to tell her I'm playing with Patty because I am afraid she would say something mean about Patty being poor and living in a condemned house.

"What's condemned, Daddy?" I asked my dad once.

"Well, I suppose it means that the house could burn down because of old wiring or just collapse because it's badly built. Why do you ask?"

"Frances says that Patty Wissy's house is condemned. She says everyone knows it." Mom overheard.

"Oh dear, John, should we really allow her to play in a condemned house?"

"I think it's fine."

I was terrified Mom would forbid me from playing at the Wissy's. All the other faculty parents had forbidden their children, but somehow Mum didn't know that. I tried to be casual.

"We're mostly outside playing Superman, Mom, on the sidewalk. Patty is Superman and I am Invisible Girl. The house seems fine; it does not seem condemned. Not at all. We even had hot dogs there."

"I really don't think you should go again," my mom said, but she had forgotten about it by the next day and let me walk over whenever I asked.

When I go over, it really seems like any other house, although it smells different. More thick. And her dad actually can talk.

Everybody calls the Wissy kids "the welfares," and everybody says they smell. Maybe the house smells but they don't smell. Patty smells nice, like talcum powder.

The haircut was done. My mother opened her compact mirror and put it in front of me. I looked like a boy. I hated it.

"What on earth are you crying for? It looks marvellous!" my mother lied.

"Frances won't want to play with me when she sees my hair short like a boy."

"But it's her fault! Anyhow, she is your best friend, isn't she?"

"She is going to make fun of me."

"She is such a little devil. You make fun of her right back. Tell her she has squinchy little eyes and she will never be pretty."

"You always tell me these things to say and then when she is right there, I can't say them."

"Why ever not?"

"I don't know. I'm not you. I get mixed up."

Funny thing was, Frances had not mentioned my short hair until this very minute. I was thinking it was probably because she knew it was her fault and she liked it that I wasn't as pretty without my long hair. But she often reacts in the opposite way of what you expect. I guess that is partly what makes her interesting.

"Ana doesn't want to play. What's the matter, Ana?" asks Miles in a fake little kid voice.

I do not like the way he is looking right into my face.

"Oh, she wants to. She's just shy, aren't you, Ana? Our shy little mouse."

She compared me to a mouse. Again. Patty would never do that. Patty always said nice things about me. "You have such pretty eyes," and "I like your shoes!" and "You're so funny!"

"No."

I am shy, but that does not make me like a mouse.

Another name she called me once, when all of us kids were in our blue above-ground pool licking our orange popsicles as fast as we could before they melted in the sun, was Charlie Brown. Francine Pinel started talking about Charlie Brown comics, which we all loved, and then Frances said, "I love Lucy the best. I'm exactly like her. You all do anything I say, you suckersssss." I asked which one she thought I might be. I was hoping she would say Peppermint Patty, because we both had freckles and she was good at baseball, and even though I had never played baseball, I thought that one day maybe I would.

"You're kind of a female Charlie Brown." I couldn't say anything for a minute because I wasn't sure how she meant it. But then, I said, "Oh. Yeah, I can see that."

Even though I did not want to be one of the boy characters, I took it at the time as a compliment. Charlie Brown was the star. Everyone in the world loved Charlie Brown. But even though I took it as a compliment, I knew it was an insult.

Why did she say to Miles and ugly Bernie: "Oh, she wants to?"

I did not want to, because I had a bad feeling. In my stomach. It's not that I knew exactly what they had in mind; how could I? But I knew it was something scary. I don't think Frances knew what they really were after. I am guessing she thought that it would be like taking a tiny sip of our mom's beer — disgusting for a moment but exciting because it was grown-up — but she had no idea what awaited us, like the fly has no idea about the spider's web, glinting so prettily in the sun.

The thought of going up there to the attic with them made me feel like I did when the doctor was about to give me a needle. The Charlie Brown part of me was very scared that I would end up going up there with them because Frances was going to force me because that's the way things had always been, ever since we were two. I always did what she wanted me to do. Like a little suck.

FRANCES IS THE boss of all of us because she can talk like someone much older, and she even swears sometimes, which is a sin for us Catholics. At this moment, she is looking right into me with her scary eyes from all the way across the driveway, which is closer to the attic than Crow's Field. Somehow, we have moved to the gravel driveway though I can't remember moving. This is really strange to me that I can't remember moving from the long grasses to the sharp gravel. I guess it is because I have been thinking so hard that I wasn't paying attention, or that those big boys had such power over us that when they moved, we moved.

Sitting on the gravel, I can see into the dark garage and to the ladder at the back, the ladder that leads up to the attic. I say seven Hail Marys in a row in my mind so that blessed Mary Mother of God will help me not do what Frances is gonna make me do. I am sure that Mary, Mother of God, will listen to my prayers now because I had my First Communion two years ago, which means that I have divine grace. The priest said so. And the Virgin Mary always listens to those with divine grace. And I actually plan to become a nun when I grow up. Our Lady and Christ, and his father, God, they really like that. They like priests and nuns. I have my own holy rosary made of pink-coloured glass that my Nanny sent me from Ottawa, and I say my prayers on it every night. Three Hail Marys and three Our Fathers. If I have been mean to Paulie that day, even more. I go to confession on Saturdays, even though I have nothing to confess.

With your help, Our Lady, I am going to stand up to Frances. Any minute now.

The problem is that Frances feels safe with Miles on account of his parents being great friends of her parents.

My parents, Joanna and John, also had many great friends at Wesleyan College. According to my mother, it was a golden time, because there were people in their crowd who later became world-famous, and some were already famous. To name a few: John Cage, Richard Wilbur, Miles's father, the super-famous, very abstract painter, Mr. Carver, Kate Rood, but most famous of all, according to my dad, was the revered Jewish philosopher Simon Levy. He was my friend Ruthie's dad, and he was a lot older than all the other dads. Ruthie joined our third-grade class and was there for two years. We started talking one day at recess when Frances was mad at me for saying she shouldn't hate her mother, so wasn't including me, and from then on we had lunch together most days and play dates at each other's houses and even sleepovers. Ruthie's dad was, according to my dad, a very important philosopher, and he came to all the parties. Sometimes he would bring not only his wife, ZeeZee, Ruthie's mother, but his best friend, Hannah Arendt. Ruthie told me that Hannah Arendt was world-famous because she wrote a book about the trial of Adolf Eichmann who was a Nazi bureaucrat in charge of the trains that brought millions of Jewish people and Gypsies and blind people and kids in wheelchairs to the concentration camps, where they were murdered. This was not that long ago, not even twenty years ago, when we were sitting on that driveway, during the war that Dad did not fight in because his father threatened to disown him if he did. I have to admit I'm a little embarrassed that he didn't fight in that war, when all my friends' fathers did. Some of them even got Medals of Honor and Purple Hearts. Usually, when the subject comes up, I mumble something about a medical exemption. Ruthie said that after watching the trial of that man, Hannah Arendt decided that Mr. Eichmann was not a devil, but just an ordinary person you wouldn't even notice, like our school principal, Mr. Henny. She said that evil people were just boring, ordinary people. Not like horror movie vampires and Frankenstein's monster. The way my dad explained it is that they are just like a small part of an engine. Something the engine needs to work properly. And, he said, "More importantly, anyone of us could have been Adolf Eichmann, given the right circumstances."

Miles and Bernie seem normal on the outside, but on the inside, the real side, they are bad. That is what Frances doesn't know at this moment. I know it for sure, in my stomach, sitting on the gravel, with them trying to convince us to go with them up to the attic. Sometimes when I have this feeling in my stomach it means I am going to have a seizure. I really hope I don't have one now, because I always pee my pants when I do.

In Sunday school, Sister Theresa said that if you are a mortal sinner, you will go straight to hell when you die, because you are a friend of the devil. One Sunday in church, the priest, Father Gomez, said that the devil tempts you to sin. I liked Father Gomez because he sounded like Ricky Ricardo on *I Love Lucy*. But after he said that it made me wonder if that meant that Eve was Satan. She tempted Adam to eat the apple. This idea bothered me. Did it mean that according to the Catholic church me and Frances were tempting Miles and Bernard?

When we went to the christening of my baby cousin, Liza, in Ottawa, the priest said, "Do you renounce Satan, in all his pomp and circumstance?" I had to ask Mom what exactly that meant, and she said, "Well, darling, it is a terrible translation, but essentially it means that Satan can be alluring. Tempting." I asked my mother if baby Liza understood those big words.

"No darling, it's just ceremonial." I didn't bother to ask her what that big word meant.

I'm thinking about how we have been warned about strange men in cars offering us candy bars or to see a puppy. Our moms and dads, our teachers, all the grown-ups. They would say that those men could act really nice and gentle and wouldn't seem scary at all, but we needed to remember they were monsters. I have seen men like that, driving too slowly in cars when me and my friends are walking home from school. There was one man that Joni Gracielle said would pay us fifty cents to pull down our pants. I thought about it for a few minutes, because you can get a lot of candy for fifty cents, but then I remembered what my mom and dad always said about strange men, and just how dangerous they are. With the men in the cars, we always run down a wrong-way street so the man can't follow us, laughing and screaming with the excitement of it. We knew they weren't just someone looking for a house number, because when we looked at their faces we saw the monster underneath the face, the monster that wanted to rip us open and devour our insides.

WITH THE EXCEPTION of Patty Wissy and Ruthie Levy, most of my friends were actually Frances's friends. They liked her way better than me because she had more zing. That's what her mother said once at a cocktail party at our house. Paulie and I were listening from the stairs. She said, "My Frances has zing, but your Ana is kind." My mother laughed and said, "I don't know about Ana being kind, but yes, your Frances is certainly colourful." My dad said, "Ana has lots of colour. It's just her colours are subtle, that's all." Dad was always defending me.

That is one of the reasons I like Ruthie Levy, because Ruthie actually prefers me over Frances. I'm not sure why. Ruthie has long, dark brown hair almost to her waist and freckles everywhere, even on her arms, and toys with her food, whereas I wolf everything down, or that is what my mom says, and it is true because when it is my mom's or dad's cooking I just want it to be over so I can get to the Oreos or chocolate ice cream or Hostess cupcakes. Ruthie is much more curious about everything than I am. She loves to argue. When she speaks, her voice is like a song that you never want to end.

My mom spotted us on the stairs, and her face went bright red. She ran up the stairs so fast and sat beside me and Paulie on the top stair.

"Darling, I hope I didn't hurt your feelings."

"No."

"I was only trying to make Frances's mom feel better about Frances."

"Why does she need to feel better about Frances?"

"I cannot tell you that, darling, I am sworn to secrecy. Just trust me."

"But you said Frances has zing."

"Listen to me. Frances is like fireworks. A quick and oh-so-impressive spark and sizzle, yes, but then, that sizzle fizzles. It's nothing but smoke."

"That sizzle fizzles?"

"Yes."

"And what about me?"

"You are a secret garden."

"What does that mean?"

Paulie always knew when someone's feelings were hurt. He gave me a piece of Dentyne gum.

I wonder what he is doing now, down at his party. I wonder if he realizes me and Frances aren't there.

Miles has moved a lot closer to Frances than before. So close that their shoulders are touching. Frances doesn't move away. I pray to God and Jesus and Mary that Bernie won't try to move closer to me. I know that I wouldn't be able to move away. I know that my body would turn to stone.

Now. Now is the time to move. Before that happens.

From down the hill, I hear grown-up laughter and kids yelping, and splashing, jumping into the water. I hear one man's loud voice telling some kind of story about eggs that made everyone laugh. I hear my mother's laugh, a laugh like no other.

Miles and Bernard look at each other. I look at Frances, and move my head as if to say, *Let's just go back*. She smiles in a mean way and shakes her head and looks back at Miles. He shrugs his shoulders and asks us if we want to go back to the cookout.

But we just sit, silently, in the heat, listening to the sounds of Paulie's birthday party.

We were used to the sounds of a party, because all the grown-ups in my parents' crowd had cocktail parties at least three nights a week. The sexual energy in the air was intense and would last the whole party. We kids didn't know what it was exactly, but we could sense it. We knew that our parents and everyone else's parents were different at the parties than they were at home. Happier, more alive, like Hollywood stars. And the sixties styles that some of them wore were far-out. The more stylish women — the women who were art instructors at Wesleyan, or who had their own pottery wheel — they wore minidresses that were bright green, with a white collar, or even better, with geometric patterns, or swirls of different colours. I would sit on the stairs, mesmerized by these women. Many of them wore big earrings shaped like circles or triangles and laughed like wild animals and their hair was either in buns or a flip. I knew from Frances's older sister that if you wanted a flip you had to wear curlers overnight, and that those curlers stuck into your scalp so you didn't sleep. Other ladies wore long dresses and silver sandals. The men had short hair, sometimes crewcuts, and blue sweaters. I didn't pay much attention to the men, really, except I noticed that all of them smoked. Some of the men smoked pipes and wore bright bow ties. All the women smoked cigarettes. When they butted them out in the ashtrays there was red lipstick all over the cigarette butts and it made me want to smoke and wear lipstick.

Me and Frances would always sing "Winston tastes bad, like the one I just had: No filter, no taste, just a, bup bup, thirty-cent waste." And then we'd laugh like monkeys. I don't think they even heard us. Some of the women, like Miles's mother, were always exclaiming, "No! He didn't! Oh, my God! You are making it up!" and "Where did you get that magnificent dress? I could just spit."

We kids drink ginger ale and Sprite and stuff ourselves with potato chips while watching the party from the stairs. Sometimes, we dare each other to sneak a sip of beer from a parent's unfinished glass. I hate the taste of beer, but I do it anyways because when someone dares you, you have to do it or they will call you a loser or, even worse, a baby.

"Come on, daredevils, we dare you."

"Yeah," chimes in Bernie. "Double dare you."

"What are you, little baby girls?"

"You don't wanna play with the big kids?"

"Too scared?"

"No," says Frances as she gets up. "I'm not scared of anything."

Oh no. This means it is going to happen. This means I have no choice.

Our parents always forgot to give us dinner when they had their cocktail parties, but we liked that because dinner was usually disgusting. Pork chops with the fat on the side of them and overcooked peas and mashed potatoes from a box. Or TV dinners with rubbery Salisbury steak and still-frozen green beans and the vanilla pudding that always burned my tongue. I hid the Salisbury steak in my shirt and the pork chops underneath the green couch cushions so I wouldn't have to eat them, because one time when I said "I'm not eating this" my dad hit me so hard on the back of the head that I couldn't see for a moment.

Mom said, "John, for heaven's sake, you're the one always talking about IQ, and you knock her IQ down ten points every time you do that. She's going to end up an idiot that we will have to support in our old age."

"What nonsense. You don't know what you're talking about." And he would light another Pall Mall cigarette and leave the room. The front door would slam, and my heart would drop to my belly because I was so afraid he wouldn't come back, ever.

Daddy still smokes three packs of Pall Malls a day. My mother says he needs the calm that cigarettes bring him because he is "a deeply agitated man" because of his shame about not fighting in the war, because when he was seventeen, he was desperate to sign up to fight the Nazis, but his tyrant of a father forbade him. For some reason, he didn't stand up to his father, like so many other boys did, and that's what I think he is ashamed of. The others, they just did. And they were even younger. They lied about their ages. Some of them died, but some of them came back heroes. Some of them saved the world from evil, and so people respected them even more than doctors or priests.

When we go to Ottawa to see my grandparents, I can see that my dad and my grandpa hate each other. My gramma looks at Daddy with love and even tears up when she sees him. She's an artist so sometimes she will do all our portraits, just in charcoal. It only takes her about twenty minutes a person and they are always right on. I like how pretty I look in my portrait. I guess that is the way she sees me. My favourite is on my bedroom wall, stuck with Scotch tape.

The cocktail parties they used to give in Middletown were the only times I heard my dad laugh or saw him sparkle. I suppose the sparkle was for the beautiful women — after all the entire faculty in Middletown was under forty — and the laughter was mostly a performance. Mom laughed easily and frequently then. I think it was one of the reasons he fell in love with her. His own family in Ottawa never laugh.

Paulie and I like it when our parents go to other people's cocktail parties because then we get a babysitter. I really like Naomi with the thighs that spread clear across the couch, and the perfectly flipped light brown hair. Paulie sits on one thigh, and I sit on the other, and Naomi makes up stories. Stories about a Moon girl, and the talking deer from Venus and tiny trolls with singing hair that live in the bookcase.

The next morning, after the tiny troll story, while sucking on an orange wedge, I told Mom that I liked Naomi's giant fat thighs.

Mom, who was wandering around the kitchen in her pink, sleeveless nightgown and bare feet, with her auburn hair flowing, protests: "Rubenesque, not giant, darling, her thighs are Rubenesque."

I also like Naomi because she laughs at all of my knock-knock jokes and tells me I'm a great kid. I like old Mrs. Wheeler too. She brings us bowls of quivering green Jell-O, with orange and apple slices in it.

Sometimes my Mom gets babysitters from the women's prison, because they are cheap. My mom and dad call them *girls*, but they are definitely grown-up. Mom says they are much cheaper than other babysitters and they are allowed out of prison to work because they haven't done anything really bad. My dad got mad when Mom said that.

"Joanna, how can you say they haven't done something bad?"

"For heaven's sake, John, most of them are only in for killing their husbands."

"Only in for killing their husbands? Only? How can you trust them with Ana and Paulie?"

"They didn't kill their children, John. Just their husbands. Who were likely beating them."

My dad does not like the arrangement, but it doesn't stop him from going to parties or concerts with my mom.

For young faculty like him it is about being seen at the right events, with his beautiful and witty wife on his arm.

Most of the prison girl babysitters are cool and funny and watch TV with us or read us stories, but there was one that scared us. Wanda had her hair cut short like a boy and greased back like my dad. She wore no makeup at all. She had bulgy brown eyes, like a fish, that seemed to look in opposite directions, and the smallest mouth ever. She had arms like a strong man, and spindly legs, with veins that looked like blue worms. She wore shorts. Her voice was harsh, with a strong Middletown accent — so that the word *bad* became *beeyad*. She had a little black doctor bag with her that scared us because we knew she wasn't a doctor. After our bath time, when we were all dry and clean and lying in bed in our pyjamas, she opened the bag and pulled out the longest white snake I had ever seen.

I screamed, and she said, "Be quiet, it's only a milk snake."

At first, I thought she was trying to convince us that what was clearly a snake was a milkshake, but then she explained. "These guys live around farms and like to latch onto a cow's titties to suck back her milk."

I thought I was going to throw up.

Paulie said, "So cool! What's his name?"

"Satan."

"Isn't that the name of the devil?" I asked. My whole body trembled because I was really scared of snakes and even more scared of Satan. I pulled my covers tightly over my body so she wouldn't see my shaking legs.

She stood in the middle of the room, holding the snake to show us how long it was. All I could think about was if she was going to put it on my bed. I felt like I couldn't breathe.

"Look into his eyes," said Wanda, voice all velvety, like a TV magician.

"I don't want to." I spoke from the safety of under the covers. "I don't think my mom would be happy about you bringing a snake in here."

"Are you going to tattle?"

Paulie spoke like a grown-up. "It's really cool, but you should put it back in the bag and lock it. We have a cat and D'Arcy does not like snakes. He could kill it."

Wanda laughed. "He's just a big baby, you know. I missed him so much so my son met me here with the bag so I could spend a little time with him."

Paulie continued, so brave for a six-year-old. "Please. Put it away. Our cat always catches snakes out back and he beheads them."

I thought I'd better say something. "He even brings us the heads!"

"Okay, okay." She started to put it back in the bag. "Hate cats! Far as I'm concerned, they are pure evil." The white snake wrapped itself around her wrist when she was trying to put it back in the bag. I gasped but Paulie stayed quiet. He had understood that Wanda could go off at any moment, like a grenade.

"S'okay, Satan, you love your little bag. Go on, Artie's bringin' you a mouse later!"

"Is Artie your son?" Paulie asked politely.

"Yes, sir."

I wanted to understand how this worked. "How's he gonna find a mouse?"

"Artie? Oh, he has ways."

I didn't like the thought of Artie bringing a dead mouse into the house and feeding it to that milk snake while we were sleeping.

"Is he coming here?"

"Youse two want a story? I got stories."

"Did you shut the bag?"

"Yes, I shut the damn bag. Okay you two, lie still and stop asking questions so I can tell you a story. One word outa you and I give ya a crack."

We couldn't believe she was threatening to give us a crack, which I was pretty sure meant a smack. Nobody had ever talked to us like that.

"Ummm, okay, okay, I got it. So, once there was a little boy named Paulie and his big sister, Ana, and they decided they would go for a walk along the banks of the Connecticut River."

Paulie spoke up again. "It's dangerous there. Mom said."

"Shhhh. Listen to the damn story."

She continued. "So, they are walking along and they're pickin' wildflowers and watching the muddy water run crazy fast and they seen something."

"Isn't it saw something?" I was really good at grammar, even when I was only eight. I think it's because I read a lot.

"I tole ya to shut your mouth or I'll shut it for you, ya little priss." Now I was terrified of Wanda.

"What they seen was shiny and black, with the greenest eyes you ever saw. You know what it was?"

"No."

"It was the black panther that lives by the Connecticut River.

And he is heading towards these two kids, because he's gonna tear 'em to pieces with his sharp teeth and …"

I couldn't stand the thought of that panther eating the two little kids. "Don't tell me anymore. Please."

"Fine. Now get the fuck to sleep, you little shits."

She left the room with her snake in the black bag. Neither Paulie nor I could sleep a wink till our parents came home, and even then, I didn't sleep the whole night. We were not used to grown-ups showing us snakes. Mom came up to kiss us goodnight, and she smelled like perfume and makeup and beer. We pretended to be asleep because that always made her happy.

After she left the room, I felt a jolt of fear, and I needed to hear Paulie's voice.

"Paulie?"

"Yeah?"

"Are you asleep?"

"No."

"Me neither. That was weird, wasn't it?"

"About the snake?"

"Yeah. Paulie?"

"Yeah?"

"I'm afraid I'm gonna dream about the white snake."

"Don't be afraid, Ana. You won't."

We could hear the wind blowing through the leaves, and I imagined Wanda meeting her son, Artie, down the street and him pulling a wriggling little mouse out of his pocket.

"That was so silly about a black panther by the Connecticut River."

"Yeah. They don't have them here. They're only in the jungle countries."

"I know."

Then I imagined the snake, Satan, eating the mouse whole.

FRANCES IS STANDING up now, facing Miles. She has her arms crossed in a way that means *I'm not impressed*, although she obviously is.

"Are you daring us? Me and Ana? We are not interested in taking the dare till you tell us what you are daring us to do."

Miles grins and pulls a Winston from his pocket. "Just smoke these cigarettes. Fool around. Have some fun."

I hear myself saying: "My mom says it's not safe up there because there's broken glass and garbage. And dust."

"She doesn't know what she's talking about."

I can't believe Bernie is talking about my mother that way.

"Yes, she does." My mother definitely does know what she was talking about. She is a lot smarter than ugly Bernie.

Frances does a grotesque imitation of my voice. "Yes, she duth." Even though I have never lisped. Our teachers always ask me first to read aloud in class because I am a good talker. I don't lisp. I hate it when she imitates me and made me sound so backwards. I talk back to her this time, mimicking exactly what my mom said.

"People who imitate have no imagination."

"Hah! Where'd ya get that from? Your mommy?" Frances always knows when I am saying what my mom has said.

Frances ruffles my short hair. "Can you believe Ana's hair? She looks like a boy." Apparently, she had just been waiting for the right moment to mock my haircut.

"No, I don't."

"Yes, you do."

"I look in fashion. That's what my mom said."

"Hah! HAH. Ha ha ha ha." She laughs way too hard, just like Lucy in Charlie Brown. "Ha ha ha ha hah ha. That is the funniest joke I ever heard. Hear that? She thinks she looks in fashion. Ha ha ha ha ha haha."

Miles looks at me for the first time, the same way Frances is looking at me.

"Hah. Well, models are flat-chested and so are you girls!" Miles is grinning at me when he says this. But then the next thing Bernie says makes me really sick.

"Doesn't mean there's nothing there to suck."

Miles elbows Bernie.

"Shhh, man."

I cannot not believe he said that. I throw up ice cream into my mouth. It is as if Frances didn't even hear it, because she is so enchanted by Miles. Truly enchanted, like in the Disney movies.

Frances shrieks. "She doesn't look like a model, she looks like Patty!"

"Patty Wissy? She doesn't even have short hair."

"And you smell like her too."

I feel my face go bright red and inform her that I could not possibly have B.O. because my mom has told me that kids don't have B.O. until puberty.

"And anyway, Patty Wissy does not have B.O."

"So, who's Patty? Another sexy little friend?" I do not like the way Bernie talks or the words he uses.

Or the way Frances is describing Patty: "She's the poor girl in our class. Lives in a condemned house. Has about eleven brothers and sisters, all nine months apart. Most of them have been to prison. Always looks stunned, like Ana."

I defend Patty. "She does not look stunned, and I don't either. You're mean."

Frances smiles. "Just sayin' it like I sees it, that's all." She is trying to sound like a character on *Gunsmoke*, her favourite show.

I try to sound like my mother. "It is simply not true."

Bernie laughs. "Simply not true."

Frances looks at Miles.

"Ana feels sorry for her 'cause she's poor."

"I do not."

"Do so."

"I like her because she's my friend."

"The two of them play baby games at recess, like pretending they are Superman. Even though they're girls. Hah!" She does the fake laugh again.

Frances looks directly at me, this time, instead of at Miles. But the way she looks at me is like it's for Miles to see.

"Come on girls, enough talking. Let's go up to your attic and get into it!"

Miles smiles and shows his slightly buck teeth with braces on them, and it makes me feel weird. I don't like the way he said "Get into it."

Frances shouts, "Into what?"

"Ho ho ho," slimes Bernie, joking that he is Santa even though it's July. "Just you wait and see!"

I say very quietly, "I don't like surprises."

And then suddenly, it's Patty, in person, the very Patty we were talking about. She is a little bit breathless, and her eyes are wide.

"Hi, Ana. Am I late?"

"What's she doing here?" Frances hisses, looking directly at Miles. I had forgotten all about inviting Patty to the birthday party. I'm embarrassed in front of Frances but not so embarrassed I would pretend I hadn't invited her, the way Peter denied knowing Jesus three times. I would never be like Peter. Patty wears the same dress to school almost every day but on this day, she looks like she is dressed for church. She is wearing a starched sky-blue dress with a real petticoat under and a little white sweater with just one button done up and black patent leather shoes and white ankle socks with a pink trim. Her dark blond hair has been curled to make a little flip. Her face is long and pasty white, which my mom says is from poor nutrition, but her eyes are light blue like the sky.

My mom always says they are "like saucers" with long curly lashes that I wish I had, because mine are straight. She has thin lips, which she purses to make an expression that seems like she is working out whether she should believe you or not.

Patty dips when she walks, like her own kind of dance, and that's what she is doing at that moment, she is dipping towards us.

"Oh, Patty! Hi! No, you're not late." I don't know what to say next because if I ask her to sit with us then she might be caught in the problem along with me and Frances, so I don't say anything more.

Patty holds out a bulging paper bag and tells me she has vegetables from their garden to give to my mother. She says her mother insisted.

She reaches into the bag and brings out a fat green zucchini.

Frances rolls her eyes and then talks phony-nice to Patty. "That's so cute! Why don't you run along and give them to Ana's mom?"

Why did Frances say "run along" like she was a mom? Patty doesn't answer her. Patty isn't scared of Frances.

"My mom is going to love that zucchini! That's so neat!"

Patty, sounding very mature, says that she had better give the bag to my mother right now. She says she promised her mother.

There is a bang of silence, and she looks right at me.

"Are you coming with me, Ana?"

Miles steps towards her, looking her up and down.

"Hey, don't go, doll. Stay out here with us."

Patty looks up at him and says loud and clear that she is not a doll, she is a girl. Just like I had said.

Bernie makes a sort of whistle and tells her she is "pretty for white trash." The only other time I had heard that phrase was when my mother used it in relation to the white people screaming and throwing things at Ruby Bridges. I know Patty's family is not like those people, and just as I am trying to figure out a way to say that to Bernie, Miles says something I don't expect. "Hey, man. Shut up."

There is quite a long silence. I see Patty swallow, like her mouth is dry.

"We are not white trash. My dad has a good job. And we are not poor. You don't know anything about us so you should just shut your mouth."

I am filled with love for Patty, and I want to say something nice, but I just look down at the gravel because I know what began before she came is not going to stop.

Miles walks over to Patty and touches her shoulder.

"Hey girlie, I promise my friend is going to be polite to you from now on."

"You remind me of Eddie Haskell," Patty says, moving away from Miles's hand. I laugh but nobody else does. *Leave It to Beaver* is my favourite show and Eddie Haskell is a slimeball.

Frances, of course, defends Miles because she likes him, "No, he doesn't. Not at all."

Patty looks at her directly and says, "Yes. He does."

Patty could tell I did not want to be there. She tugged at my arm. "Come on, Ana. Let's go. We don't want to hear their nonsense anymore."

She could just ignore the boys. I thought that was cool because I didn't know how to ignore them when they talked to me. Maybe it was because she had four older brothers?

I liked going over to Patty's house because they were all so sweet to me and we got to have hot dogs and Cokes for dinner.

Food that would never have been served at home on a regular school night. Patty and I would play Superman and Invisible Girl until it was dark out, and I had to go home. She was always Superman, and I was always Invisible Girl because I always felt invisible as a kid and if I made it a superpower it made me feel pretty good. We would put on old towels, and play for hours and hours, saving the world from bad guys, and flying over rivers and streams. Then when it was time to go, her dad would go out to their garden and pick some tomatoes and give them to me. One time he said, "It ain't been a great summer for tomatoes, but these aren't too bad."

I said, "*Ain't* ain't in the dictionary," because I had heard our teacher Mrs. Opal say that to Charlie Mcleod. I saw him flinch when I said that, but he didn't scold me, he was too nice a dad. I still feel a lot of shame about that moment, but I never told it at Saturday confession. I couldn't put it into words.

One of the things I looked up to Patty for was that though she played the Superman and Invisible Girl game with as much childish passion as I did, she was mature for her age. She was more like fifteen than nine. When it was five o'clock, she always went in for supper, and told me, nicely, that I had better get home so my mother wouldn't worry. When I stayed for dinner, I noticed that she helped her mom with the dishes and put her little brothers to bed by herself. She was never late for school, and she always had her homework done. I would sometimes copy her math homework because I found math so hard. She wasn't reckless, like the rest of us, or irresponsible. The rest of us somehow knew that no matter what we did in school our lives would be pretty good because of our parents. Patty didn't have that.

She takes my hand, which is clammy, whereas her hands are warm and dry the way they should be on a summer's day. I can see Frances is jealous.

"Come on, Ana, let's get out of here. You said we could go for a swim in your pool. Remember, I'm a YMCA Dolphin! I brought my bathing suit! Wanna see it? It's a two piece!"

That is my chance.

I stand up, looking only at Patty. To look at anyone else is danger.

"Yeah, the pool is nice and cool. We can even bring popsicles in!"

"Well, come on then! It's hotter than heck on this driveway!"

Something inside me tries to will myself to move and break through the spell I am under, but when I catch Frances's eye that is it. I can't. I cannot go against her.

"I have to stay here for now, Patty."

Frances fake-smiles at Patty. "Go on Patty, go give that bag to Ana's mother. She'll love it."

"Why do you have to stay here, Ana?" Patty eyes Miles and Bernie, understanding fully what I have only the faintest glimmer of.

Frances hisses, "Because she promised me, okay? She's my best friend so she has to keep her promises to me."

I feel sick about Frances saying we are best friends, even though it is sort of true. Well true and not true. Can you be best friends with someone you are afraid of? And when you have another, secret best friend? She was trying to push Patty away. What I knew deep inside was that Patty was a truer friend than Frances.

I almost go with her. I almost do it. I start to move.

"No, Ana."

Then we are quiet for a long, long time. I see Miles whisper to Bernard. I feel like I am trying to untie a really bad tangle, like when Frances put gum in my hair. One look from Frances and I just give up. I give up on the knot.

Patty looks at me with such hope.

"Sorry, Patty. I'll come in a bit."

"Well, I'm not going to your party by myself."

"Why, you scared?" asks Frances with that fake smile again.

"No. I just think Ana should come with me." Patty seems so grown-up.

Frances moves closer to Patty, in a kind of a threatening way. "Patty, what is the problem with going by yourself?"

"None of your beeswax, bitch."

Patty called Frances a *bitch*.

Miles and Bernie whoop in high-pitched voices.

"Oooooh, shit! Patty, wash your mouth out with soap, girl!"

Patty turns her face to them.

"I don't have to."

Patty wasn't afraid of them or of Frances, or any of the mean kids at school. That fearlessness was one of the main reasons I was her friend, along with how much fun we had playing our games, and how she actually listened to me and didn't call me stupid, the way Frances did. Also, there was the matter of me hoping to one day be named a saint by the Holy Pontiff. I understood that you had to be kind to the poor to be named a saint. It made me feel like St. Theresa. Like my soul was washed of any sins such as spitting out my mother's pork chops or being mean to Paulie. Clean and creamy with no smears. Sister Sebastian was reading us a book called *Lives of the Saints* in Catechism and I thought maybe one day I could be in that book for being Patty Wissy's friend.

"Patty? Come on, sit next to me."

She has a worried look on her face.

Frances orders her. "Just sit."

Miles looks at Bernie and nods. "Three little cuties."

Bernie laughs like a girl. "Three dollies are better than two dollies."

Frances pretends to be outraged.

"We are not dollies. Like Patty said. We are girls. Got it? Got it, assholes?"

All I think about at this point is how broiling hot it is, so hot I can see actual waves of heat in the air. My mouth is so dry. I want some cold grape Kool-Aid.

Patty looks right at the boys and says, "Who do you think you are, anyway?"

Miles thinks he's witty. "Gee I don't know. Who are we, Bernie? Do you know who we are?"

Bernie's voice is low now. "Beats me. Just a couple of horny toads."

I had no idea what it meant at the time. Neither did Frances. But I think Patty did.

She rolls her eyes at me, and whispers, "Don't pay no attention to them."

I don't correct her grammar this time. I smile and shrug.

Frances makes a face to the boys. "Patty is not cool."

Patty is blunt. "I don't like them."

Miles and Bernie laugh a fake laugh again. "Little Patty, that is rude."

"So rude for such a pretty little thing."

"I am not a thing and I'm not pretty."

Bernie slaps his hairy thighs. "Whoaaaa!"

Miles sounds like he has milk in his voice. "I think you're pretty."

Patty sounds like a teacher. "I think something funny's going on here and I don't like it."

Miles nods and looks at Bernie whose smile is suddenly so wide it shows all his sharp teeth.

One time, a bunch of us were lying on Frances's bed and she said that her sister told her that you wouldn't be a little kid anymore if you stuck a bobby pin in your down there. I did not want to do that, but she was the boss. We all sort of tried it. Me and Laura Sefera and Cathy Diamond and Francine Pinel and Joanie Curtain. It didn't feel good. It felt strange. Cathy Diamond had white-blond hair, which Frances said meant she was an albino. Her dad was a mathematics professor. She had two brothers and two sisters, and they all had that same almost white-blond hair. They weren't at Paulie's birthday party because my mom said they were "the most boring people on the planet." Cathy's hair was the most beautiful I had ever seen, but Frances was mean because really, she was jealous.

"What's it like being an albino?" said Frances, narrowing her eyes into slits.

"I'm not an albino."

"Yes, you are. For sure you are."

For some reason, Cathy's almost white-blond hair made Frances very angry. Cathy liked to say her hair was Marilyn Monroe–blond except hers wasn't bleached and it went down to the middle of her back in braids with a blue ribbon. On another day, before the bobby pin day, when we were all in Frances's bedroom after school, Frances ordered Cathy to cut her hair. She told me to go down and get the scissors from the kitchen drawer. Her mother was not in the kitchen, so I got them and brought them back up. I gave them to Frances, and she handed them to Cathy and said, "Cut." Cathy shook her head. "Nope. My mom would kill me."

Frances smiled a really mean smile. "If you want to stay our friend, just cut it. It will look way better." So, Cathy did; she cut just a tiny bit. Frances demanded more, and so she cut more. Frances said "more" again. Cathy cried but then Frances's mother, Cora, walked right in and said, "Cathy, your mom is here for you."

She noticed the scissors. "What are you kids doing with those scissors?"

Frances was not scared of her mother one bit. "Nothing. Cathy wanted us to cut her bangs, but I said no because we are not trained hairdressers."

"Good Lord. Cathy, you get your mom to cut your bangs if they're bothering you. The last person you want to come near your eyes with scissors is my Frances. She is accident-prone, to say the least."

That did hurt Frances's feelings. "I am not, Mommy."

"Oh, dear, you most certainly are."

I could hear Cathy's mom talking to Frances's dad downstairs. I had a feeling she was going to be very mad at Frances when Cathy told her the truth. Frances had this way of making parents mad. My dad got really mad at Frances one time when we watched *The Song of Bernadette* on TV. I was enraptured and I felt like I was inside Bernadette, especially when she saw the Virgin Mary and actually spoke to her. Even my parents cried at the part where Bernadette is dying of tuberculosis, and she has those sores all over her legs. She can hardly walk, she's in the worst pain, and nobody believes her. Frances said, "Bernadette is crazy, and a liar too! Hey, you guys don't believe her, do you? You don't believe she actually saw the Virgin Mary? Ha hahahahahaha," she exploded with her fake laughter.

My dad got up from the couch. "Okay, young lady, you're leaving, and you're leaving now." He pulled her by her shoulders and frogmarched her to the door. "Go home."

"Dad!" I shouted in fake outrage, but really, I was happy.

My mom said that Frances had a "mean streak." Her older sister, Lori, had one too.

I was even more scared of Lori than I was of Frances. Frances and Lori were crazy jealous of Bernice Wissy, Patty's older sister, because the boys liked Bernice because she already had breasts.

She was about twelve or even thirteen and she had a really pretty face with round brown eyes and pink cheeks. She had even started her period. Lori and Frances would talk about how poor she was and how she smelled, although she definitely did not smell. So it was really unexpected when Lori brought her home from school one day. She was three whole years older and she hated us. But this time she brought Bernice into Frances's bedroom. Frances and me and Ruthie and Francine were lying over the twin beds with pink bedspreads talking about our dream dates.

"Hey, what are you idiots doing?"

Lori and Bernice were standing in the doorway.

"We're coming in, so make room."

Lori launched herself onto the bed Frances was lying on.

"Hey, get off my bed."

"Make me." Lori was the only person in the world Frances was scared of. Bernice stood against the wall, not sure what to do. I noticed she had one foot overtop of the other. I had a very strong feeling that Lori was going to do something mean. It was because of her face and her voice, and Frances's too.

For a while, we all just lay around talking about various teachers, and other kids at the school. Suddenly Bernice looked at the time and said, "Uh oh, it's near six. I have to get home and make supper for the kids. Mama's going to work at the hospital for seven. Thanks for having me, Lori, it was really nice." She headed for the door.

Before she could get there, Lori got to it.

"You can't go till you pay the toll."

Bernice pretended to giggle. "But Lori, I really do have to go. I'm going to catch hell if I don't."

"Did you not hear me? I said you have to pay the toll. Right, girls?"

Frances yelled out, "Damned right." The rest of us, me and Ruthie and Francine, we were frozen. I think we were hoping against hope that Lori was joking, just like Bernice was.

"Everyone who comes to this house has to pay the toll."

"I am sorry, I don't even have a nickel."

"I'm not talking about money."

We all looked at Bernice at that point and from her face turning red, I think she knew. She knew that it was something not nice at all that Lori was asking her to do.

"I'm talking about taking your top off."

"Oh, no, I don't think so, I really do have to go." Her hand went for the doorknob and Lori slapped her hand over Bernice's.

"You do not leave until you have my permission."

I could hardly breathe. I felt embarrassed for Bernice, but I was too scared to say anything, in case Lori turned on me, and made me take my top off. I just didn't know how to stop it. The truth is, I was curious too. I was curious as to what Bernice would do. I looked at her face.

Her face was deep red. Her eyes looked even bluer than before.

"Lori. Please, let me pass."

I could hear Bernice's breathing.

"Take the top off. Unless you want me to take it off for you. Francie? Come here, help me."

Frances looked at me. She knew if she didn't do what Lori said she would be beaten up while she was sleeping or have maple syrup poured all over her. Bernice stepped away from the door and began to unbutton her blouse. I held my breath. I wished this wasn't happening. I wanted to be home, with Paulie, playing with Barbies. I wanted Mom to make us sandwiches with butter and hundreds and thousands sprinkled all over them. Hundreds and thousands were Mom's words for coloured sprinkles.

"Nice bra, Bernice. Now take it off."

"Please, please don't make me do that. Please?"

"What do you think, girls? Should she take off her bra?"

We didn't say anything. We couldn't. Even Frances was quiet.

"They all want you to take it off, Bernice. Why do you think I invited you over? You don't think I invited you because we're friends, do you?"

"I don't know."

"Gee, I guess you don't know much of anything. Do you?"

"No."

"Take the fucking bra off."

I really, really wished it wasn't happening. Especially because she was Patty's sister. But I was, I admit, just a tiny bit curious to see her breasts. At the same time, the fact that she looked so sad while she showed us made me feel a rock in my throat. But I still didn't say anything or try to leave the room.

I don't remember how Bernice got out. But I remember everyone laughing about her after. I remember joining in.

MILES PACES BACK and forth on the driveway. He now has a whine in his voice. "Come on, let's go to the attic. Now. It's too hot sitting here."

I tell him it's way hotter in the attic room.

"Nah, there's a window. I can see it! Anyway, it has to be cool, it's your secret clubhouse, right? For your Daredevil Club!"

"I'm not allowed up there. It's dangerous."

Patty is on my side. "Did you hear her? She said she's not allowed up there."

Miles puts his arm around Frances and says that breaking the rules is fun. Bernie asks, "Don't you want to have fun?"

The garage is not a good place because the upstairs of it, the attic, is dusty and hot with nails sticking out of the floor and garbage all over. I don't know why they want to go up there, but the feeling in my stomach is bad.

I know from the thickness in Miles's voice and the way his eyes look and the way both boys smell like burnt mushrooms that something very not good is in their heads about what is going to happen in that attic.

Frances moves away from Miles and looks him right in the eye. "Doctor? Do you guys mean doctor? We're not playing that."

I was relieved. Frances wouldn't make us go if it was doctor.

"Doctor? What? That's for kids. You're not kids, are you?" answers Miles, looking at Bernard the whole time.

I don't move. Frances walks towards me. "If you don't come with me, we are not best friends anymore. Joni Gracielle has been asking to be my best friend, so she will be my new best friend, and you will be out. Nobody will be your friend."

JONI GRACIELLE WAS a tiny girl from our third-grade class with deep circles under her brown eyes and pointy elbows. It was rumoured that her mother was a prostitute. She was obsessed with Frances and so she had us both over to her apartment one day after school and we made Pillsbury apple popovers and Joni kept cleaning everything we touched. I think her mother was still asleep because Joni kept shushing us. We talked about that for days and told everyone in the class that Joni's mother was asleep at four o'clock in the afternoon. When I drank a glass of milk, as soon as I was finished, she grabbed the glass and cleaned it in the sink, by pouring dishwashing liquid straight in and pouring hot water over it. Then she dried it with a dishtowel and put it away in the cupboard.

Frances laughed really hard. "Joni, why are you cleaning everything? Are you gonna get in trouble for having us over?"

"No, I like cleaning, that's all. I love cleaning."

"DON'T LISTEN TO her about that best friend foolishness. She's just bluffing," says Patty with a loud, even bossy voice. I can tell by Frances's eyes that she is impressed by that.

Miles shakes his head. "The three of you are babies. This is boring. Let's go, Bernie. Let's go swimming."

"Wait." Bernie holds his hand up. "Not yet."

"I'm tired of this. Come on."

"Wait, man." Bernie looks scared.

Miles sighs and sits down on the sharp gravel, too close to Frances.

"All right. Five minutes."

"What are you, stupid? I said we were coming." Frances gets up to her feet and reaches her hand out for me. I reach my hand out too and let her pull me up. Miles and Bernie look at each other, nodding their heads, eyes on fire.

Frances would have known something wasn't right, because she would have picked up on the strange combination of heat and awkwardness coming out of their words. She couldn't have missed that. But something else made her think it was going to be fun. Maybe she liked the sense of danger?

"Frances says yes! You are the coolest, Frances. See Ana? Patty? It's gonna be fun. Promise. Come on, girls, let's go on up to the clubhouse. To play cool games! After all, you're the Daredevils!"

Patty stands apart from us. "They are trying to trick you. I'm telling you. I've heard it before."

We all look at Patty and then look away.

Suddenly, somehow, it seemed like even Patty had agreed to go up. I don't know how it happened. It was like when we played tug-of-war at picnics and our side would be tugging and tugging at that rope, and really doing well, and all leaning back and suddenly, for no reason, the other side would win and we would all be lying in the dirt, face down. Frances won, she beat me, she beat both of us. But really, the boys won. Frances pretended she was the power, but she was a kid.

"So. Girls. You have to promise us something."

"Maybe," says Frances, still playing tough.

Miles asks us if we can keep a secret, and Frances says, "Yeah, of course!" I gasp, because the truth is that she never keeps anyone's secrets — she always tells. I'm the same, I have never kept a secret, even when I have sworn not to tell. Miles looks at me about the secret-keeping and I shrug because I am not sure what to say. Now Bernie squints his eyes and asks, "Cross your hearts and hope to die?"

Patty says, "I'm not crossing nothing."

How did Patty know? She knew for sure, but I only had a feeling.

Had my mother warned me about Big Boys, and not going up into the attic, or the basement with them? She must have. I'm sure she did. Because I think this was the first time I had stood my ground against Frances. It must have been a promise to my mom, but I don't remember. Resisting Frances was like hanging from the monkey bars. You could only hang for so long, then eventually you couldn't hang anymore. Your arms just gave up.

I follow a few steps behind Frances and the boys, and Patty is right beside me. The gravel on the driveway hurts my bare feet.

I somehow feel safer because Patty is here.

As we walk to the garage, I see heat ripples in the air. They look like when the wind blows on a pond. It feels like they are getting closer and closer. Now it feels like the ripples are inside me.

Frances's voice is inside my chest. "Come on, slowpoke. What are you staring at? Uh oh, are you having one of your fits? She's having one of her fits."

I want to say, "No, I'm looking at the ripples," but for some reason I can't. I can't because what I am staring at is hard to make out because the light is dazzling, but it's the Blessed Virgin Mary. She's floating in front of me with a shimmering halo around her whole self like the way she appeared to Bernadette at Lourdes, exactly like the statue in the church, with her blue and white robes, her hands held out beckoning me. "Come, little one, away from all this, come to heaven with me."

I want more than anything to take her hand, but I can't move. I can't see, except for the dazzle. I can't speak. I can't make a sound.

I hear Patty say, "Leave her alone, could be an absent seizure. My brother has them."

Frances's voice pierces, "What are you doing, Ana? Talking to Jesus?" She looks at Miles. "She ate Jesus's penis last Sunday."

"Oh yeah? What did it taste like?"

They laugh, a weird, high-pitched laugh.

"You are all rude and ignorant." Patty's voice.

Miles's family were atheists, just like Frances's family, because they were *intelligentsia*. That's the word my dad used, and that made my mom mad because, she said, "Darling we are the intelligentsia too." I guess that is true. We have about a thousand books in the house. My parents are always talking philosophy and politics with us, but we do believe in God, and everything Catholic except the part about animals don't go to heaven and babies get stuck in purgatory. The whole concept of purgatory, like a weird waiting room. And I don't understand how women can't be priests. I once asked Ruthie, when we were about ten, about that part in the Mass where it says the Jews killed Our Lord. She shook her head. "Don't you realize how stupid that is?"

"But it was Jews, wasn't it?" Then she told me something I had never known, "Jesus Christ was a Jew."

"What?? Wasn't he a Christian?"

That was the only time Ruthie laughed at me.

"Christianity is named after Jesus's last name. And we don't really know anything about the mob who hung Jesus on the cross!"

Frances shakes me.

"Come on, what is the matter with you? Shake out of it. You look like a zombie."

"What the fuck is she looking at?" Bernie sounds mean, even meaner than before.

Patty stamps her foot and tells him to never talk to her friend like that.

Frances slaps me, hard, on the cheek. It stings and echoes in my face.

"Snap out of it, Ana."

Patty pushes Frances away from me.

"Hey! You do not ever touch a person having a space-out. Do you understand?"

My teeth are chattering as if it is cold out, even though it is so hot. I am starting to see everything around me again though it's blurry.

Frances goes right up in Patty's face. "You don't know anything, welfare girl."

Patty flinches at the word *welfare.*

"I do know that. My brother Gordon is epileptic."

Miles and Bernie surround us.

"Come on, girlies. Stop your cute bickering. We are gonna give you the best time ever."

They both start pulling at our hands. Miles pulls at Frances's hand, which makes her giggle in a totally phony way, and Bernie pulls at mine with his hot, fat, sweaty hand. I hate him.

Everything is suddenly loud and ugly and the gravel cuts into my feet. My head feels like there is a dirty towel in it. We climb the old wooden ladder to the attic.

Patty Wissy lingers on the driveway, arms crossed. I look back at her. She lets out a big sigh and runs to catch up.

IT MAKES NO sense that I am so sleepy, that I cannot bring myself to sit up, to throw this blanket off. I wonder if I double-dosed the LSD — the Windowpane Matthieu had with him? He was laughing and saying, "Baby, it's just like being on a sailboat, this acid is a nice trip." I don't know if it's nice, but it is a trip. This being in three minds: the mind of the mustard flower lady, the mind of myself when I was nine, climbing up those splintery stairs into the attic, and the mind of me, here, now. Mr. Taylor, our grade twelve physics teacher, with the cute dimples, told us that there is a real thing that people in the physics world take very seriously, and it is called quantum physics; quantum physics means the *simultaneous existence of several worlds all in one world*. I remember writing that on the exam, in those exact words. Mr. Taylor explained that it was just like *The Lion, the Witch and the Wardrobe*. Those kids walked through the wardrobe and met Mr. Tumnus and went on that exciting but harrowing adventure, finally meeting Aslan the lion, who sacrificed himself to save Edmund from the White Witch. But when they walked back through the wardrobe, only five minutes had passed.

That is not exactly but sort of what is happening to me. Can't wait to tell Matthieu all about it.

I SEE DUST in the beam of light from the one broken window — thousands of little dust particles. Frances and I stand together, leaning against the broken window, and Patty sits right near the ladder. Her eyes are big and round and waiting. Her arms are crossed. Her feet are really close together. She is wearing her best black patent leather shoes. So shiny.

Miles and Bernie whisper. My knees start to shake, I don't know why. I look at Frances.

"So, what now?" she asks, pretending to be tough but I can tell she's scared. This is the first time I have ever seen her scared.

Miles steps towards Frances, and looking right at her, he says, "Now you take your clothes off." His voice shakes in the strangest way.

"I thought we weren't going to play doctor," says Frances in a weird, high voice.

Pause. Silence.

"I don't like where this is going," Patty says quite loudly.

Miles glares at her. "Why don't you leave then?"

"I'm here for Ana and you can't make me go."

Miles stares at Frances. "Did you hear me?" His voice still shakes.

"All our clothes?" Frances says this in a kind of sassy way, but her voice is shaking too, so it doesn't work.

"All your clothes."

Frances asks why in the smallest voice ever. I cannot believe how small her voice got. It is like she is a Chatty Cathy when the battery is dying.

"Because Frances is always flirting with me and it's driving me crazy."

"Take your clothes off," says Bernie. He said close like the opposite of open. "And hurry up about it."

Patty says, "No. I'm not doing that."

"That's fine," says Miles. "You can fold the clothes, keep a lookout."

"Not doing that," says Patty, with a strong voice. "I'm just here to make sure my friend is okay."

I pull off my sunset-coloured T-shirt and my white undershirt slowly. Bernard watches, his eyes like the eyes of the white snake, his breathing weird. He pulls my soft blue shorts down and says, "Now underpants." I don't want to. My hands shake so hard, I can hardly move the underpants.

Tears roll down my cheeks. I taste them. I can't move.

"Such a crybaby," says Frances.

Patty says we don't have to do anything the boys tell us to.

"Oh, yes, they do, they have to do everything we tell 'em to," says Bernie. He holds up his hand like he is going to hit me.

"Or else we'll tell their moms and dads."

Looking back, this didn't make any sense, but it scared me so much at the time I was convinced we had to do whatever they wanted.

My mom and dad could never ever know that I had taken my T-shirt off, that I was standing with my bare chest in front of two older boys. I think Frances felt the same. The way I got through it was I pretended to myself I was getting changed into a bathing suit. I pretended I was in the bathroom — that nobody was looking at me by looking down at the dirty floor of the attic the whole time.

Now we stand in front of them, naked. They're staring at us. Patty looks out the broken window and sighs like she knew that this was going to happen. Like she had been in this position before.

Miles says that he will take Frances and Bernie can take me.

I think Miles liked Frances, even though she was only eight and he was fourteen.

Bernie walks towards me. I don't take my eyes off the floor. My feet are shaking. I feel like I've forgotten how to stand.

"Ana, you don't have to do this, you know." Patty's voice is like a breeze rushing over me. I can't answer her. I'm in it now.

I remember in Catechism I promised Sister Patrick I was going to be a nun when I grew up. She was so happy she clapped her hands and said, "Wonderful!" Now I would never be a nun because I was committing a mortal sin.

"Lie down on your towel."

They have already put down two of our striped beach towels, one for me and one for Frances. They are our beach towels — my mother must have given them to them 'cause she thought they were going to swim in the pool. Those beach towels made me think of our family and times at Hammonasset Beach and singing in the car and now I had to lie down naked on one. Frances lies down first. I follow.

Miles and Bernie both take off their shirts. We are lying there, waiting. I hear my own breathing, and Frances's.

We both know now that there was no game.

Bernie is lying on top of me. He is so heavy I can't breathe. Then he starts moving around. What is he doing? I feel a sharp rock in his pants. I want him to stop moving around. I make kinda little "no" sounds and try to move him off me, then it feels like all the blood in my body is pooling near the floor. I try to listen for Our Lady, but I can't hear her and I can't see her because they told us to shut our eyes tight. I try to see her from behind my eyes, but he keeps moving. I'm going to throw up. Our Lady isn't there. She isn't coming.

"What the fuck?" Bernie bellowed. "Stop that!"

He reaches around and slaps my face.

"Don't slap her, you stupid, she is having a fit. This time it's a grand mal fit too. She'll likely wet herself. And it could be dangerous," Patty says like a teacher.

Bernie slaps me again, harder. "Fucking stop it!"

"No! You don't do that! Stop it. Stop it!" screams Patty, rushing up to us. Bernie turns to her, like she was an epilepsy doctor.

"What the fuck is she doing? Tell her to stop."

"She can't help it. She is epileptic. Just leave her alone." Patty sounded not as strong now, like she was tired.

"Why does she sound like a pig?" Bernie asks. Patty says, "Just shut your mouth. You don't know what you are talking about. She's trying to get air because they don't breathe in a fit. Just be quiet."

Bernie hisses, "Little bitch."

"Fuck this. She peed herself. What do we do? She keeps jerking. Shit, man."

And this next thing, coming from Bernie. "Hey I know, we could both do it to her. She won't even know, right?"

Miles puts his hand over Bernie's mouth.

I am awake now. I smell danger. I hear a screeching. I don't know where it comes from. I look over at Frances. She doesn't look right. Her breathing is high and fast.

Miles says, "No. Nah. We could get in bad trouble for that."

"Not if they can't tell, man."

Miles's eyes go sideways, like he is thinking. A pause, as if they are both on the edge of a diving board about to dive into water, only we are the water.

THIS IS SO crazy. I'm in the attic in Middletown and at the very same time I am lying on this field of mustard flowers, outside of Kingston, stoned on Windowpane acid. You are on that old rusty bike, maybe, biking towards me again. Is this what Mr. Taylor said was the law of eternal return? Time is a kind of loop? That blows my mind, because I always just think of it moving forward — even though we generally remember certain moments we don't relive them, like I am, except maybe in dreams. And that is what is happening now, only it feels more vivid, more present than any dream I have ever had.

The way Mr. Taylor explained it, it would mean one life would be that I did go back to the party with Patty, and then Frances followed, so nothing happened. I like that one. Another might be that they did what Bernie suggested. They did that and we screamed so loud that they strangled us so we wouldn't tell. In that life, the boys think we're dead already so they've taken off, they're running as far away as they can get, or maybe they went back to the cookout, pretending that they'd just gone to the corner store. Frances and I are lying there, dying, but Frances, she's breathing, she's coming back to life — it's only me who dies. And while I lie there, dying, I am imagining the next few years, imagining I am seventeen and I was on a date with a handsome boy and we kissed and everything was so beautiful. We dropped acid — or in my little girl's mind, had a sip of beer — and decided to spend the evening on the field, looking at the stars, but he couldn't stay. Maybe she is imagining me. And within her imagining me, I am imagining the lady who picked the mustard flowers. Although I am pretty sure she is real. Imaginary people don't ride rusty bicycles and pick mustard flowers. Maybe she is imagining me because it is unimaginable for her to die, when she is only nine. I read somewhere that kids cannot conceive of their own deaths. I love the idea that I'm imaginary. I know I'm real though, not just because of the night air on my face, or my wet bum, but because my cramps are starting. That means I'm gonna get my period tomorrow. And that is real.

Why can't I hear anything from Frances? This was the first time ever that she didn't have an opinion on something. I heard only her breathing, a breathing I knew so well from all the sleepovers we had had since we were two. But this time her breathing has catches to it. I wasn't sure what that meant.

I TAKE A big breath in. My head feels like someone is playing a tennis game inside it: thwack, thwack, double thwack.

I feel like vomiting, but I don't.

Patty kneels beside me.

"Are you okay now? Are you over your spell?"

"I think so."

Then she asks me my name and address, just like a nurse would. I give both to her, clear and fast, to prove I haven't gone retarded from my seizure.

"Who is the President of the United States?"

"John F. Kennedy. JFK!"

Patty helps me with my clothes.

"You're okay. Now let's go see your mom."

Bernie is pacing. Something isn't finished. Miles nudges him.

"I'm out."

He keeps pacing, staring at Patty with hate.

Patty looks up at them. "You guys are gonna get in trouble."

"Why? Is somebody gonna tell? Is somebody gonna fucking tell?"

Frances speaks for the first time since it all started, "Not me. Don't worry, I won't tell."

Frances's voice is shaking. I'd never ever heard her shaken like that. She is dressed already. She dresses so fast. "Do you promise, Ana? Do you promise not to ever ever tell?"

I cross my fingers behind my back just in case because to tell a lie is venial sin, and I don't know if one day, somehow, I just might tell someone, especially my mom.

"Yes."

"See? She won't, I told you. She does whatever I say. Don't worry, guys, we all promise. You don't have to worry. It's cool."

And then Patty says, "Well, I don't promise. You boys are going to catch hell."

They both look at her, and then they look at each other.

"What? What did you just say, white trash?"

"I said I am going to tell the police what you did and you will both go to jail."

The boys look at each other, nod, and Patty runs across the attic like she expects them to chase her. Then she flies. She actually flies. I see Patty dissolve into blue wind and a sort of dazzle. She flies across the room and out of the crack in the broken window. She disappears. Was that just the end of my epileptic fit? I don't think so because I'm totally out of it now. I jump to my feet, and I run to the window and look down. Patty is whole again, flying over the long grasses of Crow's Field using her long arms like wings, the way I do in my dreams.

Miles and Bernie jump down the ladder, two rungs at a time, cursing.

I see Patty disappear into the woods on the other side of Crow's Field. Miles and Bernie run after her, still cursing. They all disappear into the woods.

"Patty, you're going the wrong way! Patty! Just go to our backyard. My mom is there! Patty! Just go in our backyard!"

"No," Frances says. "No. She'll tell everyone, and we'll be in trouble."

No, she wouldn't, I think, because she's too shy around grown-ups. Especially our parents.

"Patty!" I scream as loud as I can but all that comes out is a croak. Patty doesn't look back. All I see is the back of her sky-blue dress and snow-white ankle socks disappearing into the woods.

Frances comes to the window. We look out through the smudgy broken glass.

"Well, she's gone now," Frances says in a confident voice like what happened hadn't even happened.

I'm wondering if Patty can outrun those big boys. I am trying to remember running races from school, but my thoughts are somersaulting over each other. Nothing is clear.

Frances gives me the stink-eye and demands again that I promise I won't tell my mom.

"If you tell, we will all be in trouble. Big trouble."

I look at her to see if I can tell what she's thinking. She whispers with a bit of cry in her whisper, "For being up here where kids come to smoke and drink their parents' stolen beer. For doing dirty things with older boys."

I look at the dusty floor, littered with cigarette butts and tools and old candy wrappers.

"Yeah."

She puts her hand on my face, as if to cover my mouth so I won't say anymore.

"Miles and Bernie would be so mad at us for getting them in trouble they might kill us. Get it?" Frances is trembling like when kids get out of the pool after swim lessons and their whole bodies shiver. So am I.

"They might?"

"Miles said. Didn't you hear that?" We both tremble and gaze out the smudgy window, seeing hardly anything.

I very quietly ask Frances what it was that Miles did to her.

Frances mumbles that it doesn't matter. Then she asks me what Bernie did to me. I interrupt her and say the same thing, that it doesn't matter. I'm not entirely sure. The details swirl away the way a dream does when you wake up.

She says I have to tell her, and asks me if he did it to me and made me have that second fit, the big one?

I can't answer her, because I can't speak, my teeth are chattering so much I think they will break. Then Frances makes me promise again that I will never tell. Fool that I am, I promise. Then she asks me to double promise, and I double promise. Then she tells me I am her best friend in the world, and for the first time I am not grateful that she said that.

We won't discuss what has happened for a long, long time.

WE JUMP DOWN the ladder, without even stepping on any of the rungs; we jump to the floor of the garage and the *thunk* goes right through my body but it feels good to distract my body from other feelings. Frances runs down the hill to where our cookout is, yelling for her mom.

I run the other way, into Crow's Field to see if I can see Patty.

I don't know why she's run the wrong way. I run and the long grasses sweep against my legs. I don't see Patty and I don't see Miles and I don't see Bernie. The woods are empty, and the only sound is the crickets and one woodpecker in the magnolia tree.

I think he is warning me. I hear my mother calling for me. "Ana! Anaroooohoo!"

My privates are hurting so bad — a hurt I never felt before, a throbbing like a splinter but a thousand times worse. I take another step into the woods, and I keep walking even though I have always been scared of the woods beyond Crow's Field. It is so quiet. A branch scrapes my arm, and it bleeds. I get through the woods and on the other side of the bushes, there is the river. The Connecticut River. We are not allowed to go to the river by ourselves, not ever. Especially ever since Wanda told us that story about the black panther that lived down there and would eat kids who went down to the riverbank. Even though I knew it was a lie, part of me thought it might be true. The river is not pretty, it's muddy brown and it flows way too fast for swimming. Mom and Dad said we could never ever, ever swim in there, because the current would drown us.

Sometimes there would be stories in the newspaper of dogs drowned in the Connecticut River and once, even, a kid from Hartford. I am looking for Patty, but I can't see her, just the river. Suddenly I hear, "You fuck right off. Get away from me!"

Patty's voice!

She's by the birches, and Bernie has his hairy arm around her neck. "You don't say a word, girlie, about what you saw. Right? You are gonna keep your big, welfare mouth shut."

I can still taste his disgusting breath with every breath I take; it smelled like when you go to the bathroom at the beach and the person before you took a big poo. I didn't get that taste out for a long, long time.

Hiding in the fir tree I whisper, "Get away from her, please! Just get away from her!" I pray to the Virgin Mary to intercede for Patty, to tell God to please let Patty fly away, the way she flew out of the attic.

Patty spits out her words. "You can't tell me what to do. Now get away from me. Git."

"Promise you won't tell." Bernie grabs her arm, hard.

She lets out a little shriek.

"Hey, stop running. We don't want to hurt you. We just want you to promise."

"I'm not promising nothing. Get off me. I'll get my brothers after you, they will mess you up good."

Bernie jumps on her so hard they both fall to the ground.

"Get the fuck off me!" she screams. My heart is racing so fast I think I might die.

Miles says, "Let's just go, Bernie. Fuck, man." Patty and Bernie look like a cartoon fight, rolling around and around. He is holding her dress, the skirt part of her dress, and she is trying to get away. She pulls so hard the bottom part of it rips right off.

She screams and I see her look around with this face of fear and then she looks to the river, and I see her make a choice and the choice is to swim and then she dives into the river! I cry out, "No, no. We're not supposed to." But there is no power in my voice.

I remember that Patty is a very good swimmer. At the YMCA camp we both went to, she was a Dolphin Plus; that's two levels above a Minnow, which is what I was. Her arms look so strong in the Connecticut River. I imagine that she has turned into Superman, the way she does when we play Superman and Invisible Girl. She is super-strong, and she is getting away from them. Miles and Bernie are standing on the riverbank looking at each other.

"Come back here, girlie, we're not gonna hurt you."

Bernie is wading in.

"What are you doing, Bernie?"

He reaches into the water and grabs her wrist. "Get off me!" she shouts. Her voice is strong.

"You missed out on all the fun, sexy girl. We could have that fun now, instead of you drowning."

"Let go of me you bastard."

He pulls her to shore, but still in the water, where the water was just up to his ankles, but up to her knees. He is doing something over her, and I can't see her.

No! No! No!

I don't dare move.

She is screaming but in gulps.

"Agh. You bastard. I'll kill you, you bastard, my brothers will cut off your prick, you scum! Fuck you!"

Patty gets loose from Bernie. I move just my head and yell in a whisper, "Yay, yay. Go, Patty, go. Go Dolphin!" She is swimming straight, trying to get to the other side. She is swimming strong and her arms look like the girl who won gold at the Olympics. *Go, Patty! Go, Patty!* Bernard is trying to wade out to grab her again. Miles is shaking his head

"No, no, man, you asshole, you fucking asshole, I don't even know you." Miles turns and is gone into the pines. I don't know where and the crows are angry. They are shrieking, "Caw caw caw." I see Patty's head and her dark blond hair is wet against her face, her long face. The river is moving her sideways, towards the rusted bridge, sweeping her the wrong way. It almost knocks Bernie over. I hope he drowns, but he stumbles up and then is swept down again and stumbles up again and makes it back to the bank. I see him running into the brambles. He disappears, so I come out from the fir trees and the lilac bushes.

"Patty," I say in a normal-sounding voice. I notice my feet are shaking. I am cold all over, even though it's July. My teeth chatter, chatter so much they bite through my lip and there's blood.

I see Patty's head near the bridge. I run; I run along the riverbank towards the bridge. Maybe I can save her, maybe I can.

The bridge, though, it's much farther away than it looks. It's maybe a mile away even though it doesn't look that far. Now I can't see Patty at all.

I stand still. I don't move, I don't breathe, I just pray. Why isn't Mary doing anything? Maybe I need to pray harder.

I pray again to the Virgin Mary to make the river bring her back this way, so I can catch her. *Hail Mary, full of grace, the Lord is with thee, blessed art thou amongst women, blessed is the fruit of thy womb, Jesus. Holy Mary, since you appeared to me before, maybe you could appear to Patty and hold your little hand out! Can you do that? Can you just do this one thing for me and I'll never, ever ask anything again! I'll say one hundred Hail Marys a night, I promise, I'll be so good I'll be perfect.* I look at the river, and it looks angry. No, not angry. It doesn't care either way, the river just doesn't care. I'm thinking maybe the river is really God, and God just really doesn't care. And I didn't even care if God or Mary or Jesus heard me think that.

I turn around. I have to get home. I have to get home to tell my mum and dad so maybe they can save Patty, or they can call the fire brigade or the lifeguards at the YMCA. They will save Patty. Yes, that's what I can do. There is still time, maybe. I run back through the trees and the bushes and I'm out of breath and more scraping from branches, more blood. I fall into Crow's Field.

I can't see, like I am an old lady going blind. Everything is blurry, either too close or too far.

The crows are louder. "CAW CAW CAW." I actually understand what they are saying. "SAVE ME SAVE ME SAVE ME." Is

Patty talking to me through the crows? My foot, and my privates are throbbing.

A long, very long and stripey yellow garter snake slides over my foot. It looks me in the eye, and its eyes are the eyes of Bernie, the black holes of Bernie. I remember the babysitter laying the snake beside me in the bed when I was little and me turning to cement.

I hear splashing. Is that Patty Wissy? Is that Patty Wissy trying to hold onto the bridge, trying not to drown? That means she is still alive, that means there is still time! I have to tell the grown-ups. I have to tell them now! My teeth still chatter like it's winter. I turn and run to the driveway, and I fall. My knee is bleeding from the gravel, but I get up and keep running across the gravel driveway with bare feet and down the hill to the cookout.

They all turn and look at me. Everyone except Frances, who is sitting on her mother's lap. She looks like she has been crying. Her mother is stroking her light brown hair with those golden streaks. Frances sometimes said she hated her mother, but really, she loved her. Sometimes she even called her Mommy.

My mommy said Frances only says she hates her mother because she is mad at Mrs. Kester for breaking her ankle. The story was that Frances's mom was walking home from one of our cocktail parties and she stepped in a gopher hole in Crow's Field and broke her ankle. "Like the oh-so-delicate branch of a tree. A hideous snap!" Frances's dad said about it. My mom said that Mrs. Kester was "drunk as a lord that night, I mean slurring her words drunk, making passes at every man. That talk of a gopher hole is a ludicrous lie. There was no hole, darling, she simply fell off the curb."

"For he's a jolly good fellow, for he's a jolly good fellow, for he's a jolly good fellow ... that nobody can deny." Mom is bringing the big blue cake out. The screen door slams behind her. I can't believe I missed putting the candles on the cake. I always do it. I have always been the one to put the candles on the cake and even to light them. I look over at Frances. She doesn't look at me at all. It is a big blue and white cake shaped like a teddy bear with Happy Birthday Paulie written on it in green icing. There are hundreds-and-thousands, what Mom calls coloured sprinkles, all over it. Paulie is holding his favourite stuffie, which is his doll named Happy. Happy has dirty fur all over and a big smile and kinda looks like a human boy turned into a stuffie. Paulie takes him everywhere.

After Paulie blows out the candles and makes a wish, everybody except me claps. While Paulie is cutting the cake, my mom grabs my hand and asks me where on earth have I been? I stare at the cake, as if the answer was there. I try to speak, even though I don't know what I am going to say.

Paulie laughs and says that he was not worried and asks if I want a piece of birthday cake.

"Do you want a piece of my cake, Adda?"

He says "Adda" because he has a cold.

I love birthday cake, but for the first time ever I don't feel like it. I can't talk because the air has gone out of my voice.

"Adda likes the corner piece!" says Paulie as he cuts me an enormous piece from the corner. He knows I like the blue roses and the green leaves made of icing.

I TOOK THE paper plate of cake. My hand shook so badly I dropped the plastic fork. I put the cake down on the picnic table. I knew I wouldn't be able to stomach a bite. There was something I needed to say. There was something I needed to tell everybody, but I couldn't remember what it was. I looked around at the guests, but they weren't looking at me, they were ooooing and ahhhing about the cake and how adorable Paulie was. No one at the party was worried about a nine-year-old girl not able to get out a sentence. I caught sight of Frances. She glared at me from her mother's lap. Her eyes were like butcher knives inside me. I ran into the house. I was not crying. I felt rocks in my head and a stick in my throat. I ran up the staircase to my room, to my bed with the dark red bedspread. I lay on the bedspread tasting the bitter red bedspread, praying to the Virgin Mary to please come and tell me. *Tell me something, tell me what to do, tell me what happened.* What had just happened? What did I see in the river? Was I even there? Did I hear Patty scream?

Did they do something to us? Did they? What did they do to us? Was it our fault? Was it my fault? Will I go to hell? My daddy is standing in the doorway to my bedroom.

"What's going on with you, kid?"

I couldn't answer him.

"Come on, you can tell me. What's going on?"

"I'm sorry."

He gave me a hug, and I smelled his Pall Mall cigarettes and his Brylcreem and could see all the dandruff on his shoulders, but I still loved him. I loved my daddy so much. He was the only person I felt really safe with. It didn't matter that he thunked me on the back of the head every now and then. When he moved away from me towards the door, I let out a sob that sounded like our cat D'Arcy when he's going to throw up.

"Ana? Is something on your mind?"

I wanted to tell him. I wanted to tell him and Mom so badly, more than I had ever wanted to tell them anything. But, just like Frances said, if I told Mom and Dad what happened in the attic, I would get in the worst trouble ever because we are not ever allowed up there. I promised my mom that I would never go up there. I crossed my heart and hoped to die, even. I broke my promise! My mom would know, she would just know that something dirty happened up there with those boys because my mom always knew when I was hiding something. If she told my father, I would die.

And then there was the promise I made to Frances, so the boys wouldn't come after us and kill us. That would be two broken promises, which is definitely a mortal sin. If you commit a mortal sin, you go to hell. You go straight to hell the minute you die and you burn forever.

After Dad closed my door, I waited for the Lady to come again. I waited for hours and hours, staring at the foot of my bed, praying, "Hail Mary, full of grace, the Lord is with Thee." I literally said one hundred Hail Marys, which is what Father Hanlan would have given me if I ever confessed. But the Virgin Mary didn't come.

Was she ashamed of me for being a coward? Too chicken to tell the truth? Too chicken to get help for Patty, to save her from drowning? I lay in bed and prayed for Our Lady to come back to me and tell me what to do, just like she told Bernadette of Lourdes what to do. I would dig in the dirt, like Bernadette, if she asked me. I would dig with my bare hands until there was water, and that water would be holy water that would make me and Frances clean again. But that didn't happen.

Once I realized that the Lady was not going to appear at the foot of my bed, I gave up hoping and I tried to go to sleep, but kept thinking that Wanda's white snake was there, under the covers. I was worried the snake would wait till I went to sleep, then wrap itself around my neck and squeeze me to death. I threw off my covers when I had that thought, but soon I was cold and needed them again.

Later that night, my mum and dad were cleaning up the mess from the party and talking about the other parents. Their voices woke me up.

"We are not inviting the Hobsons ever again. He actually said our house had the 'lived in' look. It was very rude of him to say, don't you think? Just because we have homemade bookcases and plants everywhere. And art, philistines simply don't understand art. And he couldn't keep his eyes off my cleavage. I wanted to say 'take your filthy eyes off my breasts or I'll knock your teeth so far down your throat you'll have to shit them out.'"

"Joanna!"

My father loved my mother's tendency to unique vulgarity, but he always feigned shock.

Our doorbell rang. It was a deep doorbell sound I could feel in my heart.

It rang again, followed by many knocks.

My dad hated it when people came to the door.

"Who the hell could that be?"

I looked out my window. It was Patty Wissy's dad. He was a short man with a brush cut and a ruddy face and a worn white T-shirt and eyes that looked like they were deep inside his face.

"Who is it? Coming!"

I opened my bedroom door so I could listen. No one could see me.

"Hullo there. I'm Jack Wissy, my daughter and your daughter Ana are friends over at Stillman School."

Patty's dad had a scratchy but loud voice, so I could hear him easily. My mom must have been nervous because I could barely hear her at all.

"Ahhh. Well, see, Patty, she was goin' to your cookout today. She was invited by your girl, Ana."

I felt like I couldn't breathe.

"She headed out about two, with a little brown paper bag of vegetables from our garden that her mother put together for youse. She promised she would be home by six, but it's past nine and we haven't seen her."

Patty's dad sounded like he was losing his voice. My mother's voice was all breathy and apologetic as she explained to him, almost like he was a child, that she had not seen Patty at our cookout, not at all, but she would ask me in the morning. I heard Mr. Wissy say, "If you could please just wake her up — my wife is worried sick."

MOM CALLS MY name from the bottom of the stairs. Slowly as possible, I walk to the top of them. My heart is pounding.

"Yes?"

"Come down here, sweetie. Your friend Patty's dad is here."

I climb down. I look up at Mr. Wissy. His face looks grey and stiff, like a mask.

"Hi, Mr. Wissy."

"Ana. Patty hasn't come home. She left the house around two today and she said she was comin' over here to a cookout. Verna gave her a bag of vegetables."

"Oh."

"To bring over. Did you see her?"

I can't get any words to come out of my mouth.

My mother says my name very sternly.

I can't look at Mr. Wissy in his eyes or at my mother so I looked out the window at the cars going by on High Street.

"No. I didn't see Patty."

"Ana, are you sure?"

I nod three times. My mother explained to Mr. Wissy that I was worried about Patty and that's why I was behaving strangely. "Kids. You know."

"Oh, yes," he replied. "I know kids." He looked at me again, searchingly.

"I had better get a move on, then, if you don't mind." He gave my mom a piece of lined paper on which he had written his name and number and Patty's name in big letters. "Just in case your girl remembers something."

After he left, my dad came into the front hall.

"She's likely at one of her other friends, for Christ's sake," said Dad, blowing smoke out of his nose. "All this hysteria."

Then there was a long silence. My dad opened the door and looked pointlessly up and down the street. My mom shook her head with her arms folded. Mr. Wissy was already at the end of the block, craning his head this way and that, stopping, starting, stopping again, as if Patty might be found between the houses on High Street.

When I went upstairs, I called Frances.

"Kester residence."

"Hello, may I please speak to Frances?"

"Yes, you may." It was her yucky father.

"Fraaaances. Telephone."

"Who is it?"

"Your friend Ana."

I didn't hear her response, but her dad came back to the phone after an extremely long wait.

"Sorry, Ana, Frances isn't feeling too well. She'll call you back tomorrow."

"Okay." I didn't have a good feeling about this, and I was right.

She didn't call the next day or the next or the next. I tried calling her every day for a week. Every day she refused to come to the phone.

My heel hurt so bad I could hardly walk. My privates hurt whenever I went pee.

When he saw me limping, my dad sat me down.

"You've got a splinter, kiddo." He fetched the tweezers and lit a match and burned them so they wouldn't have germs. He also got a needle from my mother's sewing kit, and then he held me down and dug the splinter out. I screamed and cried but once it was out, the throbbing and the pain were gone.

Frances and I didn't play together for the rest of the summer, and when school started in September, we didn't even look at each other, not once. I hung around with Francine Pinel and Ruthie for all of fifth and sixth grade. Frances hung around with Joni Gracielle and Cathy Rister and Joanie Curtain and some other stupid followers. Joni and Frances would walk arm-in-arm and sing songs from the Top Forty. Especially that dumb song "Goin' to the Chapel." I hated that song, especially when they sang it. They were not going to get married for a long, long time, so why were they singing it? When I walked by, they would look at each other and then laugh too hard. This went on for two years. If Ruthie was there with me, she would whisper, "Just ignore them. They are philistines." I asked my mother what *philistines* meant, and she told me it meant people with terrible manners. I liked that word. Ruthie knew a lot of big words. I was in awe of her vocabulary.

I did miss how Frances had a strong opinion about everything and how she always knew what to do, but I didn't miss the way she bossed me. Francine and Ruthie never bossed me, not even once. We would figure out what to do together, and we almost never disagreed. Mainly we made friendship bracelets and talked about the boys in our class and watched TV. After a while, I didn't miss anything about Frances.

Everybody talked about Patty Wissy and what could have happened to her. Somebody said she had moved to Hartford with her oldest sister, Jocelyn, who was twenty-five and already had three kids and worked as a waitress. Somebody else said they saw her getting an Almond Joy at the corner store. Michael Mayo said he saw her ghost in the schoolyard one Friday night, swinging on the swings. He said he went up real close and said her name, but she didn't respond; she just kept swinging. I told my dad and he said that Mike made up these stories because he was Irish and that's what the Irish did.

I believed that Michael Mayo really did see her. In fact, I knew he did. Especially later, when I started seeing her myself.

Her sisters Tammy, Carol, and Dawn and one little brother, Jimmy, still went to Stillman, but they avoided the other kids. At lunch and recess, they stuck together. When they saw me, they stared at me and then whispered. I thought that they somehow knew that I had lied to their dad, but they couldn't prove it.

After a while, it didn't seem like a lie. After a while, I wondered if the whole thing had even happened at all. I started thinking maybe it was a dream, and Patty wasn't there at all, and her going missing, that was just a coincidence.

I prayed every morning and every night that Patty would be found. On my knees by the side of my bed. There were handmade posters all over town, on trees, on lampposts, on streetlights, in the grocery store, and in the community centre, and in the church. The priest talked about her at Sunday Mass, in his sermon. Every time I heard her name, I went deep red and the splinter that wasn't even in my heel anymore would throb. I prayed to the Virgin Mary over and over and over, *Dearest Mother of God if you just please roll Patty out of the river and onto the banks and give her your sweet breath of life please please please*. But she did not appear. I don't think she heard my prayers. Not because she didn't know I was praying, but because I was a sinner, and she wanted nothing to do with me. I thought I would die without her.

When I started thinking too much about Patty and how the Virgin Mary hated me, I had to stay home. I told my parents I was sick, that I had a pain in my stomach, and I couldn't go to school. They let me stay home for a week and watch cartoons all morning and soap operas all afternoon and eat Vegetable Thins, my mother's favourite snack. I would leave seven crackers in the box so she wouldn't be mad at me. The first soap opera of the afternoon was *The Edge of Night*, and the grown-ups on it always looked so depressed and worried so I would leave the TV room and walk around the house on tiptoes. One day, I ate a whole box of strawberry Pop-Tarts. I didn't even like them. They had a weird chemical taste, just like canned icing. I loved them and I hated them at the same time. I hated it when I had to leave the television because that was when images of Patty in the river would fill every part of me.

One night about three weeks later, having just watched Walt Disney, I realized that I wasn't feeling the pain in my heel or my private parts anymore and I hadn't remembered Patty flailing into the river for quite a few days. For the first time since it happened, I drifted off to sleep as easy as falling into new snow. Then I was awakened by my parents' voices: "Drowned? Drowned? Oh God, it can't be. No, John!"

I threw my cover off, left my bedroom, and stood at the top of the stairs. I saw Dad standing at the window, lighting one cigarette with the one he was already smoking. Without looking back at my mother he said, "I'm afraid it is."

My mother let out a sob. I wasn't used to that, not from my mother.

"Oh, God help us. That poor girl. That poor family. I cannot bear it. Oh, John. Oh, John. Think of what she suffered trying to save herself. I just cannot ..." She walked over to my dad and they hugged, her head on his shoulder. She kept crying. My dad was doing what all the men I knew did, which was crying inside, but only showing it through a frown and smoking.

Now everyone knew what I had seen: Patty Wissy drowning. I had seen her, I had seen her with my own eyes jump into the river and swim away from Miles and Bernie, powerfully, her arms like Superman arms. I was certain she would win. I had never been more certain of anything in my life. She would outswim them and she would clamber up the riverbank on the other side and through the birch trees and the apartment parking lot and then back to her condemned yellow house where she would tell her big brothers what had happened. Her mom would wrap her in a blanket and give her hot chocolate with marshmallows and her brothers, they would run like lightning back to the river and they would capture stupid Miles and Bernie, who were just sitting around laughing, and they would throw them both into the water and watch them be swallowed by the Connecticut River.

But that's not what happened.

What happened is that she drowned.

What happened is that I didn't save her.

She was a much better swimmer than me. She was a Dolphin, and I was just a Minnow. I would have drowned for sure in that river.

That's why I didn't jump in to save her. We would have both drowned.

But there's the other thing I didn't do. I didn't tell the grown-ups. Maybe if I had told as soon as I got back to the cookout, she could have been saved. Maybe. I've heard of kids who seem like they've drowned to death being brought back to life. I've heard of that.

I never confessed what I didn't do to a priest because I didn't want to hear him tell me I was going to hell.

LYING HERE ON this soft and sinking field — is it sinking, or is it the LSD — as the sun slowly sets, I feel my heart turn to dust, thinking of Patty. I haven't thought of her for a long time. It's as if she never existed.

MY MOM CRIED about Patty, pretty much every day for a few weeks.

"Poor, poor Patty. Poor little girl. How awful. How does something like that happen? They all knew not to go into the river, every child in this town knew. Did the Wissys not warn their kids?"

"The kids are going to hear about it at school. Better that we tell Ana and Paulie first thing in the morning," said my dad.

Mom wondered if someone had hurt her *in that way* and then had thrown her in the river so she wouldn't talk.

My Dad tried to be the voice of reason, insisting that we didn't know that anyone harmed her, and we shouldn't jump to conclusions.

"She probably saw something shiny in the river and waded in."

My mom shook her head and actually shouted at Dad, "No, no, no, no. Somebody else was there. Clearly. Maybe some low-life who's been let out of jail? The police must have some idea."

That's what my mother said, like she knew something. Not everything, but something. She had feelings about things, and those feelings were often right.

From then on, when I prayed, I didn't pray to Jesus or to Our Lady, I prayed to Patty. "Patty Wissy, archangel of God, forgive me." I would say that over and over, hoping for a sign.

During one prayer, I asked her if she would be my guardian angel. Then I realized what a stupid question that was. I didn't bother to guard her when she was alive, so why would she agree to guard me when she was dead? Why would she waste her time when there were so many worthier kids who needed guarding? Who the heck did I think I was?

THAT FALL, WHEN school started, and we went into fifth grade, the teacher didn't call Patty's name when she took attendance. I was so used to her name being after Sara Varley because V is before W, but now her name was not called, and Mrs. Opal went from Sara to Michael Walters. Her desk, which would have been right in front of mine because that's how we always chose our desks, was now Abby Rapp's desk. Abby was taller than the rest of us, and bigger-boned, with a broader face and small brown eyes that seemed to be looking at something behind you when she talked to you. Abby, who would die of a heroin overdose six years later, when she was sixteen. I know because Francine Pinel called me long distance to tell me last year. I would look at Abby's desk, and I would think I saw Patty's blue-and-green plaid pencil case. Patty was tidy, she always kept her pens and pencils and eraser in perfect order in her plaid pencil case, but Abby's desk was a mess. I had always borrowed pencils from Patty, and sometimes, when I gave them back, I could see her noticing that I chewed my pencil erasers right off. She didn't like that, but she never said anything because she was so nice. She always had paper, and she had always done her homework. I never did mine, and my desk was always a mess, though not as bad as Abby's.

EVERY TIME I looked at Abby Rapp sitting in what should have been Patty's desk, my heart pounded and I felt the room spinning. One of these times, Mrs. Opal asked me to do some math on the board, so I walked up to the blackboard, my legs feeling so heavy I could barely lift them to walk, and then all was black and small yellow stars and the yellow stars became Patty's yellow hair and there was her blue hair band and she was walking and dipping towards me with that bag of vegetables in her hand and that shy smile, with the knowledge that we would play Superman and Invisible Girl soon. Nobody else knew that game we played. Her smile said she knew me, she knew me better than Frances or even my mom or dad or Paulie. She took my hand. Hers was warm, but her hair was soaking wet with droplets of muddy water. Her face was radiant. Almost blinding. When I could finally see, though, I saw the face of Our Lady, speaking French words at me, the way she did to Bernadette, at Lourdes.

"Va embrasser la terre en penitence pour les pecheurs," which our Sunday school nun, Sister Romolo, said meant, "Kiss the ground as penitence for your sins."

I'm trying to kiss the earth, but I can't move my head. I'm thinking that I have disappointed Our Lady again, just when she has forgiven me!

And then I wake up. I am on the floor, gasping for breath. Mrs. Opal is standing over me, not the Lady. Mrs. Opal has a big, square face and a big, square body. She wears orange lipstick and pearls every day. Her face has a disgusted look on it. I must have peed in front of everybody. I always do in the grand mal fits. I pee and I snort, snort just like an animal. When you pee yourself during a seizure there is so much pee and whatever you are wearing gets soaked. You never want to wear it again. You never do.

"Ana? Ana, now breathe, that's a girl. Just breathe. Your parents have been called, and they are on their way. You just lie still." I hear Frances say, "Hear her snort like a pig?" and then she and Joni Gracielle make a pig snorting sound. Nobody else does. Moses, the boy who kissed all the girls in first grade, says, "She was just trying to breathe, you stupids. When they have a fit like that the body doesn't breathe, okay? She was just trying to breathe. So, leave her alone, you morons."

Mrs. Opal, chastened that she hadn't said anything, chimes in, "Be quiet, class, for heaven's sake."

I think she is discombobulated by my seizure. I notice her hands shake and they are very cold when she helps me up.

MY PARENTS WERE very upset when they arrived at the school. My mother was especially outraged at the doctor because she had given me exactly the amount of Dilantin and phenobarb he prescribed. I had taken it faithfully every day, with my morning orange juice.

"She clearly needs more of that medication. I do not understand why Dr. Chown thought it was a good idea to lower her medication. He is a fraud."

She didn't understand that missing Patty and believing her death was my fault rendered my medication useless.

Before Patty's body was discovered, Mr. Wissy came over two or three more times, sometimes with one or two of Patty's sisters or a brother holding their handmade posters with a drawing of Patty and a description of what she was wearing. Every time he came over, I hid in my room and shook. After, Mom and I put the posters up on telephone poles and in the YMCA lobby.

I tried to tell Mom and Dad the real story a few times, especially after church, when I was most afraid of hell, but the words would not leave my mouth. Sometimes I thought it was Frances controlling me from her house, up the street. Or was it Miles and

Bernie? But then it happened. On the very last day of July after the fifth grade but before the sixth grade, Dad was taking me to swimming lessons at the downtown YMCA when he stepped on a rotting zucchini in the corner of the driveway. It was soft and covered in white mould.

"What the hell? What is that? Oh, my shoe! Damn, damnation."

He threw his cigarette to the ground, and it fizzled out in the rotten zucchini.

"And what are those rotten tomatoes? What the hell? These are new shoes! Did your mother not bother to pick them up when she dropped them? Was she hoping I would slip on them?"

"For God's sake, goddammit, Joanna!"

I didn't want him yelling at my mother again. Lately he was always yelling. When I asked her why, my mother reminded me again that his father wouldn't let him fight in the war, and the shame he felt made him angry at just about everything.

I grabbed his wrist. "It wasn't Mom. Stop being mad at Mom all the time. Patty Wissy brought them over from their garden. From the Wissy's garden." His face changed when I said that.

"What? When?"

"When we had the cookout. For Paulie's birthday." As soon as that left my mouth I knew I was in for it.

"The day that Patty Wissy went missing? Ana, what are you saying?"

I couldn't speak. Dad kneeled down so he was face to face with me.

"You just said that Patty came over to the cookout with the vegetables from their garden. That is what her dad said, that she had those vegetables from their garden. In a brown paper bag. Ana?"

I still couldn't speak.

"When Mr Wissy asked you, you said that you had not seen

Patty that day. Did you see Patty that day?"

"Yes."

I didn't want him yelling at Mom, so I had to tell the truth.

"The same day Mr. Wissy came to our door asking about her?"

"Yes."

"Why did you say you hadn't seen her?"

I couldn't speak. Tears ran down my face.

My mother was hanging up washing in the back, humming in her out-of-tune but charming way. Dad called out to her.

"Joanna! Joanna, come up here and listen to this."

It felt so good to tell the truth, even though it wasn't the whole truth. It felt like when you have to go pee so badly and you have been holding it all through class and finally it's recess and you can go.

I didn't tell the worst part of the attic. I just said that we smoked cigarettes up there and me and Frances hated them and coughed and coughed. When I told the part about the river, though, about Bernie jumping on Patty and Patty trying to swim and then disappearing, my father seemed to lose his balance.

"You heard Patty saying, 'Get off me?'"

I nodded.

"Darling, it is very important that you tell us the truth."

"I know."

"Did you see them hurt her?"

"I heard her say, 'Get off me.' That's all."

"You saw her in the river."

"Yes. Swimming. She's a Dolphin. That's way better than me. But the river was stronger."

My father's face looked white and grey, as if all the blood had drained out of it. Later that night, when I was in bed, I heard their conversation.

"John, we have to tell somebody."

"Who, Joanna, who exactly would we tell?" My mother said we should tell Monseigneur Cavan first, and then the police. My father laughed, way too loudly.

"Nobody will believe her. This is Miles Carver we are talking about. His father is one of the most famous artists in America. Do you want her picture in Life magazine? They would call her the 'little liar who tried to bring the great Carver down.' We'd lose all our friends."

I went down the stairs in my nightgown and bare feet and begged them not to tell anyone. They looked at each other, and nodded, and then they both hugged me. Mom gave me a glass of milk with a spoonful of strawberry Nestlé's Quik stirred in, then took me up to bed. I guess they must have decided that there was no point in telling anybody what I had told them, because nothing happened. Everybody, including the coroner, said that Patty had died by accidental drowning. I lay in bed, but I couldn't sleep. I slipped out of my bedroom and crouched at the top of the stairs to listen to what they were saying. My mom kept repeating that they really should tell someone, and my dad kept saying that it wouldn't do any good. There was no proof, it was just the word of a nine-year-old girl with epilepsy.

After about two hours of talking and arguing and some crying, I heard my mom fold. She conceded that Dad was probably right. There would be no point in stirring things up. It was too late. Patty was dead. Telling the police, upsetting the Carvers and everyone who knew them, what was the point in that? Journalists from all over the world would swarm around us, there would be pictures of me and of them and of the Carvers all over every newspaper and magazine. Everyone would say I was lying and they would throw rocks through our windows and spit at us. It wouldn't bring Patty back.

Nothing could bring her back.

It unsettled me when I saw the Carvers at our cocktail parties. It bothered me because Mrs. Carver looked so much like Miles. When she looked at me and shrieked, "Well, helloooo, you shy little thing!" my feet shook and I couldn't say "hi" back. I would run upstairs and hide. My mother would laugh and say, "Don't take it personally, she does that to me all the time!" Which wasn't true. They never had Bernie's parents over because his parents weren't part of their crowd.

Over the next year, I had trouble sleeping. I often woke up screaming, always thinking that Wanda's white snake was stretched out beside me in the bed, whispering to me to "go on up to the attic" in a kind of hissing whisper. My pyjamas would be soaked with sweat, and I would throw off my covers and turn on the light, but there was no snake. My mom would come in and help me into a nice dry nightie and sing me a song, smoothing my hair back until I went to sleep.

"Beeeauutiful Ana, I wish you sweet dreams! Beeeyootiful Ana. No waking with screams."

"Mom!"

"I wish you wouldn't scream. You nearly give me a heart attack. Honestly, Ana, I have a very sensitive heart."

"I can't help it, Mommy, I'm sleeping when I scream."

How could she not have understood why I was waking up screaming? I continued to wake up screaming most nights. I never had good dreams. The Virgin Mary never visited me. I realized when I thought I saw her during the seizure in Mrs. Opal's class, it was just my imagination, not like the other times, when I really did see her. She would never appear to me again because I was a sinner. But I did see Patty. I had Patty's face in my mind as if she were right in front of me, every night before I went to sleep. Whenever we passed big boys, the age of Miles and Bernie, I would hide behind my mom or dad, and I would suddenly feel cold all over and my teeth would chatter.

I started being angry at my mother and father all the time. Paulie was the only person in the family I could talk to. He would ask, "Are you happy yet?" and look deeply into my eyes. I would whisper, "No!" and he would put his hand very gently on my shoulders and shake his head. One time I just told him the truth. "I'm just not happy, Paulie, and maybe I won't ever be again." He asked me why, and I told him I was just really, really sad about Patty. He looked away and said he understood. And I think he really did. Funny, grown-ups will tell you that when time passes, you will forget about a bad thing. But time passing only made it worse for me. I wondered how I could keep living in the same town as them, as Frances. I would imagine Middletown like a room in a basement with no windows and no doors, and sometimes I would feel like I could hardly breathe.

Then one Saturday morning, when I was halfway through sixth grade, they told us that we would be moving to Canada. Forever.

THE FIRST DAY in a new house is the strangest feeling there is. It must be the way the astronauts felt walking on the moon. You are aliens and it's not your world. It doesn't smell like you, it doesn't feel like you. Especially when you are the first people to ever live in that house. It smells of new paint, and wood that was a tree not long ago, and, according to my dad, something called Sheetrock and just a new house smell. The whole street smelled of new houses — the trees were all newly planted and spindly, and there were several big gaping-hole construction sites on the street. Our house, 1578 Cataraqui Hills Crescent, was a fake limestone split-level bungalow with an open garage and a huge backyard. The first thing my mother said when we saw it was, "We need to plant ivy today, to cover that ghastly faux limestone. Then we need to plant four large evergreen trees in the back. And possibly a red maple in the front yard. But before anything else, ivy, ivy, ivy."

The builder, a man my parents called Mr. Merkel, was there to greet us. While they chatted, Paulie and I raced to our new bedrooms — Dad had arranged beds for us, but not much more. We were guarded but excited and full of hope. This was our new house in a new country. There was lots of sun coming in the living room window and it suffused the floor with a warm amber light. There was gold-coloured wall-to-wall carpet, which Paulie and I rolled on, from one end to the other. There was a flyer in our mailbox from a pizzeria called Lino's so my mum ordered a giant pizza, and we ate it on the floor of the living room on that first night. We were all happy, mostly.

On our second day I was sitting in the backyard in my baby-blue-and-white checked sleeveless cotton shift dress drinking a glass of powdered iced tea — I'd made it with about six spoonfuls of the sweet tea powder and lots of ice — when Birdie Van Der Knacker appeared.

She was tiny, about half my height, with a square face and wavy, dirty blond hair that was a kind of a beautiful mess, and red cat's eye glasses. Her arms and legs were so pale I wondered if she was allergic to the sun. She peered around the corner of our open-air garage. In a voice that was like having cold water thrown on your face, she trilled, "Hi there! My name is Birdie!"

I looked up, trying hard to arrange my face so I appeared haughty and bored, an American girl, cooler in every way and from Connecticut, a place I missed so much my chest hurt, and a place I never wanted to think about again.

"Oh, hello."

Birdie stood awkwardly on her tippytoes, swaying back and forth. I looked at my notebook, in which I had drawn so many female faces in profile that the page was almost full. Every girl had a tiny little snub nose and crazy long eyelashes. I realized, at that moment, to my horror, that Frances used to do the very same thing. After that I never drew another girl's face again. I would only draw designs, squares, and figure eights, and expanding circles. I looked down at my notebook in order to make Birdie uncomfortable because she looked like a dork. I had always been the dork in Middletown, so I didn't want to associate with dorks in Kingston. My mother appeared.

"Hello there, and who are you?"

"I'm Birdie Van Der Knacker. We just moved in a month ago. From Winnipeg."

"Well, I'm Mrs. Burns, and that is my daughter, Ana. I think you're about the same age."

"I will be twelve on October twentieth," Birdie piped.

My mother was thrilled with this news.

"Ana will be twelve on September twentieth! You're only a month apart!"

I forced a polite giggle. "That's cool." I nodded at her.

She wasn't sure what to say next. "I like your short pigtails."

My hair was finally long enough that I could wear pigtails.

"Thank you," I said in the flattest voice I could manage.

I kinda liked her, with her pointy-up glasses and dirty blond hair with bangs almost right over her eyes. She had an edge to her. I could tell her mum had forced her to come over and introduce herself. There was a silence while she struggled to think of something else to say. Then her eyes widened. She noticed something behind me in the evergreen tree.

"Oh, my goodness, is that a yellow-bellied sapsucker?"

"What?"

"That bird. The bird on the tree behind you?"

I glanced up, trying to be polite now. I told her I really didn't know anything about birds. My mother opened the screen door, and our black cat D'Arcy ran out, up towards the bushes. Mum screamed, "Don't you dare catch a bird, you nasty thing!!"

"Oh, that's terrible when they do that!" Birdie talked faster than anyone I had ever known, like she was out of breath. "And they keep them between their teeth, and the poor bird shrieks and the cat doesn't care one bit."

"It's a terrible thing to see," agreed my mother. "But they are animals and they can't help it."

"Yup, it's animal instinct, that is very true." Birdie, I found out later, always agreed with whatever adults said, even her own mother.

My mum so wanted us to be friends.

"Birdie, would you like some iced tea, same as Ana is having?" Birdie said that she would love that, which delighted my mother who gushed and ran into the house to prepare Birdie's glass.

I could tell Birdie was wondering if she had made a mistake in coming, as I had barely looked at her. But since my mum was gone, I had nobody to disappoint. So, I looked right at her, and it was like looking at a doll that you forgot you even had and how happy you felt when you found it. As soon as I actually looked at her, I knew I liked her. She smiled, revealing braces on her top teeth. She had finally thought of something to say just to me.

"So, when did you get here?"

"Yesterday."

"Oh. Nice! Did you drive?"

"Such a long drive. Fourteen hours."

"Oh gol. That is a long drive. What did you do?"

"Well, I read a bit."

"I like to read. What did you read?"

"*The Hobbit*."

"Oh, my gol!! I love *The Hobbit*! It's my favourite book!" Birdie crouched and made a monster face and did a hilarious Gollum imitation. "My preeeecious, gimme my precious, I need my precious!!"

We laughed. I could never really laugh with Frances because it was always contaminated by my need for her approval, or at least for her not to call me an idiot. Paulie and Ruthie and Patty Wissy when she was alive were the only people I could really laugh with. Now Birdie was the fourth person.

"What school will you be going to?"

"St. Thomas More. The Catholic school."

"Oh, that's too bad. I'm at Calvin Park. Protestant."

"Oh, too bad. What grade are you going into?"

"Seven."

"Me too!"

"Do you want to sit down?"

She sat on one of the lawn chairs my dad had brought from Middletown. It was odd to see her sitting on it, instead of one of my friends.

There was another awkward silence.

"Nice yard."

"Thanks. My mother is going to plant some trees." Birdie was peering at something on me. "I really like your dress."

"Oh. I hate it," I lied.

"Wanna come to my house?" My mum was standing there with Birdie's glass of iced tea.

"Oh, she would love that. Wouldn't you, Ana? You can take the tea with you!"

"I don't know. I think I have to unpack my stuff."

"Nonsense, I'll unpack for you."

Their faces looked so hopeful. Mum was hoping I would go, so I would have a friend, and Birdie, maybe, was hoping I wouldn't, so her chore would be over. But I was curious about the inside of a Canadian house.

Her house was one of three types of houses on the street. There was a split-level with limestone veneer, which we had; there was wide with white wood and a fieldstone veneer; and there was red brick with huge living room windows, which she had. As soon as we walked inside, the other-people's-houses smell hit me. This was one I had never smelled, because it was a Canadian other-people's-houses smell. It smelled like bananas and snow, and clean laundry, or that is what I imagined at the time.

"Hello!" her mother called from the kitchen. "Did you bring

the new girl home?"

"Mum, she's right here!"

Birdie's mother came out of the kitchen. She wore a bright yellow apron and she hugged me.

"Welcome to the neighbourhood, dear."

"Mum, her name is Annie."

I noticed that Birdie called her mother "mum" instead of "mom."

"Um, actually it's Ana."

"Dear Ana. What a lovely name. We are so thrilled to have your family on the block."

Birdie's mom, Aletta, was a soft and doughy woman who always had an apron on and had the kindest brown eyes. There was a framed photo of her on a horse when she was younger. She was really beautiful, like a movie star. I said to Birdie, "Your mother was so pretty."

"Thanks," said Birdie. It didn't occur to us that our mothers could still be beautiful, even though at the time they were both under forty.

When Birdie's mother, Aletta, looked at me, I felt she was actually seeing me, unlike my own mother, whose eyes always had a kind of glaze over them when she looked at me. When she looked at my little brother, however, the glaze became sparkles. I probably deserved it. I became sharp with her after what happened in the attic. I thought of myself as the gravel driveway. I almost never smiled. In fact, if I felt a smile coming, I would fight it. If I felt my voice go soft, I would give it a knife edge. Even though I was naturally a person who felt a lot of emotion for other people, maybe too much, I made myself cold — especially towards her, and in front of her. "Oh, look at that poor cat, it looks starving!" she would say. I would shrug and look away, even though inside I was dying to rescue the cat and thought about it for weeks.

IN THE LAST couple of years, I've been trying to be nicer to my mother, now that I'm seventeen. Because the fact is, I really like her company. She's kind of far-out. She isn't like the boring mothers of my friends — my friend Emilie's mother said she was eccentric. When I asked her what she meant by that, she shrugged and repeated the word, "You know. *Eccentric.*" I felt a tightness in my face when she said that. I wanted to defend my mother, but all I could think of to say was, "That's a good thing!" You don't insult my mother. Because my feelings for my mother, they're heavy and light at the same time; it is as personal as going to the bathroom and swallowing and you don't insult my swallowing.

Everybody is supposed to love their mother and father. The thing is nobody tells you what the word *love* actually means. That's one of the reasons I like dropping acid. It's helping me figure out the real meaning of words that have lost their meaning.

Birdie Van Der Knacker was my first friend in Canada.

THERE WERE HAPPY 100th Birthday Canada banners all over Kingston, which, I was told, was the original capital of Canada. Every school served every kid a thin piece of that Centennial sheet cake with a red maple leaf made of icing. There was red and white ice cream at every community centre and face painting and balloon beavers and singalongs of the new Centennial song in school every day.

Everybody in the street looked proud, eyes shining, cheeks rosy, a bounce in their steps. Or maybe that was just my imagination, but it is what I thought I saw. When I thought of America, I thought of the Pillsbury canned frosting that Frances used to steal from the corner store, shoving it into her pocketbook when the clerk wasn't looking. We would bring one spoon, and we would find a park bench and then tear open the frosting and eat the whole can. It tasted like chocolate-flavoured Mr. Clean, but we ate it anyway. We pretended we found it delicious but, really, it was all about the adventure. America was like an adventure that was just a bunch of chemicals that could make you sick.

Canada smelled to me like real frosting, the kind my mother would make with butter and cream. Vanilla. When I went to school in September at St. Thomas More, a school for Catholic kids, we were taught that Canada was better in every way than the US. This was weird for me because in Middletown they taught us that America was the greatest country in the world. Nobody even thought about Canada. In Connecticut, we were taught that the US won the War of 1812, but here in Canada, we were taught that the Canada won, with the help of the Indians and the British, and, most entrancing to me, with the help of the beautiful and brave Laura Secord, who overheard American soldiers planning an attack and so ran barefoot for twenty miles through the woods in the middle of a snowstorm to warn the British soldiers. There was even a Canadian chocolate company named after her and the Kingston shopping centre had its own Laura Secord shop, which Mum would sometimes take us to so I could buy a mint chocolate, and Paulie could buy an orange cream. At St. Thomas More, they also taught us that we abolished slavery in 1834, way before the United States did, because we were part of England. Or the Commonwealth, one of those words. Apparently, we still were, even in 1967, but the Queen couldn't actually tell us what to do. That is what our teacher, Miss Prior, said. "We are an independent nation, kids. The Queen does have to sign off on everything, but it is nothing but a formality." Canadians really liked the Queen. In fact, they loved her. You could tell because there was a picture of her in every classroom. And we had to sing a song called "God Save Our Gracious Queen" every morning after the bell. I didn't know the words, so I just moved my mouth but didn't really sing.

Canada was where Harriet Tubman, who I knew all about from our school in Middletown, brought slaves to freedom on the Underground Railroad. That made me really proud to be here. We had way more respect for the Indians too. All this was proof that Canada was where I belonged. The only thing I didn't quite understand was how come there were only white people in

Kingston. I asked some of the kids and they just looked at me like I was crazy.

But I was happy because Canada had been so much nicer to everybody than America was.

I was crushed when I found out a few years later that none of that was exactly true.

I learned that Canada called its president a prime minister, and that the first one was a Scottish man named John A. Macdonald, who they told us invented Canada.

I adored working in the Sir John A. museum, in a very flattering pioneer dress with my hair in curls, and was pissed right off when a Queen's grad student who was trying to pick me up told me that Sir John A. cared about the national railroad more than the lives of the Indians out west. He told me that John A. had written a telegram saying *I have reason to believe that the agents as a whole are doing all they can by refusing food until the Indians are on the verge of starvation, to reduce the expense.* The grad student was doing his Ph.D. on the building of the railroad and claimed he had done the research. He bragged he had seen a copy of the telegram in the archives in Ottawa, but I still didn't really believe him. I thought he was just making it up to shock me, as a way to get into my pants.

But when I thought about it later, I remembered something at Expo 67 in Montréal that first summer we were here, when I was almost twelve. We visited the Indians of Canada pavilion, which was a giant teepee, about two hundred feet high. I thought it was so cool. We went inside and the hostesses told us they were Indians from different tribes, said something about how we white people had stolen their land, and tried to wipe out their language, and even stolen their soul. Funny thing was, they said all this with a smile and a soft voice. My mother wasn't really listening to what they were saying, so she smiled and nodded. My father looked at the ground. I looked at him, because I wasn't sure if we were supposed to say something. Paulie had tears running down his face. On our way out we noticed a hand-drawn sign, *Indian children are poor and hungry*, and another one telling us *White schools are bad for Indian children.*

"Is that true, Dad?" I asked.

"I don't know Ana, there is probably some truth to it."

We were quiet for a moment, looking at the teepee and the signs. My mother pulled her Pall Mall cigarettes out of her purse and lit two, giving one to Dad. I could tell she was perturbed by those signs and her way of dealing with these things was to ignore them. I guess I learned that from her, because as soon as we left, I completely forgot about what the hostesses told us, and only a few days after telling the grad student he was full of shit did it come back to me.

"For God's sake, let's stop the sad talk and find another pavilion!"

Paulie and I ran towards the Scandinavian pavilion, pulling our parents by the hands to its glimmering, showy newness. Paulie jumped up. "Look!! Look at the Scandinavian pavilion, everybody!" We ran into the pavilion and didn't really see anything at first. But when I stopped running, and looked around while catching my breath, I saw six swans: white, and blue, and black and white swans, which seem to be swimming across a lake as blue as my father's eyes when he talks about his father. Paulie was going mental about the giant Viking ship, but it didn't do a thing for me. We got bored pretty quickly. What we were mainly interested in at Expo 67 was the food, especially the sweet or greasy things from different countries. In the car on the way home Mum snored with her mouth open. Dad drove with a frown on his face. I wonder now if he was thinking about those signs. Paulie played with his Etch A Sketch. I looked out the window and tried not to think about the Indians of Canada pavilion.

I was excited about the coming school year. I was not going to be content with being the nothing girl, the colourless moth girl. No. I was going to be the *it girl*, the American girl. And I knew exactly how to go about it. I'd always been a pretty good mimic. When I started school, I would impersonate Frances.

In the meantime, before school started, I was happy to be myself with Birdie. We would cycle down to Lake Ontario Park and swim for hours in the bright blue, very wavy, frigid Lake Ontario. My mum said that the lake was the best thing about Kingston. I was already calling her mum instead of mom.

"That opulent, pretty lake is an embrace around this town. And that is its great saving grace. Oh, and the limestone. That is why Kingston is 'the limestone city.' The ubiquitous limestone. It's quite lovely. Although I prefer the New England red brick. It's warmer. Limestone is so cold." I told her how I learned in school that limestone was made of thousands of tiny fossils and teeny little shells. She said, "Darling, that is wonderful knowledge. It still doesn't make it a warm stone."

When Birdie and I were too cold to stay in the water any longer we got out, shivering violently, knees shaking, teeth chattering, and wrapped ourselves in the giant towels our mothers had sent with us, although mine was less giant than Birdie's. Then we would climb up the grassy hill to the concession stand to buy Nutty Buddys. We would spread the towels on the grass, sit in our wet bathing suits, our hair dripping, and devour the ice cream.

Birdie loved to tell me riddles, and I would have to guess the answer. "Okay, you ready?"

"I guess."

"What is yours, but is mostly used by others?"

"Ummm — what is mine, but is used by other people?"

"Yeah."

"Pass."

"Come on, try harder!"

Nothing at all came to mind.

"Pass!"

"Your name!"

"Oh!! I knew that."

"Liar!"

"Yeah, okay. Gimme another."

"Okay. This is my grandma's favourite. What goes up but never comes down?"

I was determined to get the answer to at least one of her riddles but somehow my mind just did not work that way.

"I give up."

"Your age, silly!"

"Oh right!"

We loved collecting stray golf balls from the Cataraqui golf course, which ran along the side of our street. We would give them to the dads who played golf, including Birdie's dad, and they often gave us a quarter for them. So, one Saturday in August, we had climbed through the hole in the fence separating the backyards of folks on Cataraqui Hills Crescent from the Cataraqui Country Club's golf course. We planned on collecting lost golf balls to give to Mr. Norbert because he was the most generous. He would sometimes give us a dollar for every ten golf balls, so we could run down to the store on the corner of Johnson and the Bath Road and buy Canadian chocolate bars like the Laura Secord chocolate mint bar, or my very favourite, Cherry Blossom. I just loved the pink goo that would pour out once I'd bitten through the thick layer on the outside of the igloo-shaped chocolate. One of the best things about moving to Canada was Canadian chocolate bars.

Once we'd crawled through the fence to the other side, we ran over the actual golf course — a luminous green carpet where men like our fathers were usually playing golf — to the woods on the other side because that's where a lot of golf balls ended up. That day it had rained, so there wasn't anyone playing golf. We were dressed for adventure. I had on my blue paisley genuine Monkees shirt and Birdie had on her greenish one. We were singing "Last Train to Clarksville" sort of off-key but we knew every word. I was kneeling and Birdie was on her belly trying to reach a golf ball that was lodged under a prickly bush. Suddenly we heard a man's voice.

"Hey girlies."

We both gasped and jumped to our feet. We looked around but we couldn't see anyone. I was catapulted back to the day of the attic, heart pounding, and teeth chattering.

"How're ya doin', girlies?"

This could not be happening. We looked around frantically to locate the voice. Then I saw a flash of colour through the woods. A tall, skinny guy with brown hair slicked back and a moustache and his shirt wide open stepped out through the trees. He was holding a cigarette.

"Want a cigarette?"

We both answered, "No thank you, sir," and ran towards the shining wet green of the golf course. We ran past a dirty mattress with beer bottles around it. We ran fast, like rabbits, over the golf course where nobody was and through the narrow woods on the other side, thick with brambles. Both of us were bleeding from cuts to our arms and legs, but we didn't even feel it as we ran towards the Cataraqui Hills fence, which was at the bottom of the Harkmon's property. Suddenly, there was another guy running towards my side, his long dark hair waving up in the wind, and a short, fat one with a brush cut to Birdie's side. The first guy, with the curly hair and the bare chest and tattoos all over, he was behind us.

"Get 'em," yelled the first guy.

We were surrounded. The two guys had caught up to us, and they stood in front of us, blocking our way. They seemed to be waiting for the first guy to tell them what to do.

"Please let us go, sir." Birdie knew how to talk to grown-ups in a polite way.

They laughed like hyenas. There was only one way out. A fighting move I had seen on TV once. I ran towards the tall, skinny guy who had turned around to say something to his friend, and I kicked him between the legs, as hard as I could. He fell, and screamed, and it seemed like he couldn't move.

"I can't fuckin' move, little bitch got me in the balls."

We ran. We ran, screaming. We ran even faster than before. We were young, and light, and strong, and we ran faster than we ever would again.

When we got to the fence it was the wrong part. There was no hole, so we had to climb, almost fly over the barbed wire. Birdie went first and then I tried but I got scraped by the barbed wire. I tried again. And there was Patty. She was in her same blue dress, floating in the air, with this dazzling light around her. She reached out her hand to me, and I took it and she flew me over top of the barbed wire. I landed on my belly on the Harkmon's lawn. My Monkees shirt was ripped almost in two.

"Come on, Ana, run!" She helped me up.

"Holy, did you see that? Did you see?" I realized that Birdie had not seen Patty.

"Don't talk, just run."

We ran like Olympic sprinters to Birdie's house.

The front door was open and we barged in, gasping.

We were out of breath, panting hard for at least five minutes, face to face, both of us wild-eyed.

Her mother was in the kitchen, putting a roast in the oven. Birdie's grandmother, Gran, who never spoke a word that I ever heard, was in the living room on the couch, watching golf on the TV. She was so small it felt like she was one of the couch cushions, maybe because her hair was the same off-white colour. She had a streak of pink lipstick on her lips, which were so skinny they weren't really lips, and sparkly earrings. Birdie opened the fridge and grabbed an onion and started eating it like it was an apple. I had never seen anything like it.

"My goodness! Birdie, why are you eating an onion?"

"Just because."

"I need that onion for dinner tonight, dear."

"But ..." Her mum grabbed it from her, giving her the slyest look.

I could not figure out why in the world she wanted to eat that onion. As if eating the onion were magic. As if it would mean that her mum would never know what happened. And that what happened didn't happen.

"Where are you girls coming from?"

"Nowhere. Just the golf course."

"Why are you so out of breath?"

"Oh, we were having a race."

"Who won? Certainly not our Birdie, our little lounge lizard. Birdie hates to run, don't you darling?"

"I do like to run, sometimes, Mum, and we tied!"

"Oh, my goodness. Aren't you girls something." Mrs. Van Der Knacker's voice brimmed over with love for her daughter, and because I was with her daughter, me.

"Come on, Ana, let's go down to the rec room. But let's grab a ginger ale first."

I loved that Birdie's family always had ginger ale in the pantry. We only had crates of Mum's Tab.

In the rec room, Birdie went straight for the TV and turned

the channel till we found the Monkees show. A scary thought suddenly occurred to me.

"Birdie? Do you think that maybe those guys were escaped prisoners? Maybe murderers?"

Collins Bay penitentiary was on the Bath Road, just about a mile away from the golf course. The jail looked like Disneyland with its red peaked roof with multiple turrets.

On TV, Mike Nesmith was playing a prank on the others, something to do with eggs splatted on their faces. It was funny, but neither Birdie nor I could laugh. He was my favourite, and Davy Jones was Birdie's. I tried to giggle at Mike because part of me felt he could hear me through the TV, even though the other part of me knew that was not possible. Neither of us spoke for a while.

Birdie sounded like a teacher. "Yes, they were definitely from the Pen. You can tell they were prisoners by the hairstyles. Like greasers, from the movies," she said, very sure of herself.

"What do you think they were going to do to us?" I asked, even though I knew exactly what. I really didn't want to talk about it, but I couldn't stop myself. My voice went all high.

"Do you think they would have killed us?"

Birdie was breathing funny, in short, fast breaths. She was peering at me, trying to see something in my face that wasn't there. Her dirty blond bangs were completely covering her glasses, and she didn't bother to move them out of the way.

"Riding is gonna be super-fun next Sunday."

Birdie's mum had told my mum about Birdie's English-style riding lessons out in the country with Colonel McKibbon, so my mum had signed me up and bought me the riding pants, riding jacket, riding hat, and most importantly, the riding boots. She even bought me a crop, which I vowed never to use.

"Colonel McKibbon is bringing English Cadbury's chocolate as a reward for our cantering last Sunday. This Sunday, we gallop," said Birdie breathlessly. English Cadbury's chocolate was the best chocolate I had ever tasted. I looked forward to that. I wasn't looking forward to galloping. Birdie was fearless on a horse. She said she could have galloped all the way back to Winnipeg, and I believe she could have.

She hooked her finger around my finger and whispered, "I know things."

"You do?"

"Yes. Duh. I'm from Winnipeg."

After a bit of a silence, our eyes still on the TV, Birdie spoke. "Never forget that I'm from Winnipeg." Birdie stood up very slowly, looking like she was going to throw up.

"Are you okay? Oh, gol, your lips have gone white!"

"I think it's time for you to go home."

I felt a rock in my throat like I was going to cry. Not because she said it was time for me to go home, but because I knew she wanted to be alone to cry, just like I did. I slowly walked up her white carpeted stairs and said "bye" to her mother, who gave me a quizzical look. She knew something was up; she would probably ask Birdie once I left. The house smelled even more sharply of that roast. I put on my shoes at the front foyer and walked out into the blindingly bright afternoon. I had a skip in my step because despite what had almost happened, there was one thing I felt good about.

This time, we had won.

I COULD SWEAR the ground is sinking. Maybe while I was dozing it rained. That's what it is. A little soggy, but I don't mind. The smell of fresh rain on the grass? On the mustard flowers? One of the best. And I have my suede poncho on, so I am warm and cozy. My poncho cost forty dollars from this really cool new store on Princess Street. It's really good quality, even my dad admitted that. It's definitely real suede. I asked Mum every day for a month and she gave in and bought it for me. I was so happy, I hugged her. I look gorgeous in it, which is nice to know for when Matthieu comes back to find me. He will see me lying here dozing and think *Oh Mon Dieu what a beautiful girl!* and he will slide his big, warm hands underneath the poncho and send sparkles through my whole body.

ONE BIG DIFFERENCE between the US and Canada is that in the US we would say "seventh grade," and here, they say "grade seven."

Miss Prior had the strongest presence of anyone I had ever met besides Frances. Actually, way more than Frances. When she walked into our grade seven classroom at St. Thomas More School, she set the air on fire. Every kid in the class was both terrified of her and in love with her. Miss Prior was "drop-dead gorgeous" according to my mother. "Right out of a 1940s noir film, maybe the glamorous girlfriend of a Chicago gangster."

When my mum said that, I was a little miffed. "How do you know her boyfriend is a bad guy, Mum?"

"Oh darling, you are so literal! I'm just kidding!"

Miss Prior had rich dark hair with bangs that went over her shapely eyebrows, and long lashes made longer by gobs of thick black mascara. She painted on eyeliner like Cleopatra, with the wings at the end, and dark blue eyeshadow. On her Cupid's bow lips, she painted dark red lipstick. She wore knitted cashmere dresses that showed off her va-va-voom figure. Because I had read a lot of *Playboy* with Frances, I knew about measurements and I guessed that Miss Prior would have been 42, 28, 44. To me, that was the perfect figure, not the *Playboy* perfect of 36, 24, 36, which my mother had explained to me was "impossibly skinny, darling." Miss Prior also had shapely red fingernails that made my heart race, but I didn't know that she would change my life.

Because I was a natural mimic, I could sound exactly like Frances when I talked, and I could say the kinds of things she would. I could even walk the way she walked and sit the way she sat. I was the "American girl." For the first time in my life, I was popular, and I didn't care that it was based on sort-of-kind-of lies. I mean, I was still me, I was just acting differently. I had pretend opinions about things and finally, I wasn't afraid to express them. Or maybe they were my opinions, and maybe I was allowing myself to have opinions because I was confident they wouldn't be bulldozed as soon as I expressed them. It didn't hurt that my face was shifting from child face to a pretty young girl, and I had long bangs, or as my mother called it, a "fringe" over my blue eyes. I once heard my mother's hairdresser, Tony, remark that my eyes were the colour of her morning glories. I had light brown hair with golden glints that waved down past my shoulders, finally. I knew right away, though, that in order to really fit in I would need to learn how to talk "Portsmouth," the way my classmates talked, which was quite different from the way we talked in Connecticut, or even the way Birdie talked. It was what my mother would call "rough talk." I needed to combine Franccs's confident way of speaking with the Portsmouth tough talk. I really liked the sound of the Portsmouth tough talk. To me, it was a kind of music, much more interesting than the boring way my family spoke. As soon as I tried it, I got it. One evening, over a dinner of disgusting pork chops and crunchy rice, and a few still-frozen peas, I told my parents about Miss Prior when my mother gasped.

"Good heavens, you are talking the way those Portsmouth Village kids talk. I hear them when we go to the pharmacy there!

They're always in there trying to steal something. Ana! What is happening to you?" My dad, always the professor, said, "Actually, I hear a Scottish influence and a bit of the Maritimes. It's quite intriguing. Never cared for the American accent. For example, Americans say *aoouuuut*, and Canadians say *out*, just as it's spelled."

Mum said, "I hear *ooot.*"

"Nonsense," said my dad. "It just sounds like that to you because you spent the last twelve years in Connecticut."

"Well, whatever it is, I don't like the way she's talking. She sounds like one of the tough kids."

"And I don't give two shits," I sputtered. I could not believe I had said that. I had heard the popular tough kids say it in the schoolyard and had always wanted to try it out.

"You don't give two whats? John, did you hear that? Where on earth did you get that vulgar expression?"

"It's not vulgar. It's just the way they talk here."

My dad smiled broadly, showing off his dark yellow and grey teeth. My mum said they were that colour because of all his smoking, and because he grew up in England.

"Honey. These things are fun to try out, but I don't think the kids of other Queen's professors are using that language. Please."

I nodded, acquiescing. The truth was that I wasn't that comfortable talking "tough," even though I could imitate it so easily. My dad knew me so well.

He hugged me. I loved hugs from my dad. I felt like he loved me, or the child part of me. When my mother hugged me, it always felt like she was holding something back. Like she was trying to show me she loved me, without the actual feeling. I mean maybe she had that feeling, but it just didn't come out easily, except for with Paulie. It flowed out with Paulie, when she looked at him, when she took his hand, and when she hugged him.

What was harder than talking tough was to act tough, like some of the grade eight girls, when I was still happiest curled up with Paulie on the couch watching cartoons or movies starring Hayley Mills.

For the first two weeks or so, everyone at school was nice to me, and even deferential on account of me being the American girl. "Are you from Hollywood? Do you know Raquel Welch?" But I didn't make an actual friend. I would walk all the way home for lunch so I wouldn't be seen eating alone in the schoolyard. That meant I had about seven minutes to have lunch, which was usually Chef Boyardee ravioli from a can, sometimes cold. It was delicious. After school most days I would run over to Birdie's house and ring her doorbell, but she often had other friends from Calvin Park Public School over. She would always invite me to join them, but it never felt quite right. They were all Protestant for one thing, and they would ask me weird things about being Catholic, like "Do you really obey everything the Pope says?" I didn't know anything about what the Pope had said, so I said "Never!" and the one girl told me that that meant I was a bad Catholic. I don't know why Birdie was her friend. I got the feeling Birdie was a little afraid of her, the way I had been with Frances.

The few times I caught Birdie alone, she was practicing piano or doing homework. Her mum would invite me in for a freshly baked cookie. "But only for ten minutes, dear, Birdie has to prepare for her lesson tomorrow." That was strange to me. I never did homework. My parents were perfectly happy with B's in most subjects and A's in English and history, which I could get without doing homework. So, I was a little bit lonely. My mum kept telling me it would pass and soon I would make a real friend at my own school. I didn't believe her. I thought this was it, this was the way it was going to be forever. One day, when Paulie and I were in the basement den watching cartoons after school, I asked him if he liked it in Kingston. He didn't make any sound, but I could tell he was crying. I gave him a hug.

"I know. It's really hard, isn't it?"

"Sometimes I can't even breathe because of it."

"What do you mean?"

"I just think I'm gonna die of how bad it is sometimes."

"Are kids being mean at school?"

"No, they just ... I don't really have anyone to play with."

"You will. I promise, you will."

"But you don't. And you're older."

Comforting him made me try to comfort myself.

"It will happen for me too. That's what Dad says. He said everybody makes a friend eventually. He said we just have to find our kind of kids."

"Yeah." Paulie never liked to worry anyone. He would pretend he was all right when he wasn't. "That's right, our kind of kids."

Then I ran upstairs and found a bag of Chips Ahoy! in the cupboard and brought it down. Paulie and I went through the whole bag as we watched cartoon after cartoon, and then neither of us touched our dinner. We looked at each other when Mum scolded us for not eating her lamb chops. It was really hard not to burst out laughing.

"What have the two of you been eating? Oh Lord, you haven't been into the cookies, have you?"

"We were just talking about how we may never find a friend at school."

This seemed to particularly touch my dad.

"You will, kiddos. I promise you that if you want a friend, you will find a friend." I had a feeling my dad knew what it was to be lonely in school. Maybe from his boarding school days, when he was small for his age.

Then one day it happened. Our St. Thomas More grade seven class was on a field trip to the local bowling alley. It was on Brock Street, but we didn't know that. All we knew is we got out of class and we got to actually go bowling! I had never been bowling. The whole class climbed up a flight of stairs to the bowling alley, and the first thing Graham Morton said was, "What a shithole." We all roared with laughter. It really was dumpy, but we all wanted to bowl. So, we each fetched our worn, ugly bowling shoes and a really pretty girl named Emilie, who I'd noticed before because of her high cheekbones and her penny-brown eyes and big laugh and big mouth with the teacher, sat beside me to put on her shoes. As we laced up the shoes we started talking.

"The ugliest shoes in the universe."

"I know."

"If we didn't have to wear them to bowl, I wouldn't be caught dead in these."

"It's gross that so many other people have worn them."

"Ugly people."

"Yeah."

And then we started to laugh. She had this big barking laugh, kind of like the way some men laughed. I had a shrieky kind of laugh. We started laughing at the way each other laughed.

"Oh my God, stop. I'm gonna pee my pants."

After a couple of dismal rounds of bowling, in which neither of us managed to knock down one bowling pin, let alone get a strike, we each bought a Coke from the concession and sat down again.

"I hate bowling!"

"Me too! I hate how I suck at it."

"Me too."

She had been out of class for three days before.

"You were out sick. Are you feeling better now?"

"Actually, I wasn't sick, but I fainted and hit my head on the chest of drawers."

"Oh."

I felt excitement and panic inside at the same time.

Should I tell her? My parents warned me not to tell people I had epilepsy.

"I faint sometimes too."

"Really?"

"But mine is different. Mine is epilepsy."

"You have epilepsy?"

"That's what the doctor said."

"I have it too."

And that was it. We were bonded. I felt so safe with her that I told her how I sometimes peed when I was in a seizure, and how I would wake up and have this big hot wet stain all over my dress, so wet that it was like a whole pot of boiling water had been spilled onto me, and how it was so embarrassing. She didn't have the pee experience, but she laughed her big roar of a laugh, which made me laugh like that and all of it somehow made my seizure pee experience not so bad. That was the thing about Emilie; she made things that were really bad seem not only not so bad, but funny.

I admitted that I spent a lot of time being scared I would have a seizure in front of the class. I just loved her answer.

"Don't be scared. Just take your medication."

"Oh, I do!"

"Well then, nothing to be scared of."

Emilie was the most practical person I ever met. Being highly impractical, I cherished her for that. It's like I was the air balloon, and she was the heavy basket. I'm not sure what she saw in me, but she asked me that day in the bowling alley if I wanted to be friends and I said I did.

After that we were together every day after school, either at her house or at mine.

The best thing about Emilie, though, was that she was fearless. Like Frances, but not at all like Frances. One day in class, it was clear Miss Prior was in a mood. While we were working on math problems, she was pacing like a wolf. I had a drippy nose, so I opened my purse to reach for a Kleenex. Miss Prior stopped cold.

"What in the name of baby Jesus do you think you're doing?"

"Um, just ... getting a Kleenex?"

"Hand it over."

"Pardon?"

"Is there something wrong with your hearing? I said hand over the purse." I began to tremble from head to toe.

"I said hand it over, Miss Teenybopper. What have you got in there? Contraband?"

I had no idea what *contraband* was, or a *teenybopper*. I handed my purse over. She snickered as she reached into it.

"Ahh, candy wrappers. What kind of candy does little missy like? Cherry Blossom? Not good for your teeth! And gum. Gum is disgusting, only lowlifes chew gum." She threw my gum into the wastepaper basket. Rummaged around some more. My stomach churned. I could feel diarrhea coming.

"Oh, lipstick! Cherry red! When were you going to use that? A book of matches? What's this for? To write down the cute boys' phone numbers? Hey boys, any of your phone numbers in here? Huh?"

The boys all looked down at their desks.

"And would you look at this? Green eyeshadow? Now what on God's earth would you be wanting with eyeshadow, child? You are twelve years old, why do you want to look like a twenty-year-old hooker?"

She handed it back to me, looking right into my eyes with a kind of curiosity mixed with contempt, making it clear it was all a performance, and twirled around to walk back to her desk, as if it were a dance step. I think I was completely in love with her and actually kind of proud that my purse was chosen. A few days later, she was in that same kind of agitated mood again. Emilie leaned over and whispered to me, "Robert Zwicky is looking at you."

Robert was a tiny, freckled, red-haired boy in our class who never looked at anybody, so I gasped. Miss Prior's head swung around, and she looked Emilie dead in the eye. The whole class held their breath. "Emilie Millard. What could you be whispering about?"

Emilie didn't answer, and Miss Prior headed straight for her desk.

"Now hand over your smart little purse, Miss Emilie Millard. Come on, lickety-split." Emilie looked her right in the eye. "My father is a criminal lawyer, and he told me that I do not have to turn over my personal property to anyone ever, and if they take it, that is theft, and so if you take it, my dad said, you could be charged."

There were a few gasps and then the class went silent.

Miss Prior didn't say another word. Emilie was my hero.

I still saw Birdie some Saturdays, and every Sunday of course, at riding lessons, but Emilie was my new main friend. Birdie was always busy with her Calvin Park friends, anyway. Once in a while, she would call on a Saturday.

"Mum is taking me up to the Kingston Shopping Centre to look for cute tops, do you want to come? We're going to go to the Red Barn after for burgers and fries and a milkshake!"

Although I was tempted by how safe and normal I felt with Birdie, and her mum's kind brown eyes, their fancy car, a cute top and most of all, a strawberry milkshake, I felt the pull of Emilie's wild streak, the possibility of thrilling trouble.

"I am not sure what I'm doing yet."

"Oh, well give us a call when you know. But it'll have to be in the next ten minutes. Judy Fromm and Diane Jordan are already coming. I just wanted to make sure you weren't lonely."

"Oh. Lonely? No. I'm fine but thank you. Have fun."

"Oh, we will."

I realized she was pretending that she was worried about me being lonely because her feelings were hurt that I had said no. But it still bothered me. For about a minute. Till I made plans with Emilie. Hanging out with Emilie was sort of like skydiving. We always got into some delicious trouble together. I had lived by the rules of my parents, the church, and Frances, and now it was time to break the rules.

One hot summer evening, we headed out after a strained dinner with her parents to break some rules and have some fun. We decided to swim with our clothes on in every apartment pool we could find. We climbed the fences easily when it was dark and nobody was in the pools. We slid into the water as quietly as possible and swam one lap. If we heard anyone coming, we scrambled out as fast as we could, bare feet, sopping wet clothes, and headed to the next apartment building. One night, we swam in seven apartment pools. We were only chased out of five. Being chased out was maybe even more fun than breaking into the pools.

Another adventure I loved was on winter days when there had been a big snowfall the night before, and the streets weren't plowed. Nobody could drive. Emilie and I would stride, in the middle of the roads, all the way downtown, to the one Chinese restaurant on Princess Street, the Golden River, and we would scrounge for change in our pockets and order a tea between us.

We sat across from one another in a booth and poured the tea from the standard faded metal restaurant tea pot into both white cups and then grabbed as many white sugar packets as possible and tore them open with our teeth and poured them in. Then creamer after creamer after creamer. We usually hadn't had lunch, so we were always hungry. Sometimes, though, if he was feeling guilty from drinking the night before and losing his temper, Emilie's dad would have tossed her a five-dollar bill so we would order egg rolls and chow mein. After, when we were paying, we would choose a chocolate bar. Emilie always chose an Aero, and I always chose a Cherry Blossom.

On the Saturdays that Birdie and I did hang around together I could sense she was puzzled by how different I was than the girl she first met. I was still working at being a Portsmouth girl, even if it did make me slightly uncomfortable, because if you didn't talk Portsmouth, you were labelled "a suck." There were three kids in Miss Prior's class who were "sucks": Magdalena Bobrowski, Henny Harmson, and Barb Baker, and I did not plan on joining them. I even shoplifted Crispy Crunch and Kit Kat bars sometimes just to feel not sucky. And once some blue Maybelline eyeshadow. So, I had actually broken the law, and when someone has become a criminal, there is a different aura about them. Birdie felt it. There was sometimes an awkward silence when we were together, and she would start speaking Dutch to her mum or her brother. When she did that, I would mumble an excuse and slink out of there. It was hard to admit to ourselves that we weren't connecting anymore because we were actually trying.

In April of grade seven Miss Prior commanded each of us to write a speech that would "change the world."

"What for?" asked Emilie with her *my father's a criminal lawyer* voice.

"Well, Miss Aren't-You-a-Smart-One, there happens to be a city-wide public speaking contest coming up in December, and I believe that you load of misfits and delinquents will wipe the floor with the others. Why? Because I have rigorously trained you in two disciplines. What? What? What two disciplines?"

Magdalena was the only one who raised her hand. Reluctantly, Miss Prior called on her.

"Miss Bobrowski?"

"Grammar and public speaking, Miss Prior."

"Exactly. Thank you, Miss Bobrowski."

"You have not mastered either discipline, of course, but at least most of you flea brains can put your thoughts into words in a persuasive way."

Magdalena looked outraged. She was not a flea brain, she was planning to be a doctor, and she never got less than a ninety-five on anything. Emilie raised her hand.

"Yes, Millard." She called us all by our last names except when she was mad.

"You have no right to call us flea brains," said Emilie.

Miss Prior looked abashed.

"You're right, Millard. I apologize. More like hamster brains."

The whole class roared at that one. Jerry D'Entremont especially, with his strange, staccato laughter.

Emilie got out her notebook and wrote down exactly what Miss Prior had said. Not because she was going to take it to the principal or anything, just because she wanted to scare Miss Prior.

Miss Prior gave Emilie a crooked kind of smile, which showed she was just a little bit scared of Emilie and continued. "When you kids are at recess, you are the best speakers in the world. You are unrestrained, and your voices are free and full, and you talk to each other in full sentences. I may not like the words you use or the appalling grammar, but I want you to write a speech with that same feeling of freedom. I want you to write what infuriates you. I want you to write what delights you. I want you to write what is wrong with the world, or right with the world, or the time you almost died, or the time you saw a ghost, or when you spent the holiday with your grandmother, or how you hated camp, or loved camp, what you think your future holds, I want you to be yourselves, and write the way you talk."

Graham Morton, who was twelve but looked nineteen, with wild hair completely covering his eyes, always the troublemaker, spoke without raising his hand.

"Miss Prior, if our grammar is good, can we use curse words in our speeches?"

Miss Prior was a grammar fiend. Split infinitive, causative, past participle, future past, cataphoric, I even knew what *cataphoric* meant at the time though I don't now. She hammered grammar into us every day. I think it was because she knew that if the Portsmouth Village kids spoke with proper grammar, they would have a much better chance at life. I have never forgotten her lessons, partly because she was so beautiful and so scary I couldn't not listen.

"Mr. Morton, you may write what you want, the way you want. When you hand it in to me, I will cross out the curse words, but other than that, you write the story you want to tell."

Graham stood up. "Can I write about my old man beating the shit out of my old lady and me?"

The rest of the class gasped, but Miss Prior didn't even seem embarrassed by what Graham had said. She thought about his question for a moment.

"Graham, if that is what you truly want to write about, then that is what you will write about. And, please, see me after class."

"Am I in trouble?"

"No, Graham. Not at all."

Magdalena raised her hand. "May I write about the Holy Spirit?"

Miss Prior smiled, showing her slightly buck teeth, which somehow made her all the more beautiful.

"Why Miss Bobrowski, the nuns would love that."

I could tell by the tone in her voice that Miss Prior thought that writing about the Holy Spirit was sucking up, and she didn't like suck-ups. She hated suck-ups even worse than troublemakers.

Magdalena twirled her fine, dark hair around her fingers, looked down at her notebook, took a deep breath, and wrote something.

Magdalena had alienated most of the class early on when she told us that she was actually a Polish princess. Which would mean her father was the King of Poland and her mother was the Queen. But we saw them when they picked her up after school and they certainly didn't look like any king or queen. When she announced that, Graham Morton snorted loudly. Claudia Evangelista quietly sang, "Liar, liar, pants on fire." Emilie whispered, "Prove it." I giggled at those reactions, but I actually did believe her. Even though she had crooked teeth, there was something about the way she carried herself. And the fact that she was by far the smartest person in the class. She invited me over to her house after school one day to meet her cat, Malika, and try a sweet Polish omelette. Even though I hated eggs I said yes because I was curious to see if she had a throne, smuggled over from Poland, or a crown full of rubies hidden away somewhere. We sauntered slowly up her street, Campbell Crescent, where there were three styles of houses, only slightly different from the three styles on Cataraqui Hills Crescent, because they were all a bit smaller. She took my arm and asked me if I had ever spoken with the Holy Spirit. After struggling with whether or not to tell her the truth, I decided I might as well.

"I have spoken with the Virgin Mary, but not the Holy Spirit."

She ignored the amazingness of the fact that I had spoken with the Virgin Mary.

"You haven't felt the Holy Spirit move inside you?"

A part of me realized that Patty, maybe, had become my Holy Spirit. And I did sort of feel her inside me. Sort of. Maybe all kids who die become part of the Holy Spirit.

"Let me tell you about the Holy Spirit!"

"Okay. Sure."

"The Holy Spirit, Ana, is the part we like best! The Holy Spirit is the great mystery, the unknown element of the Trinity." She was talking like a catechism teacher, but I didn't mind.

"What's the Trinity again?"

"Silly. You remember: 'Father, Son, and the Holy Ghost.' Don't you say that every time you cross yourself?"

"Oh, yeah. Right. They never tell us exactly who the Holy Ghost is."

"Promise you won't tell anyone this?" She looked at me sternly, and her face made me think of an eagle. I promised.

She raised her right hand. "Cross your heart and hope to die?"

"Cross my heart and hope to die." I promised, crossing my heart with my left forefinger. I shouldn't have promised because try as I might, I just couldn't keep a secret. I don't think I had ever kept one. Magdalena leaned into me.

"The Holy Spirit is our cat, Malika."

I know Emilie would have said Magdalena was crazy and just laughed in her face, but I tended to believe what people said. Perhaps her cat was Magdalena's Holy Spirit. Maybe we each had our own Holy Spirit. Mine was Patty.

"What makes you think that?"

"I can feel it. Malika is not like other cats. She has a giant spirit, bigger than a lion. When I am sleeping, she sometimes stands on my chest, guarding me from the devil. Because the devil is roaming, roaming around looking for children to claim as his own."

"Do you really think so?"

"I know so."

THE MINUTE I got home, I called Emilie and told her everything. I felt slightly remorseful because I knew she would tell everyone in the class, which she did, first thing on Monday morning. People were pleased to hear that Magdalena was crazy because everyone was jealous of the fact that she might possibly truly have been a Polish princess and she never got below a ninety-five in anything, and actually cried like a baby when she once got a ninety on an English test — a test on which I scored ninety-eight, though I knew enough to tell everyone I got a seventy. On top of all that, Magdalena's other crime — from the girls' perspective — was that she was very pretty, almost like a movie star, despite her teeth.

In small-town Ontario working-class circles in 1968 to declare yourself good at anything was social death. You had to pretend you honestly believed you were the worst at absolutely everything. If you were getting nineties in math, you had to say it was sheer stupid luck. Magdalena never did that. If you were the top student in English, you had to shrug and say, "She must have been drunk while she was grading, I didn't even read the book," which is what I always said when I got an A on a book report. I had learned the rules fast. If you had a beautiful face, like Magdalena, or a perfect figure, like Barb Baker, you had to say you had boils on your back and pretend to be stupid, and never, ever talk to the boys so you wouldn't make the other girls jealous. You also had to befriend the ugliest girl in the class to prove you were nice.

The last thing any girl wanted was to alienate the other girls in the class. If you did, your life in middle school was over.

If you had ambitions to move beyond Portsmouth Village, where the school was, where most of the kids lived, you were a conceited traitor. Nobody mentioned Toronto or Montréal, let alone New York or London or Japan or Africa. Basically, no other place in the world existed but Kingston, which, after all the initial frenzy and fun of the Centennial year, I was beginning to see was a dreary prison town of 50,000 people, halfway between Toronto and Montréal. Yes, it is on a spectacular Great Lake, which apparently is the bluest lake in the world, and yes, there is also Queen's University, which brings in hordes of students from wealthy Toronto and Montréal families as well as abroad from September to April, making the town a little brighter and wilder, but really it is just a prison town, with ancient grey limestone everywhere. The mentality was the same. The oldest prison in the country, Kingston Penitentiary, is right there, plonk in the middle of Portsmouth Village, just a block away from our school. It was different from the fairy-castle prison, Collins Bay pen, which we could see from Cataraqui Hills. It was big, dark, and dangerous looking. Old, and crumbling and cold. It was maximum security, which meant that the inmates had done the worst things you can think of. Things that nobody wants to think of. Miss Prior told us that there were nine prisons within the city limits. Quite a few of the parents of the kids in my class were prison guards. Some of the other parents were actually in prison. I think Graham Morton's dad probably was, but I never would have dared to ask him. But even though part of me could see it was a grey, depressing small town, another part of me felt it was pure magic.

I still do.

Miss Prior was obsessed with public speaking, so everything became about this public speaking contest. First, we had to write out our speech and hand it in, and then Miss Prior would give us suggestions in red ink about how to make it better, with lots of underlines and exclamation points.

I didn't know what to write about. I was like an empty room. I became so desperate for a subject to write about that I asked my parents for advice. My mother got way too excited.

"Why don't you write about D'Arcy? You love D'Arcy, darling! Look, just write everything you know about him. That is the way to start — then you can always refine."

"That is the stupidest idea ever," I grumbled, while at the same time thinking it was a pretty good idea. I loved our cat like he was my second brother. More, actually. The way he would sit on my bed and look right into my eyes with his emerald eyes! The way he could jump up onto my bed so gracefully. I didn't think he was guarding me from the devil, but I loved stroking his soft black fur, and the way his purring felt underneath my hand.

I sat at our kitchen table with the green plastic tablecloth and wrote everything I could think of about our cat, D'Arcy. I was taking my mother's suggestion but not admitting to myself that it was her suggestion.

I started with a title. I called my speech "The Tale of a Cat," which I thought was quite witty, though I wondered if everyone would get it. Feeling clever made me feel good about writing about D'Arcy. I wrote and wrote. I liked the look of my handwriting even though it was slanted backwards because I was left-handed. I wrote about how my dad gave him that name because he admired an English author, "the Earl of D'Arcy." I wrote about how D'Arcy purred so loudly you wouldn't believe it, it was like a lawn mower, and how he caught a rat one time and dropped it on my father's bare feet. Me and Paulie said, "Ewwww, that is so gross!" Dad said, "This is D'Arcy's ultimate show of respect and loyalty. It would be like me buying the best roast beef and dropping it off at your friend Birdie's place. He is just a cat being the best cat." This helped Paulie and me to understand, even though Paulie mumbled that he felt sorry for the rat. He mumbled it because he did not want Dad to hear him say that, but he did have to say it.

I described how D'Arcy slept right on my chest and would dig his claws into my belly while purring. My mum explained that he didn't get enough milk from his cat mother because he was taken away from his cat mother too early. I wrote about how D'Arcy loved smoked oysters and fried chicken, and hated car rides, always meowing in this sick, low way the whole car ride and it drove us absolutely crazy. Then I knew I had to end it because the speech could only be ten minutes, so I jumped from the car ride to "I hope you enjoyed 'The Tale of a Cat.'"

My mum stepped into the kitchen, looking pleased. "You've been writing like mad, Ana! Can I have a peek?"

"Not supposed to show parents. It has to be all our own words."

"Let me at least read it, darling!"

"Nope." I knew I was being rude but couldn't help it.

I am pretty sure she read it when I went to sleep that night.

On Monday, we presented our speeches to the class. Miss Prior was all black eyeliner and red lipstick and curves under a lavender cashmere knit dress, wearing high heels that clacked on the floor loudly when she walked. "Okay, you ragamuffins, let me hear your speeches!"

Emilie glared at her. She did not like being called a *ragamuffin* when her mother, Cecile, went to so much trouble to make sure Emilie was dressed in stylish clothes sent by her great aunt Manon all the way from Montréal.

"I'll start, Miss Prior, if you would like to apologize for calling me a ragamuffin."

"Oh, well, I am sorry if you were offended, little girl. What is your speech about, Millard?"

"Grave robbers."

Emilie proceeded to deliver her speech, which was a thrilling account of a group of professional thieves robbing the graves of the Medici family. She had done a really good job.

Most of the kids really didn't have much to say. You could tell they wrote their speeches in ten minutes. Even the good ones were on boring subjects like their favourite hockey player. "Gordie Howe is the greatest hockey player of all time." Then they would tell us the number of times Gordie Howe scored or whatever. Others were about the boring history of Kingston or the War of 1812. "We won, we burned down the White House!!" — the opposite of what I learned in Connecticut. The ones about history were copied word-for-word from the textbook. I whispered to Emilie, "Miss Prior is not going to like that." Emilie rolled her eyes. Almost all the kids recited their speeches in the most awkward, halting way possible, even though they were memorized. Except for Mike Mayo's, Emilie's, Barb Baker's, and, of course, Magdalena's, they were really hard to listen to. Excruciating. Magdalena delivered her speech on the Holy Ghost as if she were a teacher giving a lecture on science, with great authority and conviction. She did not mention her cat but only told us about what it says in the Bible about the Holy Trinity. I think that was because she didn't want people to think she was crazy. She spoke every word slowly and clearly, but about two minutes into her speech those who were listening were rolling their eyes and pointing their forefingers at their temples and making a circle, which meant crazy. I didn't do that because it was just rude.

I'm not sure why Miss Prior chose me to go last, but she did.

"Burns, your turn." She used her harshest voice. I didn't mind, because I was proud of my speech. I walked up to the front of the class and began.

"This speech is called 'The Tale of a Cat.'" I looked around the room. "Get it?" Nobody blinked, so I continued, my face going red.

"Our cat is a black cat with white paws and his name is" — but then the room started spinning. "His name is D'Arcy, on account of" — the floor looked like the ceiling and the walls were coming closer. People's faces distorted, and sounds were way too loud. My calves had that heavy feeling I sometimes got when I was going to have a seizure. I would just die of embarrassment if I were to have a seizure and wet myself and snort like a pig. The illusion of me being cool would be shattered forever and everyone would look at me differently. They might even make fun of me, behind my back or to my face. Then I would go back to being uncool Ana, my Connecticut self. My real self.

I looked up at Miss Prior. "I'm sorry but I'm feeling dizzy. I don't think I can do it."

The class was silent.

"Too dizzy? What a load of horse manure. Everyone is scared of public speaking, my dear, so you take a breath and you continue the speech you have taken the time to write, or I will pulverize you."

I was in shock. Nobody had ever argued with me when I told them I was feeling dizzy because they did not want to deal with a seizure, even though being dizzy did not always mean that I was going to have a seizure.

"Now, begin, Burns, or you get a zero and a fat lip."

Unlike Emilie, I was scared to death of Miss Prior. Even though I knew she would never actually pulverize me, my fear of her wrath was stronger than my fear of seizure, so I relented. After a long pause, in which I tried to control my breathing and my swirliness, I began again. After a few minutes, my feet stopped shaking and I was able to look around the class instead of just at one spot on the floor. I felt good, like I was gliding down a hill on my bicycle, and I speechified until the end. The whole class clapped, especially Miss Prior. Miss Prior said, "Brava, you are going to the finals. I detest cats myself, but that was a lot of *fun*, quite well observed, and surprise, surprise, very well delivered. Dizzy my foot."

It was the first time anyone said I had done something well. I was, in a way, the happiest I had ever been. But the Holy Ghost punished me for being happy and having a swelled head. A few days after that, something serious happened with Birdie. Something that proved to me that I was not a better person than I was in Middletown. It was a false spring day in March. One of those days when it is suddenly so warm you only need a sweater, after months of twenty-below-zero weather and blinding snowstorms. The ice was melting, and there were happy little streams everywhere, running into the gutter. You could hear the birds. I saw a robin red breast, perched on the tippy top of the linden tree in our backyard, singing so loudly I had to cover my ears. I was happy, but restless. I wanted some action. I wanted something interesting to happen. So, I got on my bike and rode over to Birdie's.

Birdie was watching golf on TV with her dad in their little TV room off the kitchen, and reading Nancy Drew, *The Mystery at Lilac Inn*. I think this was only the second time I had ever seen her dad because he travelled all over the world for his work fixing airplanes. He was having a glass of what I think was Scotch, a nasty-smelling alcohol drink my dad liked too.

She looked up and then back at the TV.

"Oh. Hi." It seemed like she really didn't want to see me. I wondered if she was hurt that I hadn't called her in a long time, or maybe she just wanted to hang out with her Calvin Park friends. Whatever, I knew I could win her back.

"Hey. You want to go biking? We could bike down to Bath Road and get our favourite chocolate bars. I've got money."

Without looking up, she mumbled, "I haven't biked in a while."

I knew she didn't like biking. Even though she had a beautiful, brand new, blue bicycle, with three speeds, whereas mine only had one speed. I tried to be an encouraging friend. "Come on. We'll just go slowly. We could walk them up the hill."

She looked at her dad. He looked a lot like Birdie, same merry eyes especially and even the same glasses. Main difference was that he was very tall. I envied Birdie having a dad who was away all the time, because of the presents he brought when he came home — the most exotic presents imaginable, Japanese dolls with real silk kimonos, or Indian lady dolls with saris. He told her he thought bicycling was a splendid idea, because in his opinion, she needed to get the heck out of the house.

He came outside to check that her bike was working okay, and off we went.

I loved my green bicycle. I would ride round and round our crescent. The reason it was called Cataraqui Hills was, first, that it was beside a Cataraqui, which is another word for golf course, and second, that there were two very steep hills, which meant one really hard upward climb, and then flat for about twelve houses at the top, then the funnest downward ride ever.

I suggested we take a spin around the block. There were still several huge construction sites, new houses still several months away from being finished. We had been warned again and again not to go near them.

"Let's go round the block three times! Let's see who can go faster!"

"I don't think so."

"Come on. It'll be fun! Don't be a scaredy-cat!"

Birdie did not say a thing for the longest time. Then she agreed. "All right, I'll try."

"The number one rule is you can't touch your brakes."

"What about the construction sites?"

"You stay on the road, you curve around when it's time, it's easy. Why would you go straight into a big hole? You have a straight-A average, you are smart enough to know when the road turns."

We tried to cycle up the first hill but we both had to get off our bikes at the steepest part. From the top, we could see two different construction sites.

"I think I'll walk down."

"You can't."

"Yes, I can."

"Wussssy."

"I am not."

"Prove it."

"Okay. But I'm going to use my brakes if I need to. I'll do it once and then I'm going home."

"Fine. Whatever. If you want to play it safe."

"Why are you being mean, anyway?"

I didn't answer that because I knew the truth. The truth was that I was channelling Frances, the way she would act with me. I didn't really like myself for being like that; at the same time, I couldn't seem to stop.

We cycled on the flat part past the Harpers', who all had short, curly red hair and glasses and lived in the biggest house on the block, with actual pillars, and three big evergreen trees out front, and Dr. Raimond's, who had a walleye and brown hair in a crewcut and lived in a big house that my mum said was a "ghastly English Tudor imitation," and the Fernie's, who had the daughter in a wheelchair so they had a big ramp, and then over to the other hill. We stopped at the top and peered down. There were three construction sites and spindly newly planted maples and cedars on the side. Even I was a little nervous.

"You wanna go first, or should I?"

"I'll go."

"Good! That's so great, you'll be so happy you did!!" I don't know why I was talking like a gym teacher.

She looked around.

"I haven't done this in a while."

Her voice was shaky. I guess she was scared, but she didn't want me to know. She looked back at me and then got up onto her seat.

"I'm waiting." Why was I being like that??

"Well, you can wait another minute." *Good for her, sticking up for herself*, I thought. More than I ever did with Frances. I vowed to be nicer.

"You're my friend. I'll wait as long as you like." When I said that I felt my left ear fill with feeling like I could cry out of my ear. Because she was my friend.

And she went. She flew down that hill, hair blowing behind her. I cheered her on. And then, suddenly, she started to scream. It seemed like she had forgotten how to control her bike. I yelled, "The brakes, Birdie, the brakes!" I don't think she heard me because of the wind and her panic. Her back looked so straight and stiff and then she stopped screaming and she was silent. Instead of curving with the road, away from the construction site, she rode right into it.

She was too scared to scream, but I screamed all right. I screamed and screamed.

It was strange how she stayed upright on the bicycle as she rode right into the construction site — if anything her back got straighter and straighter. The bicycle flew out from underneath her, and Birdie somersaulted over rebar and blocks of cement until I couldn't see her. She must have been trapped in the pipes they build under the basement.

I was breathing so fast the air was suddenly like ice. I threw my bike to the ground, leaving it in the middle of the road and ran. She wasn't under the pipes, but she was in the part where the basement of the house was going to be. There were already stairs, so I got down easily.

She was unconscious. I had to wake her up.

I put her head in my lap. I talked to her. Softly, like my mum used to do when I was sick.

"Birdie. Wake up, sleepy."

I smacked her cheeks lightly, like I'd seen on television.

No response.

"Birdie, please, please, just wake up."

She opened her eyes for a second. She seemed to be looking just beyond me. What was she looking at?

"Birdie! Why didn't you stay on the road? Or use your brakes?"

Her eyes closed. I shook her shoulders. "Please Birdie, open your eyes!" But she wasn't waking up.

I was so scared she was going to die. Was it my fault for saying she shouldn't use her brakes? Why did she listen to me? I had a can of ginger ale in my purse. I popped it open and took a sip, and then I poured it over her.

She opened her eyes again. So briefly.

Her leg was angled like a doll that had been thrown in the garbage. I think there was even a chalk-white bone sticking out. She had cut her other arm on the bricks and the copper wires. There was blood everywhere. It was so red. Nothing is as red as blood.

"Wake up!" I screamed.

She whispered something. "Mum and Dad."

"I'm going! Just don't die on me! Okay?"

She passed out again. It was so strange, because when somebody is sleeping, you can always wake them up by shaking them or talking loudly in their ear. When a person is passed out, you can't wake them up. Or if you do, it's only for a second.

I walked away. My legs were so heavy it was like walking through mud. I walked past Birdie's house to my own and walked up the side to the backyard, where I sat in the green lounge chair where I had originally been the first day she met me. I sat there and I closed my eyes. I could feel the devil's red scaly hand around my throat, his long black nails digging into the flesh. I tried to make a sound to call my mother and father, but nothing came out. I tried to open my eyes, but it was as if the devil had nailed them shut. I could not open my eyes. Suddenly, there was a bright light shining through my eyelids. A bright amber light. Through my eyelids, I saw Patty. She was right in front of me, with a halo, like the Virgin Mary. She was pulling the devil's claws from my throat. Her face was so close to mine, one green eye and one blue looking right into mine. I saw water rising. Rising over her face. I saw her choking, gasping for breath, all the while looking right into my eyes.

A weird sound like when racoons fight in the backyard came out of me. I jumped off the chaise and ran as fast as I could to Birdie's house. The door was open, so I ran in and there was Birdie's dad still watching the golf and her mum in the kitchen humming while opening and closing cupboards. I thought I could smell peanut butter cookies baking.

"Ana, hello. Where's Birdie?"

"She's ... she's ... drowning ... she ..."

"Drowning? What?"

"Over ... there ... over" — I could hardly breathe, I was hyperventilating.

Both their faces changed like the sky right before a thunderstorm.

"Ana. Can you take us to where Birdie is?"

I ran out, and their screen door slammed behind me.

Birdie's mum called an ambulance.

I was running so fast it was like my feet were springs and Mr. Van Der Knacker was running behind me. The construction site was only eight houses away, so we got there pretty fast. I pointed. The bicycle lay all twisted. Her green helmet had fallen into the site.

"Oh, dear God," said her dad. "Birdie. Good Lord have mercy."

I noticed his breathing was faster too. He clambered down the stairs and he sat with her.

"Can't move her. You should never move anyone who has been in an accident like this. Could break their neck."

I began to cry.

"Birdie, it's Daddy. You are going to be just fine. The ambulance is on the way; don't you worry a bit."

I went to get my bike, which was still in the middle of the road.

I wheeled it back to the site and watched as her mum and the men from the ambulance scrambled down into the unfinished basement of the house that would be occupied by the Carsons and their six boys in a few months.

"Ana. Just go home and tell your parents what happened."

My mother was at the dining room table with the worried face, which meant she was doing bills. My father was in the basement with the football game on. My brother was in his room with a friend. I went into the kitchen and opened and closed the fridge and then went to my room and lay on my bed and stared at the orange corduroy curtains. They found out what happened later that night when Birdie's mum called to say that Birdie was going to be fine, just a broken collar bone and a broken hand and a sprained ankle, and some cuts to the face. A miracle. I thought to myself that I must have hallucinated that white bone. She wanted to thank me for being Birdie's friend and helping. Mum made me get on the phone.

"Hi."

"Hi, Ana. I just wanted to let you know that Birdie is going to be fine. She does have a broken collar bone, and a broken hand, but generally she is not doing too badly. The doctors are amazed. I wanted to thank you for helping our Birdie out."

They didn't know that the whole thing was my fault. Birdie hadn't told her.

My mum looked me right in the eye.

"Why didn't you tell us?"

I opened the fridge and peered into the freezer compartment.

"Do we have any ice cream sandwiches?"

I then ran to my room and threw myself on my bed, face down. I did not understand what was happening to me and I felt powerless to stop it.

I heard my mother calling out to my father, who was downstairs marking student papers and watching baseball and drinking Scotch.

"John? Jawwwn?"

I knew they would talk about me.

I cried most of the night, and when I dreamed, I dreamed of Birdie cycling, sitting up so straight, cycling into the wires and cement. In the morning, I shuffled to the kitchen. Mum was sitting at the table drinking instant coffee.

"How is she? Mum? Mum. Is Birdie dead? Did Birdie die?"

"No, no, no, goodness, darling. Aletta told you last night, she's going to be fine. Don't you remember speaking to Aletta?"

I didn't.

"Birdie is at the hospital, probably for a while. Broken collar bone, broken hand. Terribly bruised face. Her dad said we can visit in a week or so."

Mum sat down across from me and looked me in the eye. "How on earth did it happen?"

"I don't know. I don't know why she didn't just brake. Her brakes were fine. Her dad even checked her brakes before we left. I guess she panicked."

Mum took my hand. "How are you darling? That must have been very scary for you."

"Yes."

What I didn't tell Mum was that what scared me the most was that I might have been responsible for another death. Another death of a true friend.

THE SKY AFTER sunset is maybe even more beautiful than the sky during sunset. It's the pink and the red and the mauve, but really, it's so much more. It's something even I can't put into words. That's why I'm going to hang out here for a while longer. I want to see the sky turn midnight blue. And then the stars? We can't even see stars in town.

AT ST. THOMAS More school it was time for the Finals. I wasn't sure what Miss Prior meant by "the Finals" exactly, but then she told the class, "Tomorrow is the day of the Finals. Tomorrow is the day our school is competing with every Catholic school in Frontenac County. They send the best from every grade, my friends. We are competing with the best. Are we ready?"

A smattering of "Yes, Miss."

"Oh, I know we are ready. Miss I'm-Too-Dizzy has a smashing speech and if she doesn't win the gold I will eat my hat."

The class laughed. I was in shock. A "smashing speech"? It was? What exactly did she mean by "smashing"?

"Get that dumb rabbit look off your face, Burns, you are going to win this!" She looked directly into my eyes. I looked away, giggling nervously.

"You think this is a joke?"

"No, Miss Prior."

"Who here thinks this is a joke?"

Graham Morton put up his hand. I could see Miss Prior's soft spot for Graham getting gushier, even though she was pretending to be strict.

"Mr. Morton. You regard this as a joke?"

"Yes, ma'am."

"And why is that, Mr. Morton?"

"Because all the speeches suck."

"That is a matter of opinion, Mr. Morton. And your opinion is wrong. Now go back to sleep."

He was right, of course, about most of them. Some in the class tittered, and Graham leaned back in his desk and looked right into Miss Prior's eyeliner eyes and grinned. Somehow even though he said he hadn't ever been to a dentist, he had perfectly even, white teeth. Miss Prior rolled her eyes.

"It is not a joke. It is about bringing honour to our school. Let's take a moment to think about honour, and what it really means." The class was silent for about thirty seconds, some of us thinking about honour, most of us thinking about recess.

"Now. About your atrocious essays on *The Red Badge of Courage*. You are going to rewrite them until they are respectable. This may take two, three, or seven rewrites. What I want are your own original thoughts. Not something you copy from the study guide. I want you to trust your own responses. And you know what? You will not graduate grade seven until I am satisfied. I will flunk every one of you if I have to. Understand?"

Even though most of us inwardly groaned, we kinda loved it when she was tough. We knew it meant she liked us.

The next day was the Finals. We were told to wear our Sunday best, so I wore a green velvet dress and Emilie wore a brown empire waist dress with white polka dots. We had bought them together at Steacy's on Princess Street. I was quite embarrassed that I had not developed breasts yet, but there was no way of hiding what wasn't there. Emilie had already started her period. She had breasts, even though they weren't big. She said I should not be hoping to get my period, because it was nothing but a pain. I still prayed for it every day, even though I didn't get it for two more years.

Yellow buses parked in front of the school and dressed-up kids piled out, talking and laughing, looking the same as us but different somehow. There were three grade seven classes, and four grade eight classes. I was more nervous than I had ever been.

I heard one speech after another, most of them boring, all about Canada's new flag, or "reach for the stars," or Centennial year, or their great grandparents immigrating from Ireland because of the famine. I thought I might actually faint from boredom. Then I heard my own name called: Ana Burns, grade seven, St. Thomas More, Rita Prior. I looked at Miss Prior. Me? She nodded and violently gestured towards the podium.

She hissed, "Get up there NOW, Dizzy!" I noticed that my feet were shaking again when I walked up to the podium. It was as if I had forgotten how to walk, and I was just going through the motions, like someone just learning.

I looked out at the audience, my mother's bright red face and my dad in his beige raincoat that really needed a wash and his lake-in-a-rainstorm grey-blue eyes showing me goodwill, cheering me on. Mum actually waved, with her long red nails and her big red face, which mortified me. I actually frowned at her, and then I was mad at her for making me forget my first line, which I had spent many hours and days memorizing. How could I forget my first line? I spotted Doug Martin in the corner, whispering to Michael Garland, and I felt the support of my class, which was nice. I dove right in. "I want to tell you the tale of a cat named D'Arcy, who changed our lives forever. D'Arcy is black and shiny with three white paws and a white kind of bib. Anyways, um, we found D'Arcy, um, uhhh ..." (I couldn't remember the next part! *Where did we find him?*) Oh. Right ...

And then another voice came out of my mouth. "Um, well, I love my cat and everything but seeing as there are so many priests and nuns here, like people who speak the truth with God,

I want to tell you about something that happened to me once that I never actually confessed."

I look at the faces and they look like cartoons. Nuns, priests, parents, kids from other schools, all crowded into the hot auditorium, looking at me, but without real eyes. Their faces started to swirl. But it didn't feel like seizure swirling. It was a different kind of swirling, an *everything is going to change* swirling.

Miss Prior looked confused, and she was shaking her head at me, as if to say, *No, no, just stay with your cat story!*

I was about to go back to "The Tale of a Cat" when I saw Patty in the crowd. But she wasn't like the others, she was bright and shining. The more I looked at her, the more three-dimensional she became, whereas the rest of them were fleshy swirls of cartoon characters, even my parents, but Patty had a light blue hair band and her dirty blond hair in a slight flip and her long face and deep-lidded blue eyes. She was peering right into my heart and giving me strength.

"When I was seven, I went to a camp called Bearmac. At the end of camp, I was given the Miss Good Samaritan Award, but I didn't deserve it."

Miss Prior would be furious. She loved "The Tale of a Cat." I was too scared to even look at her because I knew I couldn't stop myself.

The words just poured out of me like when the lizards and bugs pour out of the princess's mouth in that fairy tale because she didn't give the old woman water at the well.

I couldn't stop and change to "The Tale of a Cat" even though the paper was right in front of me and I had memorized the speech, practicing in front of the mirror for hours and hours. I didn't understand what was happening, but since I had no choice, I gave in. I started to feel I was in warm water, being moved along by the current.

I fixed my eyes into Patty's eyes, and yes, it was her. She was willing me to tell this story. The force of her eyes was the current, moving me through the water.

I let go of the paper my speech was neatly written on. It dropped to the floor. Words I didn't plan fell out of my mouth.

"ON THE THIRD day of camp we had been divided into different cabins. My cabin was called Evergreen. 'Okay Evergreens, your time on the jungle gym,' Shannon yelled. Shannon had a voice hoarse from always shouting. She had been shouting at campers since July first, and it was now the middle of August, so her voice was almost just a frog croak. 'One two three, RUN! Get up on that jungle gym! You have forty-five minutes before swim time!' So, we ran. I wasn't fast like the others, but I wasn't slow either. Somewhere in the middle. I always liked being in the middle because then I wasn't noticed. I was a really shy kid when I was little. So, this jungle gym was like Disneyland in my eyes: It was big and so blue and just shimmering. I was in love. Why? Because I loved climbing. It seemed my legs and knees and feet and arms and hands knew what to do before I did. I just clambered up, like a monkey, faster than most of the other kids, except the one loudest girl, Janet. 'Come on you slowpokes, last one to the top is a dirty rotten egg,' she yelled in her bossy voice. We made it a race and one girl, Laura, who was the winner in all the running races, she reached the top first, and she cheered, 'I'm the greatest!' Janet did not like that one bit. 'Hey. You. You think you're so smart? You think you are cool? Well, you are not smart and you are not cool. You are fat and ugly. And you know what? I own this jungle gym and so whatever I say goes. And what I say is that you have to get off. Now! None of us wanna see your ugly face, okay?'"

I took a deep breath and continued. Strangely, my voice was clear and strong and, strangest of all, calm.

"We all froze. I was so scared that Loud Girl was going to notice me and kick me off too, that I was shaking, my feet were even shaking, so violently I could hardly stay on the gym. My hands were sweating so much that they were slippery. I didn't even think of talking back to her, even though I was pretty sure that a kid couldn't own a jungle gym. I prayed to the Virgin Mary that she wouldn't kick me off. At that moment, staying on that jungle gym felt like the most important thing in the world. Even though I felt sorry for Laura, and I really did, the thought of defending her, or leaving the jungle gym with her to show I was on her side? That didn't even occur to me. Or any of us. Laura looked around at the rest of us, I knew hoping for one of us to be on her side, but we all looked away. Loud Girl bellowed, 'I said NOW, what's wrong with you, are you deaf?' And very slowly, Laura climbed down. It seemed to take forever, even though it was probably only five minutes. I watched her walk away slowly towards the lake."

The blurry shapes of the crowd cleared, and I could finally see the faces. The pudgy, pale priest from Cathedral school, tired looking parents in shabby coats, bored, fidgety sisters and brothers of the speech-makers, my own, mortifyingly bright-faced parents, Miss Prior, looking like my image of Cleopatra, with her eyeliner and her haughty expression. No Patty. I was in the real world again. I wasn't sure what to say next. Was I finished? Should I go back to "The Tale of a Cat"? Miss Prior interrupted me before I could embarrass myself.

"Clap for God's sake. What's wrong with you people? Were you all born in barns? Clap!"

I looked around till I found Patty but as soon as I looked her in the eye, she disappeared, just like on *Star Trek*, when they discombobulate to go somewhere else.

For one long second nobody except Miss Prior was clapping, then my mum and my dad started to clap really loud and then Paulie.

My mum and dad didn't count, but Miss Prior did. She was clapping so loudly it was like cymbals crashing together, and she was looking around while she clapped, with her dark eyebrows arched, like a dangerous film star. She was glaring at people so fiercely that they finally clapped, as if they were unsure of what they had heard. The kids in my class clapped because I was in their class, but quite weakly, because if you weren't a celebrity, or sports star, that's what they did. The principal and the other teachers and the nuns and priests clapped politely, with no oomph at all. Clearly, they didn't care, one way or the other. To my amazement, one nun I didn't know clapped just like Miss Prior, as if I had given the best speech in the entire world. And she kept going when everyone else had stopped, even though the other nuns were giving her the stink-eye. She was taller than anyone around her, and she had waxy yellowish skin and the biggest red hands I had ever seen on anyone.

I felt the walls moving, as if I was on the Tilt-A-Whirl, the slow one in the park that the kids have to push.

The jury of priests and nuns left the room for ten excruciating minutes and then came back with three pendants: gold, silver, and bronze. Somehow, I dared to hope. I don't know why. I looked over at Miss Prior, but she was avoiding my gaze. My parents were looking at the floor.

The priest who was the head of the jury must have watched a lot of TV game shows because he sounded exactly like the host of *The Price Is Right*, with a sort of over the top and wavy kind of voice.

"And the bronze medal gooooooоes to: Michael GARland for his EXcellent speech on the founding of the city of Kingston.

Very well researched, young man. You have a future as a history teacher!!" Michael shlumped up to receive his medal, murmured his thanks, and shlumped back to his seat, where his friends swiped the medal and started throwing it around.

The priest continued, "The silver goes to Miss Magdalena Bobrowski! Yes, Magdalena, it's you, unless there is another Magdalena in the room. I don't think so! Not here in Kingston! Yes, Magdalena snags the silver for her ultra-moving speech on the Holy Spirit; we appreciated her serious and solemn reflection on one of the great mysteries of the Catholic church, which, of course, is the only TRUE church, right everybody?" Magdalena walked up in her noisy party shoes, her head held high, her hair swinging and gave a little curtsey while accepting the award. Emilie looked back at me and made a throwing-up gesture.

Miss Prior looked over at me and rolled her eyes. I smiled a tight smile.

He continued, "And finally ... are you ready everybody? Are you ready for the BIG moment?"

I knew I was crazy to hope, but for a moment, I did, mainly because Miss Prior seemed to like the speech so much, and Miss Prior was always right.

"The gold goes to Elmira Leuwen, from Cathedral School, for her knock-out speech on the great work the Catholic church is doing with our native people. Bringing the word of Jesus Christ to each and every Indian we can, providing the best education in our beautiful residential schools, so that our Native kids will come outta there with perfect English, a real understanding of right and wrong, and a good trade."

I looked at my dad, remembering what we had seen at Expo 67. "*White schools are bad for Indian kids*" and "*Indian kids are starving ... they need their families.*" My dad just looked at the floor, shaking his head. Everyone else in the crowd cheered for Elmira. But not Miss Prior and not the clapping nun.

The crowd parted for her as she walked up to the lectern to receive her gold plaque. She walked like an old lady, slightly bent over with her head down. The bent over part was to hide her boobs, which were way too big for a twelve-year-old, and the head down was because she was shy. Elmira was a six-foot-tall girl with long, greasy, reddish hair that covered most of her face. She wore the Cathedral School uniform even though everyone else was in their Sunday best. She gave a long, prepared thank-you speech, thanking her parents, the Sisters at Cathedral School, her grandparents, and the fine nuns and priests doing the Lord's work at the residential schools.

"Suck up," Emilie mouthed from across the room. I appreciated that, but I was too nervous to nod my head. My teeth were chattering as if I was suddenly very cold, though my face was burning.

I ran to the girls' washroom so I could throw cold water on my hot and flushed face when the very tall clapping nun pushed open the door.

Her voice was shrill and she grabbed my arm too tightly.

"Dear child, would you like to know why you didn't win?"

Something told me I wouldn't get away with being snarky with this nun. Maybe because she was just strange and not like other nuns.

"Um, Sister, do you mind? That hurts my arm."

"Would you? Would you like to know?" She gave me the creeps, and I wanted to get away from her. I could see my parents waiting for me, through the glass door at the end of the hall.

"Oh, um, there are my parents. Sorry I gotta go," I said a little sharply. She lurched towards me and held my shoulders tightly. I could feel her desperation. She had bad B.O. too.

"Because your speech was about how you wished you had spoken up."

"No, it wasn't. It was about this girl being kicked off the jungle gym."

"And they don't want anyone to ever speak up." She didn't register what I had said. She continued in the weird whisper. Her smell was making me gag.

"I didn't speak up either. After I saw what I saw. At first, I thought that I could not have seen what I saw, or heard what I heard, it was not possible. I thought it was the devil sending me a hallucination, to turn me against Father Douris."

The devil? Now I was interested. Maybe Magdalena was right, maybe he was roaming around. The nun continued, like she was a car with no brakes at all — careening towards me. "At the school in Spanish, Ontario. Where I taught sewing and English to Indian children for two years until I saw what I saw. More than once. I saw it, child, but I never said anything. I never said a word. Because I knew what would happen to me if I did! The same thing that happened to them! I made up a story about my mother being ill and I left. And what's worse is, I will never say anything. Because I am a coward. Just like you, only you were a child, and —"

I turned from her and ran, as fast as I could down the hallway to my parents, who both hugged me and told me how well I had done. Later in the car, my mother asked, "What was the Sister talking to you about?"

"Oh, nothing, she just said she liked my speech."

"I just hope you don't blame yourself for not standing up for that girl who was kicked off the jungle gym, Ana. That was not your responsibility."

"Yeah. But Frances would have."

"No. No, Ana. Frances would have been the one kicking her off."

THE FIRST TIME I spoke to Frances since the day Patty drowned was when we were both fourteen, just three years ago. My dad had been invited to the University of Connecticut to give a talk about his work with certain plants, and Mum thought it would be fun if the whole family went and we drove the extra thirty minutes or so to Middletown to see everyone again. I refused to go at first, because even hearing the word *Middletown* made me feel like throwing up. But the pull of Frances had me. What was she like now? Was she better looking than me? Was she more popular? Would she still have power over me? We piled into the old black and white Rambler, and off we went. Mum and Dad in the front, me and Paulie in the back. Mum and Dad chain-smoked the entire way. Mum didn't like the car windows open because the wind messed her hair, so Paulie and I had trouble breathing, but neither of us minded. We were used to it. I was glad it was such a long drive because it gave me time to prepare. The closer we got, the more nervous I felt. Every stop I would run to the bathroom mirror to redo my makeup. I had become an almost pretty girl. Not a dork anymore. I wore Levi's jeans and a white, gauzy top that looked really good. I knew I was not the same girl who left Middletown all those years ago. I was pretty sure she would treat me differently.

Next thing I knew, we were in Frances's parents' living room, the same living room I had spent so much of my childhood in. Their house smelled exactly the same as I remembered. The same couches, the same paintings, and those three little dogs were still there, sleeping on the couches. The grown-ups regaled each other with vicious but fascinating gossip about old friends. Frances was on the phone with somebody, so she hadn't even said hello. I felt like a total idiot for coming and desperately wished I had stayed in Kingston with Emilie. Mrs. Kester brought me an orange juice with a maraschino cherry in it. I sat on the couch, petting the dogs, wondering if they remembered me. Suddenly Frances was there, standing over me.

"Come on, let's go to my room." No hug, no *hello, welcome back!* Just an order. She hadn't changed a bit. She looked stylish, in a hippie kind of way. Her jeans fit just right, she had a ring on every finger, and a mauve kind of top you might see on a model. She had bare feet, like in our barefoot summers.

I followed her up the stairs and without turning around she continued, "My mother's going to get drunk, and she makes me sick when she's drunk. She once even tried to neck with our babysitter."

I thought *here she goes, lying again already*. I remembered how I would always pretend I didn't know she was lying and realized I would have to pretend again.

"Eeee, that's terrible. How embarrassing."

"Ya think?" she sneered.

Her bedroom was still pink, but now there were posters of the Rolling Stones and the Beatles, and some hippie kind of prints, the word LOVE written in that crazy way. I sat on one of the twin beds. Her room smelled like patchouli.

Her eyes, which looked into mine in a mocking and assessing

way, were still crinkly brown and her light brown hair, now long and straight and parted in the middle, gleamed with blond and red highlights. She still frightened me, so I tried to talk my way out of that fear. I told her in detail about my life in Kingston, my friends, and Canada in general. I liked telling her how much better it was than Middletown, Connecticut. She suddenly began stroking her hair, with a stunned look on her face. At first I didn't understand, then I realized that I had been stroking my hair, giving away my fear of her. I had been caught out. She was mocking me. I wished I could just disappear. I sat on my hands and resolved not to give away any more weakness. I noticed a huge pile of dirty underwear on the floor. She noticed me noticing.

"Hah. Laird thinks I'm such a slob."

"Who's Laird?

"My boyfriend. He's nineteen. I am so annoyed because he's on his way to this really far-out music festival, with our other friends. Woodstock. Peace and love and drugs and sex and it's three days long. My parents said I couldn't go. Such assholes. Jimi Hendrix and Janis Joplin are playing. And the Grateful Dead!"

I had heard about Woodstock, just like everybody else. I didn't want her to think Canadians weren't cool.

"Oh yeah, my friend's older brother is going."

She walked to her window, which looked out onto the yard. I remembered the camp-out in that yard after one of my seizures, when she and Joni Gracielle told me that I had snorted like a pig. Thinking about it made me queasy. With her back to me, she said, "It was gonna be so great. Laird and me and Laird's brother Will, and his girlfriend, but my stupid parents said no."

"Do you still hate your mother?" I regretted it as soon as I asked her.

She denied ever having said that, but I clearly remembered her saying that all the time, because I had been so shocked by it.

"You're imagining things, Annie. Always loved my Mommy. They are just trying to protect me. It's gonna be so wild. Too wild for me."

"Sorry, must have been someone else."

"Yeah, I guess so," she said, hitting the word *guess* as hard as she could, so hard it hurt. She got up and turned on a big fan in the corner. It was one of those fans that turn slowly back and forth.

"This rich friend of ours, Elizabeth? She has actual air conditioning in her house. Like a movie theatre. Can you imagine?"

"That would be amazing. Our house gets so hot, I can't sleep sometimes. The only thing that helps is a cold shower." I felt like we were kind of flowing now.

"Hot? In Canada? You're pulling my leg, right?"

I was tempted to say that it snowed all summer, to get one up on her after the hair stroking put-down, but sarcasm never came easily to me.

"Yeah, just as hot. Maybe hotter."

"I don't believe that. It's Canada. People live in igloos and eat snow."

I knew she was playing me; she knew that not all Canadians lived in igloos and that it wasn't cold all the time. I wasn't sure how to react. She was bored with me already, I could tell. She was distracted. I definitely got the feeling she did not want me there. I would have given anything to not be there.

I used my best teacher voice. "Where we are, in Kingston, Ontario, the weather is pretty much exactly the same as Connecticut. If you went way up north, it is a lot colder, but they do still have summer, even above the treeline. And it's light, twenty-four hours a day."

"Ohhh okay then. Why are you going red in the face? Wait a minute, you always had a tomato face, right?"

This was not going well.

"So, do you have a boyfriend?" she asked, without any interest.

"I've had a couple, but not right now."

"Laird is so cool. And he's totally in love with me."

"That's nice."

"Except he always wants to do it, you know? Even when I don't feel like it, at the beginning and end of every date. In his stupid car."

A really awkward silence. I had to say something.

"That sounds gross."

"What? Are you kidding? It's amazing. It's an amazing feeling when a guy is inside you, it, like, fills you up."

"I thought you just said —"

"You are clearly a virgin."

I did not know what to say. I was not going to talk about those things with her. I could feel myself going red in the face again, just like my mother.

"Hah, funny when a tomato face blushes. Double tomato."

"I guess."

A long silence followed while she walked around her room, fiddling with little figurines on her dresser.

"Do you ever see them?"

A certain *something* came over her face. Like she had been ambushed.

"Who?" she asked, although I knew she knew exactly who I meant.

"You know. Miles and — I can't even say his name. The other one."

"Yeah, I see Miles sometimes."

"You do?"

"He has this really cool band, the Ruffians, and Laird is actually a friend of his."

My heart pounded at the thought she still saw him.

"Doesn't it make you uncomfortable? Seeing him?"

"I don't really think about it," she lied.

"You don't ever think about what happened?"

"I really don't want to talk about it."

Her voice became aggressive. I could feel myself shrinking.

"Oh, okay."

Frances walked over to her bedroom door and locked it. I suddenly remembered Bernice Wissy, not being allowed to leave until she showed us her breasts.

"It took a while for me to not blame you, Annie."

"What?"

"You were pushing so hard to go along with the boys. Pushing and pushing me. I had a very bad feeling about what they were wanting, but you kept saying 'come on, let's go.' I couldn't resist you. I'm still mad at you. I really did not want to see you."

I felt like the ceiling was suddenly on the floor.

"Umm ... What? Whoaaa. You aren't serious. Is that how you remember it?"

"That is how it was."

Was she messing with me, reversing the way things were? I searched her face and decided that she was not messing with me, she was telling what she perceived as the truth. I had to tell her my truth. Which was the truth.

"Oh. That is really funny, I actually remember the opposite."

"What?"

"You were the bossy one and you wanted to go with them and play whatever game they pretended they had in mind. Obviously, you didn't realize what it really was. But I kept saying no, shaking my head, and stalling. Surely you remember that? I even had a seizure."

She looked at me with hatred, her eyes like stones. "You have really twisted things, haven't you? Don't you remember? I was fucking scared of those boys! My sister had told me what boys like that were after. In enough detail to terrify me! You forced me to follow them up into the attic. You threatened me. I remember it so clearly. You wouldn't be my friend if I backed out. To tell you the truth, I've blamed you for my messed-up relationship with sex."

I looked her right in the eye and I did not look away. "That is not at all how I remember it."

"I have an infallible memory," she said calmly. "I score perfect on all school tests, one hundred percent on almost all of them."

I didn't doubt that. My hands and feet shook. She still had power over me. I hadn't changed or grown a bit. I was so disappointed in myself. For a moment I considered answering her in the toughest Portsmouth kid, foulest-mouth way I knew: "You fuckin' suck ass bitch cunt one more word out of you and I will fucking cut your throat from ear to ear." I had it all ready, but my good manners won.

"I guess we will have to agree to disagree."

I asked her if she ever told her mom.

She said she had told her immediately, right after it happened. I couldn't breathe for a moment I was so shocked. I hadn't told my parents for the longest time because I had promised her that I wouldn't. What a stupid fool I was. I was so mad at my young self that I pinched the flesh of my forearm as hard as I could. I took a moment to recover, and then I asked her about her mother's response.

"She laughed and she said that would teach me for going up to the attic with big ugly boys."

"Wow. Did you tell her what they actually did to us?"

"Of course not. That would upset her."

"Did you tell her that they talked about killing us?"

"You are the only other person in the world who knows that."

"Did you tell her about Patty?"

"Patty who?"

"Patty Wissy."

"She was that girl from our class who drowned! From the poor family with eight kids? They lived in the condemned house, and they all smelled of overcooked hot dogs. What about her?"

"Do you remember, she was there?"

"Where?"

"In the attic. Leaning against the wall."

"Patty Wissy wasn't there."

"Yes, she was. She was definitely there. She threatened to tell so they chased her into the river. I saw it with my own eyes, I'll never forget her trying to swim, and then her head, going under."

Her eyes widened.

"Annie, you are mixing up two events. Patty Wissy was not there."

She was trying to throw me off. She was really getting under my skin.

"It's Anastasia now. Ever since I moved to Canada," I said, even though it was a lie.

"You're Annie in my house."

That felt aggressive, and I flinched. She was still doing that Frances thing, trying to make me feel smaller. She came over and put her hands on my shoulders.

"Maybe you are misremembering because you had that fit while it was happening. I remember Bernie freaking out and slapping you and Miles telling him to stop."

"It was Patty who was telling him to stop. Miles didn't say anything. He was too busy with you." Her face turned a deep, dark red. The parents exploded in laughter downstairs.

"We were nine years old." We both said that, but not exactly at the same time. It gave me hope that she was warming towards me. But she stood up and headed for the bedroom door.

"I gotta go meet a friend. You can do whatever you want."

She held it open for me.

As I walked through the door she leaned into me and whispered in my ear, "Patty Wissy was not there, you Canadian yokel." I didn't answer because there was no point. I didn't know how I was going to spend two more days with her. It seemed impossible. So, I didn't. I stayed close to Paulie and my mum and dad. We slept in a hotel, so that helped. Paulie and I sat quietly in a corner, whispering, while the grown-ups talked. Frances was busy with parties and sleepovers anyway. I only had to see her at the end.

When we said goodbye, we knew we would never see each other again.

WE HAD TO wear uniforms at Regiopolis-Notre Dame. I hated the idea at first but then it was sort of a relief because I really didn't have a sense of style — that was the part of Frances I couldn't imitate no matter how I tried. The bright white Oxford cloth shirts and the hunter green cashmere sweaters looked good on me. Made my eyes bounce. I needed help in working out exactly how short my kilt needed to be to not be labelled a loser. Emilie knew all that as her older sister, Brigitte, had been at the school for two years by the time we got there. "Exactly three inches above the knee, girls. Okay? Bare legs and green knee socks, even in winter. Does not matter how friggin' cold it is, bare legs, got it?" We headed downtown to Steacy's department store to buy the uniforms and to stock up on high-quality green socks. Emilie could tell me which greens would go with my cashmere sweater, and which would clash.

Grade nine was pretty good. Emilie and I made a new friend, Michele Guinaud, who had just moved to Kingston from Québec. Her family only spoke French at home, but Michele spoke perfect English, with a gorgeous French-Canadian accent, which is why the other kids avoided her. If it had been a France-French accent they would have loved her. But they were weird about

Québec-French accents. Emilie and I loved her accent, and when we imitated it, she didn't take offence, she just laughed, and imitated our boxy accents, which made all of us laugh. She told us that French-Canadians called us Anglos "square heads." We could both see the point, especially Emilie, whose mother was originally French. Michele had short dark hair, flashing brown eyes, and these cute dimples when she smiled, which was all the time. We helped her with her English homework, and got her to help us with French, which meant doing it for us. She always brought two ham sandwiches for lunch, and she was more than happy to share when Emilie or I had forgotten our lunch, which was often. She didn't know anyone else at the school. We were a happy threesome from the beginning — and sometimes a foursome when Hilary joined us. Hilary had the cutest shag haircut and a perfect doll face. She missed school a lot, but when she did come her boyfriend, Sandy, rode her to school on his motorbike — we never got a good look at him, but we got the feeling he was a bit older than her, maybe even eighteen or nineteen. She was reviled by the other girls because there was a rumour that when she was out once for eight weeks it was because she had an abortion. She told everyone it was some kind of kidney problem, and though we believed her, no one else did. We believed her until we heard from Wendy Asher, who literally was too stupid to lie, that her best friend's mother was a nurse who knew another nurse at KGH (they would never perform an abortion at Hotel Dieu!) who told her about Hilary's abortion: Apparently Hil had to actually give birth because she was five and a half months along, and it was bad. Even if it was true, we felt sorry for Hilary, with all those mean girls gossiping about her like a bunch of hissing snakes. She was sweet and pretty and she liked our jokes.

So even though we weren't in the in crowd with the kids who had all gone through Cathedral School together, we weren't in the absolute out crowd either. I said "Hi!" to people I knew in the hallways, like each person was my favourite person in the world. My smile was fake, but I didn't really know how to change that. There were dances for every occasion: a Valentine's Dance, a St. Patrick's Day dance, a Sadie Hawkins dance. I even got asked to the dances once or twice, by the same very quiet boy, Gordon, who was in grade ten. All that meant is that we met at the dance, and without exchanging a word, danced the slow dances. When the dance was over, Gordon disappeared. He never looked me in the eyes once. After that, I usually said no when he asked me because Emilie, Michele, and I preferred to go without a date, so that there would be the possibility of meeting a really cute, popular guy — like Pete Anderson, the quarterback of the school football team and the most popular guy in the school. It's funny how delusional we were, imagining that Pete had smiled at us in the hall, or Pete was checking us out in the school cafeteria. He wasn't. His girlfriend, Holly, was the most beautiful girl in the school, and the head cheerleader. At the dances, we would mainly just stand along the walls, looking available to dance. Gormy boys we barely knew would ask us to dance, and we would always say no. We didn't care at all that it might have hurt their feelings. Once in a while, a cute guy would actually ask one of us to dance. Sometimes Emilie, sometimes Mich, sometimes me.

After the dances, we would go back to one of our houses and clean off our makeup and get into our jammies and make popcorn and talk about the dance and the other girls — who was crying in the washroom, and who looked like a slut, who was drunk, and who was really sweet and what boys we had our eyes on. We would talk and talk right until dawn, and then sleep until two or three, which drove our parents crazy.

It's funny, the bad reunion I was to have with Frances at the end of the summer after a happy grade nine should have been a warning. *Ana, get ready, because the storm is coming.* Maybe Frances put a curse on me.

Sure enough, Regiopolis-Notre Dame became a hellscape for me partway into grade ten.

One morning in November, three or four fairly large pimples appeared on my forehead and my left cheek. At first, I thought I had been bitten by a mosquito, but they weren't itchy like mosquito bites. They were sore. I stared into the mirror for about an hour trying to work out what to do about them, and then went back to bed, telling my mother I was sick with the stomach flu. I couldn't possibly go to school. Later in the day, when Emilie called to ask why I'd stayed home, I told her what happened.

"I know exactly what to do."

"Really?"

"Yup. Worked for my sister. Like a charm. Get over here now."

I raced over to her house, and into her bathroom. She sat me down on the toilet and tried to squeeze each pimple, which inflamed them so they each grew to the size of a large cockroach.

"Okay, okay, that didn't work but I know for sure what will completely get rid of them. Noxzema!" She rummaged around in the cupboard over the sink and found her sister Brigitte's Noxzema.

"Noxzema? Are you sure?" I was filled with hope. Emilie was a problem solver.

"I've never been more sure of anything. Now stay still."

Emilie spread the Noxzema all over my face, with especially large glops on my actual pimples.

"Keep this on overnight. Do not touch your face or wash it off under any circumstances. I promise, they will all be gone by morning."

"Promise?"

"Absolutely."

I was so frightened I was willing to believe anything. I had never had a problem with my skin, though my mother would tell us stories of being "ravaged, just ravaged by acne when I was thirteen." Once I passed thirteen, I assumed that I would not get it but now I understood the difference. Mum got her period — "We call it the curse, darling, because that is what it is" — at thirteen, and I had just begun mine at fifteen. Dr. Stalker said that when girls begin to menstruate, "all heck breaks loose with the hormones, and that causes acne in some of you." When I washed off the Noxzema the next morning, the pimples were still there, as red and huge and hideous as ever. But now there were ten.

I called Emilie. "There are ten now. TEN."

She laughed. "Sorry. I really thought it would work. It worked for Brigitte. I've never had a pimple in my life."

"It made them worse. I can't come to school."

"You have to! We are doing our Shakespeare presentation, silly! It's worth twenty percent! I can't do it without you; I've memorized my part! Annie!!"

So, I smeared Maybelline tan foundation all over my face in an attempt to cover the ten pimples. It came out kind of orange, but it did a good enough job that I felt I could go to school. Then I applied black eyeliner under my eyes and extended it way out on each side because I would be playing Cleopatra. Our English presentation for Father O'Connor's Shakespeare study was the scene of Cleopatra's death by a poisonous snake from *Antony and Cleopatra*. I was Cleopatra, and Emilie was Charmian, her servant, because she had almost no lines, and Emilie didn't like to memorize. Emilie wore her sister's long peach-coloured granny gown and we both wore black velvet capes from a box of old Halloween costumes we found in Emilie's garage.

We walked confidently, even joyously, up to the front of the class when our time came. We had rehearsed the scene till it was perfect, so we were feeling good. I especially loved saying "I am fire and I am air, my other elements I give to baser life." Somehow, my embarrassment over my face disappeared while we were doing the scene, and both of us were line-perfect. Not one of the other students listened to a word, but we didn't care.

"Marvellous work, you two. What a pair of talented young thespians you are!" shouted Father O'Connor when we finished. We pretty much danced out of that classroom.

But by December the acne transmogrified from the Noxzema ten to twenty, then thirty, then forty, then fifty-seven enormous, red, raised, angry, unpoppable cysts, which ravaged not only my face but under my chin and my neck. I was a monster. Even my parents found it hard to look at me. I could tell. Everybody at school noticed, I caught them wincing when they looked at me. And those were the polite reactions. After gym one day, I heard one of the cheerleaders, Carole, whispering to the others, "She didn't even wash her face." I wanted to tell her why I didn't wash my face; it was because I had spent an hour in the morning, carefully applying the prescription acne medication the doctor had given me, and I didn't want to wash it off. Besides, my face didn't sweat in gym class. But I didn't tell her because I couldn't bring myself to speak. Only Emilie and Michele didn't seem bothered by my face, and I was beyond grateful. "It's going to go away, Ana, I promise you! It happened to my cousin, just like you," Michele tried to reassure me, but I honestly thought it would last forever. Teachers would avoid looking at me, and worst of all, a group of wild, feral boys in my grade started going after me. They were a frenzied squad of low-life losers who somehow frequently managed to corner me when I was alone. They would surround me and make throw-up noises, they would bark like dogs when they saw me, and they would call me "Ugliest chick in the school." Every day was a battle: I woke up, ate the orange slices and the dry piece of toast Dad made, and mentally prepared for attacks. One rule I made for myself was to keep my head held high and to pretend I did not hear them. I vowed to myself I would never say anything back. Because I knew it would only give them fuel. Sometimes I thought about that little girl, Ruby Bridges, I had learned about back in Miss Lawrence's class in Connecticut: how she walked through so much worse, with such grace and perfect posture and ferocious spirit. I tried to follow her lead and fixed my eyes about five feet over their heads and pretended they did not exist. If she could do it, and she was only six, I definitely could do it. I was fifteen. I would never let them think they were having any effect whatsoever.

I laughed about it when Emilie and Michele looked like they were sorry for me, or mad at the boys on my account. "I really could not give one shit," I would say, although they knew I was lying. I never told Mum what was happening, but I know what would have been her advice. "Rise above it." I didn't tell Dad because I would have felt ashamed for him to know I was such a loser. I think it would have shamed him. He liked winners, he always said so.

"Ana, Paulie, always remember: Nothing succeeds like success."

I didn't tell Paulie because he would worry so much about me that he would have his breathing problems again.

Ignoring the attacks was a way of coping, but it did not stop them. Like any predator, the boys could sense not fear, but the soft, tender thing that quivered beneath the fortress I had erected. They would circle me, bark at me, physically trap me.

"Ugly dog, you make me want to barf. Woof woof woof, come on, bark for us."

"So fuckin' ugly. Why are you so fuckin' ugly?"

"You should drown yourself in the toilet, dog."

I did not change my pace, nor my expression. I walked with

perfect posture, as if there was a book on my head, looking straight ahead — they did not exist. They would pull out every trick to elicit a response: They made vomit sounds, they would bark like attack dogs, and they would surround me.

"Hey. Back off, please."

"Ooooh, it talked. I didn't think dogs could talk!"

I did not want them to see my infected face turning scarlet. I walked as quickly as I could to my next class, which, on that particular day, was Religion, taught by a simple-minded nun, Sister Betty. I sat at my usual desk, behind Holly, the most beautiful girl in the class. Scandinavian blond, huge blue eyes, perfect complexion, husky voice, perfect figure, and actually very nice. She was the head cheerleader for our abysmal football team. She never winced when she said hello to me.

Sister Betty, or Sister Simple, as Mich and I called her, was teaching the class. She was tiny, shorter even than Adele, who was the shortest girl in the school, and she had buck teeth, which showed every time she talked, in her nasal, Kingston voice.

"Who can explain the Immaculate Conception?"

Holly raised her hand.

"Yes, Holly?"

"The Immaculate Conception refers to the fact that the Virgin Mary became pregnant with Jesus without, well, um, it wasn't the usual way." The whole class broke out in uncomfortable laughter.

"No, Holly. The Immaculate Conception is about Mary, Mother of God. It means that Our Lady was born without sin, from the moment of her conception!"

Troubled by this idea, I raised my hand. I could see her avoiding my eyes because I talked too much in this class. I was the only one who cared to engage. When it was clear no one else was going to put their hand up, she rolled her eyes and called on me.

A few of the kids in the class snickered and made eyes at each other as if to say, "Oh no, she's talking again."

"Yes, Ana?"

"Aren't all babies born without sin?"

"Oh no, that's where you are wrong. Every human is born with the sin of Adam and Eve. Except Mary."

"I'm sorry, but I don't think that's true, Sister. I have a baby cousin and she is definitely innocent. Nobody could call her a sinner."

"Young lady, you need to read your catechism."

"Babies can't be sinners, Sister."

"We are all born with sin, Ana. Jesus dying on the cross made it possible for us to be forgiven and to go to heaven when we die."

"I really don't get that. Did God actually say, 'Okay, my son, if you allow yourself to be tortured and beaten and then die slowly on a cross, I will forgive all of humanity for any sin they commit. Murder, war, anything goes.' I just don't see that." A few of the kids laughed, which boosted me a bit, but Sister Simple glared at me and continued the class. I thought of her as a robot of the church. Not a single thought of her own. I don't know why I bothered to argue, she clearly was not willing to think. But I did argue, almost every class. Being engaged with ideas I didn't agree with was far preferable to the hallways.

"Hey dogface, we got an idea. To get rid of your disease. You should pour gasoline on your face and set fire to it. We'll bring the gas and the lighter."

It was like they were reading my mind. Every time I looked in the mirror I wished I could set fire to my face.

MY MUM SAYS that when humans are children or teenagers, one year is like ten years in an adult's life. I believe that. Life is so good now. I'm in a groovy school where everyone likes me, my skin is pretty good, thanks to tetracycline, and Neo-Medrol, and lots of makeup. I have cool, smart, arty friends, and a lot of cute guys are after me. It's almost like Ana with the monster face is another person. I am just not that cowering person anymore. I mean, why didn't she just fucking leave the school? Honestly, I'd like to go back in time and give her a kick. But I can't, 'cause when I go back in time, I *am* her.

Oh no, my eyes are getting heavy again and I have that sinking feeling. Really? Do I really have to go back?

EVEN AFTER MOSTLY sleepless nights replaying the previous days' torment in my mind and trying to come up with *what would have been the ideal response,* I would wake up with a pathetic sort of optimism. It might be better today. I would think, "Hey, I could maybe get a small white paper bag of those little chocolate snowballs from the candy counter at Zellers after school while I'm waiting for the Johnson Street bus to take me home." I loved the way the marshmallow inside the snowballs was so creamy and the way the sprinkles on the chocolate look like snowflakes. Sometimes I would hold them in my mouth without chewing so that they would melt, and then I would swallow the treat down whole. Snowballs in the white paper bag were often the highlight of my day. Also, it's not like every single person at Regiopolis-Notre Dame Secondary School hated me — I did have my girlfriends. At school and out of school.

Like Birdie. She was my friend through the bad times and she's still my friend. Just the other night, we drove downtown in her parent's Camaro; Birdie always drives because it is her parent's car, and I don't have my licence because of my seizures. We use the car lighter to light Player's cigarettes, which we smoke one after another, even though neither of us likes the taste. We sprayed our necks and wrists with my Xanadu perfume in the hopes of running into some cute hippie guys. We zoomed down Princess Street to see if anybody cool was around. We don't ever consider guys with hair above their shoulders. That means they go to the Royal Military College or work at a bank. Yucch. But those were the only guys strolling Princess Street. No thank you. So, we went to Harvey's and ordered fries and a milkshake each. Birdie parked the car right on Princess Street while we ate our fries and slurped up our milkshakes. The fries were hot and salty, and the milkshake was thick and chocolate and beyond good. We felt beautiful and cool, and we knew that one day we would be so beyond Kingston.

At Regi, though, back in grade ten, I felt like a sick animal being hunted, even though some days weren't too bad because of Emilie and Michele, and our poor, reviled friend, Hilary. Thinking of my friends made me feel better. *My girlfriends, they like me.* We howled with laughter a lot. Hysterical, pee-your-underpants laughter, and even though we sort of cared what the popular girls thought of us, in a way, we didn't. Emilie remained my friend even after her friend from her grade school, Terri Filler, told her she would be a lot more popular if she dropped "that Ana with the face." I appreciated her loyalty, but I wished she hadn't told me.

I counted the cysts on my face every morning, in the hope that one morning, there might be only forty. Then the next, thirty-seven, and so on and so on. "You'll grow out of it," my mum said, but I didn't believe her. Instead of clearing up, like Dr. Stalker said it would, my face was getting worse every day.

I saw this nature show about hyenas attacking an injured lion. They had ugly faces and aggressive whimpering and eyes with no kindness. From then on, that is exactly how I thought of my tormentors at Regi. A pack of mangy hyenas. They attacked me every single day too, sometimes three or four times. With my blistered, pus-filled face, and my slightly different way of being in the world, I was perfect. They dedicated themselves to breaking me like other boys dedicate themselves to basketball, football, or hockey. Full time, full on.

The worst thing they did was to throw dogshit at me. It had been only words penetrating me before, now it was dogshit, splatted all over my green blazer. How could I not respond? Emilie wanted to report them, but I begged her not to. I knew it would get a thousand times worse if they thought I had reported them.

"Don't worry, I'm fine. I'll think of a way to get them back."

"What are you going to do? There's so many of them."

"I don't know, but there must be something."

"You sure you don't want me to report this? My dad says it is assault, and they could go to jail."

"No, please. It really will not do anything."

"Yeah, you're probably right. My dad also said that."

TO MAKE MYSELF feel better I sometimes imagined I was Saint Sebastian, with the thousand arrows stuck in my bare torso. But the thing is that the dogshit was, in a way, my fault. I actually deserved it because of what happened when I got picked up hitchhiking one morning. I brought it on myself. Dad had offered to drive me that day, on his way to work.

"But only if you can be in the car at ten after eight, Ana, I cannot be late for my eight thirty class."

"Thanks, Dad, but I'm just too tired," I said from the warmth of my bed. "I really need to sleep more. Maybe tomorrow."

"You'll get the bus, then?"

"Yup."

"Okay. I've left a cut-up orange and a strawberry Pop-Tart for you."

The bus to Regi drove up the Bath Road, bringing the country kids to school. It would stop for me if I waited at a certain spot. There would be apple cores and banana peels on the floor, spit balls thrown at me, vomiting noises, books grabbed from scared grade niners and torn to pieces. The boys at the back pointing at me, laughing like lunatics at what? What did I do that was so funny? I thought my violet toque looked nice on me, sort of like Juliet's cap in the movie *Romeo and Juliet*.

On that morning, for the first time, I visualized what getting onto that bus would mean. I saw it all play out and decided that I would never take the school bus again.

EVERYBODY WAS HITCHHIKING, or "thumbing" rides two years ago. That was before all the abductions and murders of girls started to happen, their naked bodies found wrapped in garbage bags, covered in twigs and leaves in muddy, shallow graves in the woods. I guess it was probably happening all along, but we hadn't heard about it. It was late February, icy and stupidly cold. My blue leather coat was way too thin. I refused to wear the sensible warm one my mother bought me because I was sure it made me look fat.

"Darling, no clothing can make you look fat. Either you are fat or you aren't. And you are not."

"It does."

"It cost me forty-five dollars!"

"I'm sorry. I can't wear it."

"I give up."

Standing on the side of the Bath Road in twenty-five below weather and a howling wind, my hands were numb, but I had no choice. I had to get to school. I took my mittens off and stuck out my thumb. Whooooosh, Whooooosh. Every car ignored me. I was going to be late. This would be my fourteenth late slip. I cursed my own laziness. Why hadn't I just got out of bed and gone with my dad?

No car stopped. It was as if I did not exist. I would have to walk. That would take me an hour and a half. Another detention with Father Hennessey. So boring, watching that classroom clock, gazing out the window at the darkening sky, pretending to read, aware of the other kids whispering about my face.

I hate every driver who whizzes past me. I'm so cold I feel like I might faint and I'm holding the books I didn't open last night, plus my pink purse with makeup and crushed cigarettes. I don't know what to do.

A dusty red Datsun pulls to a stop in front of me. Joy. I run to the passenger side, dropping my books in the snow. I gather them up and open the door with my free hand.

"Hi. Thanks so much."

It smells heavily of smoke inside. Export "A," which is the brand the tough boys all smoke. An acrid, musty, motorcycle kind of smell. I spot the green pack with the Export "A" lady wearing her tam on the dashboard. I look over at the man, younger than my dad but definitely a grown man. He has reddish-brown hair, kind of long, and a beard. He has green eyes too. They crinkle when he smiles.

"Hey there. Make yourself comfortable. It's cold out there."

"It sure is. Really cold. My hands are frozen."

"Go ahead and warm 'em up. Where're you headed?"

"Regiopolis-Notre Dame? It's just off Division. Downtown?"

"Oh yeah. I know where that is. Hey, aren't you late? It's five minutes to nine!"

"I missed the bus."

"I'll get you there as soon as I can."

"Thanks."

An awkward silence. All I am thinking about is warming my hands.

"What grade are you in?"

"Tenth." I reverted to the American way of saying this.

"Weird year. I remember."

"I guess."

When we got near the school, I asked him to pull over.

"Oh, you're embarrassed someone might see you?"

"No, no, not at all, I just ..."

"You know, you are gonna be real pretty when all that acne goes away."

"If it ever does."

"Oh, it will."

"How do you know?"

"Never seen a mum with acne."

That doesn't help me at all.

"Anyway, I'd better go."

"Can I ask you something?"

"Yes?"

"May I warm your hands before you go?"

This creeps me out.

"Oh. Hmm. I don't know, I don't really —"

He grabs my hand. It's still cold, and so I actually don't mind him warming it up with his two hands.

"So, what is your name?"

I was told to never give my name to strange guys.

"I'd rather not say."

"Fair. Mine is Mikey."

Mikey? What grown man has a name like Mikey?

"Hi Michael. I'm good now. I'd better get going, I'm gonna miss first period." I go to open the passenger door, but he holds it shut. I can see the blue veins and the hairs on his hands. I'm getting a little nervous.

"Hold on, beautiful."

He takes my face in his hand. No one has ever done this before. It feels so good. He pulls my face towards him. My heart is racing. I could turn away, but I don't, and I am not sure why. He kisses me. My first kiss. Fifteen, and this is my first kiss, kind of nice but revolting at the same time. The smell of cigarettes on his breath makes me feel sophisticated, but his thin lips were pressing mine too hard and his tongue is a fat worm trying to burrow into my mouth. The other part, the part I had never experienced before, is a warm feeling spreading down my legs. I didn't quite know if I like it or hate it. I think maybe both.

"Stop!"

"Doesn't it feel good?"

He then unbuttons two buttons of my Oxford cloth white shirt and slides his hand over my bra. What is that feeling between my legs and why does it make me want to stay here with someone who disgusts me? I make myself move away.

"I need to go." He moves his hand away and buttons up my shirt.

"Okay. Sure. Whatever you want. You want to go, go."

He brings his face about an inch from mine, looking right into my eyes. He has pale eyelashes I don't like at all. I gather my stuff and I reach for the door handle. Again, he tries to stop me.

"Wait a minute."

"What?"

"We'll see you tomorrow morning? Same time?"

I was unnerved by the feeling in my private parts.

"I'm not hitchhiking tomorrow. I'm going with my dad."

"Well, the next day then."

I get out of the car. I'm feeling uneasy. I walk away. He calls after me.

"You meet me at the same spot, okay?"

I SHRUGGED AS if to say "I don't know, maybe." A part of me I didn't recognize wanted to feel the warm feeling again even though I knew it was very wrong, a mortal sin probably; Mary, mother of God, was maybe watching and crying tears of pearl. I thought of her tiny hands, outstretched, as if to say "come to me, my lovely girl, I will love you even with your fifty-seven acne cysts. To me, you are beautiful." But Mikey had said that too. I was confused, so confused, and it made me feel squirmy and grimy.

"I'm not sure if I can," I yelled, and as he drove alongside me, I glanced at the back seat and noticed a baby seat. Oh my God. Was I stupid or what? He had a baby! He was married! He was way older than I thought. He could be twenty-eight or even thirty! This was bad. This was the worst thing ever. I started to shiver, but it wasn't from the cold.

He stopped the car beside me and offered me something. A battered-looking book.

"There's a book I want to give you."

His eyes were glazed over. Filmy. I did not trust him. In fact, I suddenly hated him.

"What's the book?"

"*The Lord of the Rings*. By J.R.R. Tolkein. I think you'd really like it."

I sneered. "I read it when I was thirteen. Aren't you too old for that book?"

He grinned a fakey grin, showing his crooked teeth. "Hey, never too old for a masterpiece."

I run towards the school, which looks like a fairy castle if you never went there.

I notice one of the boys who occasionally barks like a dog when he sees me. Danny Richmond, right there, leaning against the big old maple tree with a full view of the car, smoking, watching me. He is tall, and very thin, with a hunched back and curly brown hair and freckles and although he is not one of the worst, he isn't nice. The tree's branches are bare. I turn to look because I can't help it because they are somehow so beautiful in the morning light, but when I look, he barks and tosses a penny at me. It hits me in the face. He whistles. It's hot and it's greasy and I pretend it didn't happen and I run. I'm not running because I am scared or crying. Danny Richmond is a primitive dork like all those boys he hangs with. I'm running because Father Hennessey will give me an hour detention for every five minutes late. That's already three hours.

As I pull the heavy wooden back door of the school open my mind is racing. First it is the absolute knowledge that Danny will be telling everybody in the school what he saw, and that he will be exaggerating, telling them he saw us "doing it," and second, the certainty that I have committed a mortal sin and will go to hell. Will the Virgin Mary forgive me? She is already mad at me for not saving Patty. She never appears to me anymore, I think, even though I pray to her. I don't think she listens or intercedes with Jesus on my behalf. Will her sweet hands ever reach for me to come unto her again?

I wonder if I should confess to Father O'Malley when I go to Confession on Saturday. I kissed a married man. Who I didn't like. Who I even hated. I couldn't go into detail, to a priest. But you can't lie in a confessional. That is a real sin, maybe even a mortal sin.

I couldn't wait to tell Emilie or Michele, or even Hilary,

because Hilary had experience with older men. Maybe not the baby seat part, but the part about how much he liked me, and how he kissed me. After all, when most of the school considered me the dog of the school because of my ravaged face, it was gratifying that an older guy liked me enough to kiss me, even if he was a loser.

I rummaged through my purse, feeling the blue Maybelline eyeshadow that was coming out of its case, and loose Player's menthol cigarettes that actually made me sick when I tried to smoke them, and a bottle of aspirin for my monthly barbed-wire-ripping-my-insides-apart period cramps and a wand of mascara, and a pack of matches from Lino's pizzeria, and half a Caramilk chocolate bar, a box of tampons, and an old tube of Mary Quant pink lipstick. I quickly applied some lipstick before I went into the school. I know, what a joke, putting lipstick on a face with fifty-seven acne cysts? But it made me feel better. And it did make my blue eyes pop, Emilie even said so.

Within two hours of Danny seeing what he saw, the boys who had previously just barked at me and made puking noises would be asking how much I charged and could I suck their cocks. I figured from that question that Danny definitely had seen Mikey's hand on my breast.

Maybe I was a whoredog.

Maybe they were right.

I didn't like being called one. I really wished Danny had not seen what he had seen. I kicked myself that I hadn't looked around before I let Michael kiss me. This is why they have thrown dogshit on me, and this is why it is all my fault.

When those hyenas hunted the sick lion? She tried to run away, but they surrounded her and several of them jumped on her back and literally began eating her alive.

That's what I felt was happening to me at this point.

They weren't going to stop. None of them made any of the teams, so eating me alive was their sport. The guys who played football or basketball, the popular guys, they just ignored girls like me.

About two hours after I left Michael's car, in third period, I was sitting in French class, and a note was passed to me. *I would like to screw your tits.* I crumpled it up, walked to the front of the class to the garbage can, and threw it in. To hand it to Sister Marianne was unthinkable, because if I was branded a snitch the whole school would turn against me, although looking back I wish I had let someone in charge know.

I did take a few more rides with him. Mainly because I had missed the bus again, but also a little because of that feeling between my legs and also because it was just so nice to have somebody tell me I was pretty.

"Would you please let me off right here?"

"What, you're still afraid one of your friends will see you with me?"

"No."

"Sure you are."

"Just let me off here, okay?"

I opened the door, wide just in case.

"Do I get a thank-you kiss?"

"For what?" I said in the voice reserved for my mother when she was being intrusive.

"For picking you up. You funny kid."

"I'm not in a kissing mood."

"You let me know when you are. Because I'd like to kiss you again."

"Bye."

"Can I get an IOU?"

"Are you kidding?"

"What?"

I nodded towards the baby seat.

"Oh. Cora's seat? Her mother and I are separated."

"My friend Emilie, her older sister, Brigitte, says I should not trust you at all." I had told Emilie when we were at her house and Brigitte heard us talking. She came into Emilie's bedroom with a very serious face, telling me that I must never, ever, take a ride with that guy again. She told me that older guys like that are after one thing only, and he might drive me out to the country and rape me. She told me that this happens all the time, and that I was incredibly stupid to trust this person. She actually threatened to tell my parents if I ever rode with him again.

"Does this Brigitte know me?"

"No."

"Do you trust me?"

"I don't know." I felt a hard spiral of hatred towards him in my forehead. He pulled me to him and even though I was repelled by his touch, I didn't resist. He kissed me deeper than ever with his fat worm tongue almost right down my throat. I made noises I had never heard myself make, and then I felt a hard knobby thing in his lap. It woke me up and weirded me out. I wondered what in the hell was going on with him. This would definitely be the last time I rode with him.

"I gotta go." I opened the door and looked around to make sure none of the hyenas were gathered. Then I got out and walked my most queenly walk. My hatred for him became sharper and sharper, giving me a headache.

After the first period we gathered at our lockers. "How come you missed the first two periods?"

"I slept in."

"You didn't let that creep pick you up again, did you?"

Long silence. I didn't want to tell them the truth, but I had to.

"I missed the bus."

"Any married guy who picks up fifteen-year-old girls should be shot."

"He's separated."

"Right. Is that what he told you?"

"Oh mon Dieu! Quelle petit fille naïve," shrieked Michele.

Emilie said that if I didn't promise to never see him again, she was going to tell Brigitte that I was taking rides again and Brigitte would tell my parents. I tried not to cry when she said that.

I promised them I was never going to take a ride with him again. They were right that it was reckless, and the worst thing, besides being too old, and quite ugly, was that he had some kind of deformity.

"Ewwww. What kind of deformity?"

I started to tell them about the strange, hard knobby thing, and they started to laugh so hard I was not able to finish. They laughed so hard they actually slithered to the polished school floor. Emilie had to rush to the washroom. They laughed the hysterical kind of laughter where you can't catch your breath, the kind of laughter you talk about for years. "I have never, ever laughed so hard in my life." I just stood there with a puzzled look on my face.

After their laughter died down, which took a while because they would bring up a word I had used like *knob* or *hard* or *deformity* and the laughter would start up again. But each time it was a little bit weaker till finally they held hands and looked at each other.

"Shall we tell her?"

"Tell me what?"

"What that deformity is!"

"Yes, please do tell me! Or maybe I don't want to know."

"Oh, you want to know, Ana."

"Guys! That is so mean! Just tell me!"

Michele said, "Oh mon Dieu, you tell her, Emilie, I gotta go to class."

Emilie took my arm and guided me into the girl's washroom, and then into a stall.

"Promise me you will never ever mention 'hard knobby deformity' to anyone again."

"Okay, I promise."

There was a long theatrical pause.

"It's a hard-on."

"A what?"

"That is the word for when a guy's penis fills with blood, and it feels hard."

"Oh. Why does it fill with blood?"

"I can't believe you never learned this. Don't you remember from health class?"

"No. I mean yes, of course, but I didn't think it was ... I don't know."

"No wonder. You are lost in space in most classes. When you're always dreaming in class you miss really important stuff! Okay, so, when a boy is turned on by a girl, the penis becomes hard and erect so it can go in the vagina and then they move it back and forth — that's intercourse — until the guy ejaculates. He ejaculates sperm, which then swim up the cervix to the egg and sometimes make a baby!"

I looked pretty dazed.

"Jeez, how could I have been your best friend all this time and not know that you did not know the most basic things?"

When she left, I tried to pee, but nothing would come out.

I did not want to leave the bathroom because it felt like my childishness would be everywhere in the air and people would just know as soon as they saw me. The only relief was that I knew they wouldn't tell my enemies. My secret was safe with them, although they would tease me without mercy every day for a month.

I was ashamed about not knowing something so basic. But that shame was nothing compared to the shame I felt about being the school monster. And the shame I felt about those times I lay in bed and felt like I wanted to die. Because suicide was a mortal sin. And even though I did, from time to time, have a vague — I would never really do it — death wish, I was not going to hang myself, like funny, lively, sweet, red-haired Gerry. Our friend Gerry, who they called *faggot* and *homo* and *cocksucker*. Wonderful Gerry, who they never let up on, who they carried to the boy's washroom and held down screaming while they stuck a broom handle up his anus. He pretended to think the whole thing was hilarious, despite the fact that he was quite seriously injured. His imitations of the attackers were spot on and wickedly insightful as usual, but we couldn't really laugh because he had been hurt so badly.

"Why aren't you laughing? You girls on your periods, like me? Bet my cramps are worse than yours."

He then very sheepishly asked us if we could spare a few Kotex to absorb the bleeding. We each kept a box in our lockers and gave him several when nobody was around. There was one day when all four of us were wearing Kotex. We did laugh about that and sent notes back and forth in class. *How red is yours right now? Gotta change the Kotex soon. I think I'll throw it in their faces.* But also serious notes. I ripped a page out of my science notebook and then ripped it in half and wrote: *Gerry, they have to pay for what they did to you. It's basically a form of rape and it is not okay. It's a crime!* Then I folded it twice and passed it to Gerry who was sitting two in front of me.

He wrote back. *Ana, have you met the Kingston police? No way, Ana. Because nothing would happen to them beyond a warning — or maybe a congratulations. I am serious. And then they would get worse. They might even try to kill me, and they would definitely get away with it!*

I was very lucky they never went so far with me. I think it was because they knew they probably would get in trouble if they attacked a girl, whereas they were given high fives for attacking Gerry, because Gerry was effeminate.

I loved Gerry's voice and every single thing he said. He always made me and Emilie and Michele, and sometimes Hilary, laugh so hard. He was the kind of funny that when you tried to repeat something he said to someone else, it just wasn't funny coming out of your mouth. It had to be Gerry. I wish every day that I could have stopped him from hanging himself. When he was studying whatever book it was that showed a person how to hang themselves, I wish I could have run into his basement bedroom and thrown my hands up and shouted, "Stop! Stop, Gerry, they won't feel bad when you kill yourself, they will see it as a triumph. They will laugh about it, honestly, I know them. The others will feel bad, really terrible for about a day. They will light candles and write cards and give pious speeches, then the next dance or football game will come along, and they'll forget all about you and it's like you were never here. It's only your family that will suffer. And me and Emilie and Mich. Even Hil. No one else. Your family will suffer every minute of every day until they die. So do not do what the ugly voices in your head are telling you to do. They aren't real. You have invented them. Do not take orders from them! You? The Gerry I know would never, ever let them win!"

But I didn't get the chance because I did not know he was going to do it. I didn't even get a feeling. Slept right through it, just like his parents and sister did. I really didn't think Gerry would let them win. The way he would laugh about it, and casually refer to it as "my gangbang with the hundred-year-old broomstick!" And the nicknames he gave each of them: "Stupid tit, stupid piece of shit, and stupid dick brain" and "Ugly, uglier, and face like my arsehole," which were beyond funny at the time, because they were so accurate. He may have been gentle and sweet, but he had the sharpest wit. When they muttered at him in the hallway — "You liked that broom, faggot, how about my rifle next time?" — he would come back to their insults with the funniest put-downs. "Your teeny, tiny little baby toy gun, Petey? It didn't even squirt in my mouth, let alone shoot." It was funny at the time because Pete's face went blood-red. I don't even remember most of them, because I am not funny, but at the time they were perfect, and they actually shut the guys up for a few minutes. I would be like "Gerry, how do you think so fast? It would take me a week to think that one up!" He would shrug and say, "It's called timing, kid, and if you study me hard and learn me well, you're gonna be a big star too." We loved that line and repeated it for weeks.

A few months after the broomstick attack, Gerry was in an unusually reflective mood. We were sitting on the back steps of the school, smoking Kool cigarettes. We had graduated from Player's to Kool. The menthol made it a bit easier to take the harsh smoke, and there was magic around menthol. It was autumn, and the maples had shed their leaves, so we were looking at a brilliant carpet of red and orange and yellow leaves, all a little wet and fragrant after a light rain. We were shivering in our Regi blazers.

"Look," he said, blowing perfect donut holes of smoke, "we are in a Catholic school, right? And sinner that I am, I am a big fan of Jesus Christ. He was the coolest. And what they are telling us every day is that the guy suffered. What they did to me? Nothing compared to that."

"I don't know, Gerry. I think it's pretty bad." Michele put her arm around him.

"Me too. In fact, I still think you should report it to the police." I exhaled and coughed a little.

Gerry gave me a deadpan look. "Like I said, have you met the Kingston police?"

Emilie laughed. "The Kingston police? Are you kidding?" She continued in this resigned, defeated voice, not like her usual strident, confident manner at all.

"I told my dad about it, I mean I didn't say who it happened to, but I said I had heard about a kid in grade nine and I asked him if the kid should go to the police. You know what he said?"

Gerry knew. "I bet they would laugh."

Emilie hugged him. "I'm sorry, but yeah. My dad knows them really well, he goes to breakfast with the chief of police at Morrison's every Saturday morning, and that's what he said."

I felt my blood simmer and then boil. "Fuck that. That is outrageous."

Emilie shrugged. "Believe it. Gerry. Look. High school is only three years after this. You can get through it. Anyways, you have us."

"It's true. I do have you guys. Nerds that you are. And I ace all my English papers, every one, nothing less than ninety-five, bitches. I am going to be a writer, a journalist. And one day I'll write about it. A big fat article in *The Kingston Whig Standard*. Then *The Globe and Mail* and then *The New York Times*. And I will name every name."

We joined in with gusto. I don't know who said what, but what we basically said was, "Take that suckers! Take that, ya suckers, you shit-eating assholes, you disgusting bacteria, you scum that is lower than foamy spit on the ground, depraved cockroaches. Take that!" And we fell on the lawns and rolled around laughing, holding our bellies. I got grass stains on my Oxford cloth white uniform shirt, and Michele actually peed her pants, and Gerry teased her about it every chance he got, whispering in her ear, "Do you need the litterbox, kitty kat?" She would blush and smack him playfully. We loved him, and he loved us.

We did not think Gerry would surrender. But in thinking about it, we decided that he didn't surrender. They killed him.

The moment I heard about Gerry is the moment I stopped believing in God. I didn't go to school for a week. I just lay on the floor of my room, under my bed, face on the gold wall-to-wall carpet. My parents didn't bug me about it; they didn't even mind when I didn't come to dinner. My dad did come in once in a while and crouch down beside me. He didn't say much, only "This is as bad as it gets, kiddo. I am so sorry."

I did not believe in God.

And yet I prayed.

I half-prayed, half-vowed I wouldn't let them win like Gerry did. I reminded myself of what Mum always told me, that I'm from fighting Irish women. Before they came to North America they were living in ditches in the Irish bog because of the British evictions. But they held schools in those ditches. They educated their children. And when there was a chance, they got the hell out of there. They survived the passage to North America, watching their friends and loved ones die of dysentery or cholera, watching their bodies thrown overboard. They survived the plague, they survived the Spanish flu, and I will survive.

I would not bow down, I would not bend over, I would not leave the school. I belonged there and I had a right to be there.

Lying in bed at night, I did some planning. Especially on winter days when there was a white-out snowstorm raging outside my window. On the spring-like days, when we could hear the snowbanks melting into thin streams of water running into the road, and the sun shone, I was full of hope. But on the bad days,

I would lie there and feel like a volcano about to erupt. I could not tolerate another day at that school.

I think my dad sensed things weren't great at school because of the way he would study me in the evenings.

"You don't look happy, Ana, do you want to talk about it?"

"I'm fine."

"Is it school? I know how bad it can be, believe me, that boarding school I went to in England was torture."

Dad talked about his time at Stonyhurst a lot. Sometimes he would say it made a man out of him, as in the whole boys-don't-cry rule, and sometimes he would say it was the worst time ever. According to Dad, at his school, if you showed the slightest sign of weakness you were beaten until your face was unrecognisable. If you woke up with a fever and a cough, you were pushed out the door by a Jesuit priest and ordered to run ten miles, even in the rain, or a snowstorm. My dad once told me, when we were at a cottage on Sharbot Lake, outside looking at the thousands of stars, "A boy I knew actually died that way. A pale, very thin fellow, Rog. Hilarious wit. Everything he said had us on the floor laughing, and rarely at someone's expense, other than the priests. I suppose a bit like your friend Gerry. I remember him waking up one winter day with a fever, gabbling to nobody, and the priest tossed him out the door and said, 'Five miles, Brayson.' Never saw him again."

"But Dad, didn't you ...?"

"Oh goodness, no. You didn't ask. You did not question priests. We were upset about Rog, but we kept our mouths shut. We did play pranks, like catching mice and sneaking into the kitchen and putting them into the stew for the priests but never dared protest our treatment.

"We were treated like trash and like future kings at the same time, really."

"What do you mean by future kings?"

"It was taken for granted that we were going to rule the world when we grew up. And not only did we have the right, but we had the obligation to rule the world. Because the rest of the world was depraved, ignorant, and in desperate need of our guidance. Such rubbish."

I knew what it was to be treated like trash, but not like I was someone who was going to rule the world. Somehow, hearing about Dad's time at his boarding school made me sure that I would survive. I would make it to the other side. It helped considerably to imagine taking revenge. So, I would imagine it almost nightly in delicious and immensely satisfying detail.

I CLIMB THE steps to the school and open the giant, creaky wooden door. It's so dark in the school, I can't even see at first. It takes a few minutes for my eyes to adjust after all the bright sunlight outside. I hear singing down the hall, it must be music class. The old oak floors have just been mopped, and they are damp and glistening.

I head to the chapel. It will be empty at this time of day. But there is a nun, kneeling at a pew in the back, deep in prayer. I nod to her though she doesn't register me. I head right to the statue of the Virgin Mary, her tiny hands outstretched, her face serene. I light a candle and put a dime in the box. I pray. I pray for her to give me the strength to destroy. I can feel her encouraging me; her eyes are no longer plaster painted blue; they are alive and communicating with me. It feels like an electric current through my body.

Treading carefully, I make my way down the hallway to my locker, and there they are: the hyenas, teeth bared, drooling, huddled in a group near my locker, waiting for me. As soon as I am within spitting distance, they start. Their spit is all over me, dripping from my hair and my face, and then they start in with the barking and the fake vomiting They throw dirty pennies at me and taunt me with the hoarse, sexually charged whispers of "whore dog" and "cum dumpster." They all have eyes, but their eyes are glazed, not seeing anything. One of them, I will never say or even think their actual names, grabs my arm and says, "Hey whore dog, wanna get ass-fucked?" They all laugh and make more vomit noises.

I turn around with a Snow Queen smile and then, lightning fast, I pull a sharp shining steak knife out of nowhere and my books fly through the air. The hyenas scream with laughter. "Awww you want us to be scared?" They are excited that they think they have finally got me stirred up, that I have finally engaged with them; after one year and many months of pretending they don't exist, I am looking right at them.

They are hissing vulgarities, "Come in my face, baby, do it now," and then, one by one, my books hit them in the face, knocking them to the ground. They are stunned into silence for a moment, but then they start to scream obscenities at me. I silence them with my gleaming silver knife. It is gratifying to see their ugly smug faces with the featherings of moustache explode into blood and pulp. I am an angry archangel having my vengeance against demons. I cut and cut and slice until they are lying on Regiopolis-Notre Dame's century-old wooden floor, blood spraying. The fat one with the white-blond hair is begging for mercy. "Please, Ana, we didn't mean nothin', we like you." Ha ha. The tall one with the bush of light brown hair, he is crying for his mother, and I am laughing.

"She's not here! You'll never see her again, loser!"

I kick him hard in his teeth and they fall into his mouth. He chokes on his teeth. I can hear his ragged breathing. I stand over them all as they writhe in terror on the floor. "Tell me, assholes, why on earth would you want to live? You have nothing to offer the world, nothing. The world hates you and nobody, nobody will notice when you are gone. Oh, and by the way, Gerry will be there to see you on your way to hell with a giant horse whip. Yeah, the sweet kid you called faggot, the one who killed himself? And you found it so funny?"

I swear, as I lie in bed imagining all this, I hear Gerry laughing.

IMAGINING THEIR FACES as they fell was my nightly salve. I knew that by even imagining the scenario I was "shaking Satan's hand," but I didn't care.

It was the only way that I could actually get out of bed in the morning.

MICHELE AND I skipped lunch and breakfast because we were in a contest to lose ten pounds before the end of school. The loser had to buy the winner a milkshake at the Jiff across the street from the school. We wanted to be thinner because summer was coming, and we wanted to look good in shorts and cropped tops and even bikinis. We wanted bellies as flat as the sidewalk. I was 129 pounds and Michele was 137 and Emilie was 156. I may have been the thinnest, but I had the fattest legs. If I had to live with a hideous, frightening face, at least my body should be perfect, or close to it. I stopped eating. I would have, maybe, a cookie, or an apple and a glass of milk for the whole day. And I was feeling good. It was happening. The weight was falling off. Emilie was on a sensible diet, three healthy meals, no snacks, no sweets, so it was taking her a lot longer. Michele lived on ham sandwiches with glops of mustard and mayonnaise. She had them for breakfast, lunch, and dinner. Today she hadn't brought any lunch. It was hot and sticky, which was weird considering it was the first of June. We were still wearing the heavy wool skirts because Regi didn't have a warm weather uniform. The air was thick with the humidity and sweet with the fragrance of flowers and blossoms and green leaves and there were bright yellow dandelions all over the expansive, green Regiopolis lawn.

Nearing the end of the lunch hour, we were both making dandelion necklaces. We made a neat slit in the stalk of one dandelion with our fingernails, and then we threaded the next one through that slit, and on and on, till there was a beautiful dandelion necklace. Both of us already had over twenty dandelions in our necklaces, but every day the one who had the most would get a Passion Flakie from the vending machine in the cafeteria. They could have it for dinner as long as they had nothing else. We loved Passion Flakies, a commercial pastry with fake white cream and fake red jam in the middle but we didn't care, we found them delicious. If there weren't any left in the machine we would settle for a Jos Louis, which looked like a chocolate hockey puck, the chocolate colour almost purple, and inside was a dreamy chocolate cake and white creamy filling. They were very good but nowhere near the pleasure of a Passion Flakie.

THE BELL IS going to ring soon. Michele pulls her Kool menthol cigarette package out of her purse, and she lights one up and gives it to me for first puff. I love that menthol hit, how it softens the nasty tobacco taste. I look around to see if any of the cool kids are watching, but they have gone into classes.

I feel strangely happy.

It is spring in Kingston, so it is hard not to feel lightened by the brightness of every dandelion, the intoxicating fragrance and the soul-exploding colour of the lilacs on the grounds of the school, the towering maple trees all in full pale-green leaf. I feel in love with my own hands and how the sun has warmed my knees, and the fact that we both have copper pennies in our new penny loafers is perfect.

And then — you know when there is music playing and the power goes out? That's what I suddenly feel like inside. Sick to my stomach. Extreme foreboding. The air that was bright and promising is now sharp and menacing. There is a sinister hum in my ears. There is a threat. A very serious threat. The bell rings. It penetrates my bones. I am kneeling at the stone statue of St. Francis of Assisi with my hands on the little dog at his feet.

"Come on, Ana, we gotta go or we'll be late. What are you doing? Are you praying to St. Francis?"

"My calves. Somehow my calves feel so heavy and I feel like I ..."

"Take a deep breath. Just try to breathe," urges Michele, who stepped into a maternal role easily, being the oldest of five kids. "It's from missing breakfast and lunch." She puts her hand on my back. "Maybe put your head between your legs."

I try to breathe deeply, but there is no point. It would be like trying to stop a tsunami. And putting my head between my legs will do nothing. Once the process has started, nothing in the world can stop it.

"Can't stop it."

"Stop what?"

"Sorry. I'm so sorry. Can't stop it."

"Are you feeling sick?"

"Going to have a seizure. Oh no. Sorry. I'm so sorry."

"Oh no. Ohhh ... no, oh ... Mon Dieu. Should I ...?"

Like a bomb exploding in my head and I am falling, flailing backwards into the fire, a fire raging somewhere in the middle of the earth. The sound is deafening, blotting out everything else, I am falling, spinning backwards, heavy, the spinning propelling me down, down deep into the evil, waiting dark, into the fire at the centre of the earth. My hair is burning. The smell of burning hair chokes me. I am choking, not breathing. I can't breathe. My eyes are on fire, melting. I can't see. I can't hear. Where are the voices of humans? I am so far away from life. I am dead now. They will never find me deep down in the middle of the earth. Dirt packed around me, packed solid, no light. I don't want to die yet. There is no way out, I am done, no way out wait, wait there is one way out, only one way out, yes, and that is to scream! To scream myself up and into the air.

I hear a creamy whisper.

"Scream yourself up, Ana."

It sounds like Patty, exactly like Patty. But I can't. Can't scream, can't breathe, suffocating in the earth, the middle of the earth. I'm dead already, I think I am gone, all this dirt, this earth over me, around me, in my mouth, my nose, so far so far from the grass and the trees and the birds and the dandelion necklaces, so so far and moving farther, farther away!

"Scream yourself up, Ana. Scream yourself up and out into the air! You can do it, come on, deep breath, and scream, scream yourself alive!"

I can see her, Patty, she has burrowed down into the earth. She is all dazzling light!

I try and fail, I try again and cannot, but the third time I do it. I take a huge breath, huaaahhhhhhhhhh, and I scream, oh I scream, I scream with every cell of my fifteen-year-old body. I scream out the fear and the rage and the past and the future. I scream so loud and so long that every clock in the school stops, every conversation, all movement, all breathing. I scream myself up, up through earth and out into life.

A FALLING STAR. So beautiful. What does a falling star signify? Maybe that Matthieu will be back soon to drive me home. Or that lady. I hope not. She will be so disappointed to find it's only me, and not a litter of foxes. I don't think I want to stay much longer. And there is no pay phone anywhere near here to call my parents. I want Matthieu to come back now.

SHARDS OF SUN through spring-green leaves, sharp blue sky, cartoon clouds. Robin singing. My eyes are open, seeing. Car honking. Siren sounding. Someone laughing. Smell the dandelions and the mowed green grass. It's real. I am real. I came back. I am lying in the arms of Michele Guinaud. Can smell Michele's deodorant, mixed with her perfume. That spray deodorant.

"Ana? You all right?"

"I think so."

"You had a seizure. Your face was purple. Like an eggplant."

"I'm sorry."

"Oh, mon Dieu. I'm just glad you're all right."

"Feels like I've come back from the dead."

"Looked like it too, Ana. Freaky."

"Huh. Weird, that's what my name means."

"What?"

"It's uh ... you know ... the word for, like, coming back from the dead."

My mum always tries to encourage me when I feel like giving up on something, anything, by reminding me that my name, Anastasia, means resurrection.

Electric shocks in my head create a kind of random music. As Michele helps me up, I feel the heavy wetness of wool. My green tartan skirt is soaked with hot urine; some of the grade nines are smoking behind the tree, they see me rise, they laugh and make snorting sounds. I learn later that I was making that sound as my lungs tried to pull in air. They can see a giant, dark, wet spot spreading on my skirt. I know they will never let me forget it. School nurse, apple juice, vice-principal. My parents arrive in our blue convertible. The top is down. My mother is wearing a sky-blue flowy scarf on her head. She gets out and I think she is a ghost; she isn't real or maybe it's me. Maybe I am the ghost. Maybe I am not here. Maybe I never breathed. Maybe Patty came and flew me away to wherever she is. Maybe I died this time.

My mother's voice, so clear and throaty, "Sweetheart!" My dad's face twisted in worry. I get in the car, slowly, like a very old person. My mum cranes around to look at me. *Please don't look at me, please, please don't look at me.*

"How are you, darling?"

"I'm feeling fine."

"You had a seizure."

"Yeah, I think so. I think I knew it was coming." The electronic music still pinging and ponging in my brain.

"How did you know?"

"Because of the aura I get, and I knew because, well, I hadn't had any lunch."

"Why? Why hadn't you had any lunch? You know you can't skip meals with these attacks. We gave you money."

"I'm on a diet, and we were smoking a menthol cigarette, Michele and I." There was no point in lying now.

"You weren't smoking."

"Just one."

My mother was shaking her head. "I don't understand why you didn't have lunch."

"Trying to lose weight for summer."

"That isn't the way. You must have lunch. Just give up sweets, that is all you need to do."

My dad asks me to promise them that I will have lunch from now on. I promise, though I have no intention of keeping it.

The car turns up Division Street and drives past the strip mall and the fast-food restaurants towards the Bath Road.

My father, who never liked the Catholic church, says to my mother, "It all started with that bloody fasting before Mass. The first time she fainted was in church, remember?"

"I did give her orange juice."

"That is not breakfast!"

"There might be an exception for children. I'll ask the priest."

"I don't give a damn what that old fraud thinks. Our kids will be having breakfast before Mass from now on. If they keep going at all."

"He is not a fraud. He is a man of God. And there is no point blaming the church, John."

"I do blame the church."

I screamed, "Stop it. Stop fighting. It's my fault for not having lunch or breakfast."

"You must have lunch," Mum repeated.

"You already said that."

Even though I am aggravated by their squabbling, I feel somewhat calmed, reassured by being in the car with my dad driving. I feel safe. I was not safe at school. I cannot ever go back.

Mum lights a cigarette. The smell of the smoke is nauseating and comforting. Dad already has one going.

I HAD NEVER experienced such loneliness. It felt like it might swallow me. My dad drove into our open-air garage and turned off the ignition. He turned around and looked at me.

"Hey Ana. How are you feeling now?"

"Okay. Pins and needles in my head."

Mum made her voice as soft as she could. "We're taking you to the doctor at five o'clock. Dr. Stalker has agreed to see you."

I felt like there was a crabapple in my throat.

"Fine."

I walked slowly from the car to the house, feeling like nothing was real. My feet and hands were still trembling.

I sit across from Dr. Stalker in the examination room, trying to avoid his eyes. I am hoping I won't have to undress.

"Well, Ana."

I startled at the way he said my name, so loud and clear.

"I hear you had a seizure."

Dr. Stalker is sort of like Mr. Rogers. He makes everything better. I look at the floor. This is so embarrassing. "Yeah."

"How do you feel now?"

"Not too bad."

"You look fine!"

Dr. Stalker has the best bedside manner. He has tried his best to treat my acne.

"I just want to get rid of these pimples."

"Your face is looking clearer, Ana."

"I don't think so. I mean I don't know if Neo-Medrol is working."

"Oh, I think it is. I can see it is drying your face out very nicely!"

"I just wish it would get rid of the big ones. They're so big."

"Ana?"

Startle.

"In the next appointment I want to talk to you all about the acne and really see what we can do for you. Is it okay if we talk about the seizure today?"

I did not want to talk about the seizure. I wanted to pretend it had never happened.

"Yes."

"Ana. Do you remember anything?"

"Some things. But not right before and not right after."

"Ana, your friend says you were seizing for at least ten minutes."

"I was?"

"That's a long time, Ana."

"Sorry."

"It's not your fault. I know we had taken you off your Dilantin and phenobarb, but I'm going to put you back on. Do you agree with that?"

"Yes."

"We don't want another seizure like that, do we?"

"No."

"I will write a prescription for you, and your mum and dad will pick it up today at the pharmacy."

"Okay."

"After that, I would like you to go home and get some rest. Will you do that?"

I nodded, still not meeting his eyes, which I knew were trying to look right into mine. I couldn't look back. He told me he was sorry that the seizure had happened, and reassured me that the medication would work, but only if I took it faithfully, and did not miss meals as low blood sugar was clearly a trigger for me. I promised him I would faithfully take my meds and that I would never miss lunch again. Then I made a weak joke. "Cross my heart and hope not to die!" He laughed, with the brightest expression in his eyes.

"That's a very funny joke, Ana." He continued, "If you make an appointment for next week with Miss Melnyk at the front we can see about the acne."

I nodded again, trying to stop myself from crying with gratitude.

"Okay, Ana?"

Startle. Shock in the brain. Like tiny little warriors are having a tiny little sword fight in my brain.

"Okay. Thanks, Dr. Stalker."

I was so happy I didn't have to undress.

I HAD VIRTUALLY no friends. Emilie and Michele and even Hilary had slowly but surely backed away because, I guessed, they were afraid I might have another grand mal seizure while I was with them. I might turn dark purple again and grunt and snort like a pig and pee a lake of hot urine. I might bite my tongue in half or asphyxiate on my own vomit. And they would be expected to hold me while I thrashed around like a dying animal. It is a terrible thing to witness. I wouldn't have blamed them if they never saw me again. They weren't cruel or even cold to me when I did call them; they were polite and almost warm, but when it came to spending time together, they always seemed to be busy. In the few weeks that were left at school, I didn't see nearly as much of them as before. At lunch time, Emilie had gymnastics and because she was on a diet she couldn't be around someone who had a big lunch. My dad made me a peanut butter and jam sandwich for lunch every day now. Emilie would walk to the end of the grassy area and eat nothing with her friend, the one who had told her she'd "be a lot more popular if you ditched Ana." I hated her, with her long thin face and her pointy red nose that always seemed to need a Kleenex and her long thin body, all legs and elbows. She looked very content to be back in Emilie's orbit.

When we passed in the hallway, she would look any which way but at me, afraid to catch my eye. Did that mean she felt guilty? I don't think so. I think she just did not like conflict. Our two eyes meeting could very well mean a little fire of guilt in her gut that she would not be able to put out.

I was an empty shape, like the ones drawn in chalk by police on a sidewalk where a crime has happened. I found myself sometimes wishing I had died in that seizure; at least it would have spared me this humiliation. The only thing worse than being that lonely was my parents knowing how lonely I was. And Paulie. He would casually ask me, "Wanna watch TV?" but I saw something terrible in his eyes: pity. He looked up to me as the paragon of social success, so he was bewildered. How could Ana not have any friends?

It was very close to the end of the school year. My parents, I could tell, were concerned about me. On a typical Saturday night my dad would creak open the door to the den where I was watching *Mannix* on TV, or if I was lucky, *Get Smart*, and quietly ask, "Where's Emilie this weekend?" I would answer as cheerily as I could, "Oh, she's busy!"

The one time we did get together in that period after the seizure, it felt like we didn't flow together anymore, as if the seizure had mucked up our friendship. Sitting at a bus stop with her, about two months after the seizure, we were on our way to a movie downtown. She had a cast on her arm because she had fallen off a horse at Janis O'Connor's birthday party and broken her wrist and hand. It pained me that she was invited to the party and I wasn't. A very small, very terrible part of me was a little bit buoyed that she had fallen off a horse. Served her right for betraying me. Lots of people had written with Sharpie on the cast. Big hearts, encouraging messages, silly poems, and slightly lewd drawings. I was hurt that she didn't ask me to write something.

She peered at my eyebrows with a distressed look on her face. "You need to pluck your eyebrows. Badly."

"Oh, yeah, I guess I do."

"It's practically a unibrow."

"I couldn't find the tweezers, actually."

"Well, get your mum to buy some."

"Does your arm still hurt?"

"Yes. It's hell trying to sleep."

"That sucks."

"Oh, and there is something else I have been meaning to tell you."

I did not like the sound of this. Her face had this I-hate-to-tell-you-this-because-it-is-going-to-hurt-your-feelings-but-I-just-have-to look.

"Please don't."

"Okay then. Some other time. But it's something you need to hear."

I decided to be honest, instead of polite.

"You know what? I don't want to hear it. Not ever."

The bus came and we sat on it in silence till our stop downtown in front of the Capitol movie theatre, which a local businessman named Richard Barber owned. His son, Riley, was apparently a local drug dealer but he also worked as an usher there. He tried to sell us some hash but we both declined, telling him that we already had some.

The movie was *2001: A Space Odyssey* and it saved the day. We both felt awe and amazement, and we talked about it for hours afterwards. It felt like we were friends again. I helped her with her popcorn bag and her purse because her right hand was useless.

"We should hang out again soon."

"Yeah. Though my dad is always taking us places lately, just spur of the moment. I can't really make plans."

This felt like a lie, but actually it was true.

Emilie's big, jovial dad, Hamish, the tough lawyer with the crewcut and the sparkle in his eyes, would often spring an idea on them. Emilie continued, "He'll be like: 'Hey, get on a pretty dress and get yourself into the car. We're going to Toronto with Mayor Gelkie's family and we are going to see the Leafs! And then a concert at the O'Keefe. And then we are going to get the biggest juiciest steak ever at Barberian's steak house!'"

Sometimes they would stay for two or even three nights at the Royal York so Emilie's mother, Cecile, could go shopping for clothes at Eaton's. She said you just couldn't get anything worth wearing in Kingston. She preferred Montréal shopping, but Toronto was still better than Kingston.

Michele was also always busy, but in her case, it was with her new friend, Jeanne, who had moved to Kingston from Trois-Rivières. She said it was a great relief to speak French with someone and the one or two times I hung out with the two of them, they would shift into speaking French every few minutes, so I did feel like I was a pity friend, even though I knew it was not the case. I was amazed how the French words seemed to fly out of their mouths and swoop through the air together like crazed, giddy birds. When I saw the joy on Michele's face, I felt I understood her for the first time. Birdie was at the camp she spent every summer at, riding horses, swimming, and making lifelong friendships with girls from all over North America and even Europe. And even when she was in town, we only hung out once every few weeks. No teenage girl wants to spend time with her own worst nightmare — and a face that looked like mine was every girl's worst nightmare.

Most of my weekends were free.

It was on one of these weekends in late spring that I met him.

My parents were getting ready for a cocktail party at the

Lane's, and my mother was dressing up. Her hair had been done at Julio's downtown, so it was teased up in an outdated big puff in the late sixties style, and she was wearing her jade drop earrings and a sea-green dress. She looked quite nice, and I told her so.

"You look nice, Mum. I really like that dress on you."

"Aww, thank you, Ana. I try my best, but with Ariana Lane at the same party, there really isn't much point!" Mrs. Lane had the reputation of being the most beautiful and brainy woman in Kingston, so all the women tried extra hard with their appearance when the Lanes had a party. All Mrs. Lane had to do was to throw on a simple dress or pantsuit and a smear of lipstick and she looked like a movie star. The men flocked around her, and I think it hurt the other ladies' feelings.

"You're as pretty as her, Mum," I said.

"Thank you, sweetheart. I do think that Julio does a very good job, even if he does talk my ear off." I forced a laugh about Julio's talking.

"What are you up to tonight, then?" she asked, not really listening for the answer. But I answered anyhow, almost relishing in my loserness.

"Making myself some Pop-Tarts for dinner and then watching TV, even though there is never anything on on Saturday night. *The Lawrence Welk Show* is for losers. Or hockey."

The only consolation was that all the popular girls were also watching hockey because no matter what was happening, what fancy party or event, the boys always retreated to a rec room to watch *Hockey Night in Canada*, and the girls would follow, sitting on their boyfriends' laps, trying to cheer with enthusiasm when their boyfriend's team scored a goal, and arranging their pretty faces to look sad if their boyfriend's team lost.

I suddenly had an idea. Felt like a sparkling, silver balloon in my head.

"Actually, after dinner I'm seeing a friend downtown," I lied.

"Oh, that's marvellous, Ana. Which friend?"

"A girl from school. Lisa. You don't know her."

"That's lovely. I'm sure you'll have a good time."

My dad poked his head in.

"You're seeing a friend?"

"Yes, Dad. Don't act like it's a miracle."

"I'm just happy to know."

"That is fantastic news, Ana."

"What ... that I'm doing something besides watching TV?"

Mum looked at me directly for the first time that evening. "What exactly are you doing, sweetheart?"

"The Fair is on. At the Memorial Centre fairgrounds."

"Oh, yes, that sad, dirty local fair, with the rickety rides. Please don't go."

"I'll be careful, I promise."

"Make sure the rides are safe, Ana."

"What makes you think the rides aren't safe?"

"We used to take you when you were kids, remember? One of the rides stalled or broke and someone fell off. Also, bit of a criminal element there, you know."

"John, really?"

"The folks who work there. The carnies, they ... tend to be ..."

"I won't be talking to them, Dad. Just Lisa. We'll just go on a couple of rides. Maybe play those games where you can win a giant teddy bear."

He reached into his pocket and pulled out a ten-dollar bill.

"Do you need some money?"

"Ahh yeah, that'd be ... great. All I have is two dollars from babysitting."

"Take ten. Buy some cotton candy and hot dogs, and whatever strikes your fancy."

"Oh John, surely cotton candy would be the worst thing for her skin!"

"Dr. Stalker said it doesn't matter at all what I eat," I said aggressively.

"I don't agree. I had the same condition when I was your age and what I ate definitely made a difference," said my mother with the most annoying superior look on her face.

"I don't even like cotton candy, okay?"

"How are you getting home? Would you like us to pick you up?"

"Lisa's mum will be driving us," I lied. It surprised me how easy it was for me to lie.

"That is lovely. What does her dad do?"

I told them that it was male chauvinism to be asking that, but if they really wanted to know, the fact was that her dad sold refrigerators. I have no idea how I came up with refrigeration, but it seemed to convince them, though it did not impress them.

Dad played "Für Elise" on the piano, cigarette dangling out of his mouth as he waited for Mum to do whatever last minute thing she did before going out to a party. Maybe a spray of 4711, her favourite perfume. Maybe rehearsing clever things to say. It was a mystery.

About twenty minutes later she appeared.

"Finally, Joanna, good God."

She ignored his lament and held out her freckled arm. She was wearing a chunky bracelet I had never seen before, and her nails were long and sharp and vermilion. I felt like they represented her jealousy of Mrs. Lane. "Shall we?" Dad took her arm and they seemed to float out the door and into the car, they were so happy. Happy to be going out, happy they were so good looking, and mostly, happy that their lonely daughter was going out with a friend. Paulie was at a friend's for the night, so

I was alone in the house. It was kind of a magical feeling, until it wasn't.

Stepping out the door at around seven thirty, the sun still high in the sky, it felt as hot as it had at noon. Maple and birch trees in front of the houses, in full green leaf, dandelions all over the lawns, and colourful imported flowers planted in every garden, zinnias, impatiens, and the neighbours' hollyhocks. Japanese maples, apple trees, hundred-foot evergreens, kids everywhere, on the sidewalks, on their little bikes, shouting with kid joy, it was all good. Nothing could be bad on an evening like this. I spotted the sweet six-year-old neighbour boy, Danny, and said a jaunty hello. He was a tiny boy, delicate with large, wide-apart eyes and long, straight eyelashes. He moved constantly and quickly, just like Paulie used to. When I babysat him, we would play Superman, just like Patty and I had. He was always Superman and I was "Supergirl." On that evening, Danny asked me innocently if I had chicken pox on my face. Even that did not throw me off. I simply told him the truth, that I had pimples, and they would go away one day.

"When you gonna get rid of it?"

"Soon!"

Danny looked beyond me and his pretty eyes lit up.

"Hey, Errol!" Danny ran to a friend coming out of another house with a big soccer ball.

"Can I play?"

Part of me wanted just to stay on the block, watch the kids, pick dandelions, maybe make a dandelion necklace. But the other part of me was insistent. *You have to have an adventure. It is going to be fine. You love the Fair. Especially the Haunted House. It's so fun to scream like that, and nobody minds. You love the Fair, you love the Fair, you love the Fair*. My biggest fear was of running into someone from school. Did not want to be caught alone. *If it happens, which it won't, just lie, that's all*, I reminded myself. I'd say I was meeting Sue Ann Burley, who was less than four feet tall and hunched over, with glasses that magnified her eyes. Nobody talked to her, so I could say I felt sorry for her, so I cancelled my amazing plans for the night and asked her to come on to the Fair. I had the lie all nicely packaged and ready to go.

I reassured myself I'd play a game or two, go on a ride, buy a hot dog, and come home. Just to say I did something. On my own. It was going to be fine.

I walked up the same hill that Birdie almost died on, with a pang of missing her, and down Queen Mary Road, past the apartments, and then up the Bath Road and over to Princess Street and past the Woolworth's and the Wilmot's Dairy, where we sometimes went for fruit salad sundaes, and down Division past the garages and the grotty convenience stores and a Red Barn. Their song drove me crazy. "When the hungries hit, when the hungries hit, hit the Red Barn." Sometimes I couldn't get it out of my head. I was tempted to go in and get myself a burger and a shake, but I thought I had better save my appetite for the wonderful, greasy, sugary fast food on offer at the Fair. I kept putting one foot in front of the other, imagining the best things that could happen and the worst, and there it was, the Fair.

Kids on every seat of the roller coaster were screaming, laughing, yelping. The Ferris wheel, so high in the sky, stuck, as usual, for ten minutes. The delicious smells of cotton candy, fried everything, the B.O. of crowds, the tough carnies, and syrupy drinks. One of my favourite smells in the world. I bought a set of ten ride and game tickets and walked in. I even loved the trash all over the ground. There were lots of families; the kids were frenetic with excitement, and the parents were busy making sure the kids did not get lost.

I felt just as excited as the kids did. First thing I did was get on the Ferris wheel. I daydreamed about being on a Ferris wheel a lot, especially when I was bored in class, or being taunted and harassed at school. I imagined I was on the very tippy top of a giant Ferris wheel, looking down at the world, at the whole of Kingston and Frontenac County, and Regiopolis was only a very small part of that, and those boys were just tiny little specks. Specks that I could crush like mosquitoes. It was true, what my parents had said — it did not exactly feel safe. There were troubling sounds and it felt like something was loose, but part of me thought *if my carriage flies off the Ferris wheel and into the night sky and over the city and lands in Loughborough Lake, that would be a beautiful way to go*. And I just wouldn't have to deal with the embarrassment of being lonely.

So I was in my seat, waiting for the ride to start, when a giant biker guy, with long, wavy, dark hair moving with the breeze, sun-weathered face, green eyes that felt like spotlights on me, stepped into my carriage, and sat down right next to me, as if he knew me. I looked at my feet, terrified. I had heard scary things about the Satan's Choice bikers that hung around Kingston. They apparently had a clubhouse, out near Quattrocchi's farm market, that had no windows or even doors. People said there were fights, and drugs, and even killings there. The prisons were full of Satan's Choice members because they committed so many crimes. My body trembled. His hips were actually making contact with mine. This made me supremely uncomfortable, so much so that I could hardly swallow. He waved at a friend on the ground, a tall, lean fellow with a pretty face like a girl and black curls down past his shoulders and violet eyes.

I made a plan. As soon as the ride was over, I would get out of his sight as fast as possible, so he wouldn't really register me. A creaking sound signalled that the wheel was about to move. He wore dirty jeans, a cut-off leather vest, and cowboy boots. His arms were strong-looking, and deeply tanned, with a tattoo on each that I couldn't make out. I wasn't sure, but I also thought that I saw the face of a grinning red devil with horns on the back of his jacket when he turned around to wave at his friend. I started remembering stories of kids our own age who had somehow crossed them, like not paying them all the money owed for a block of hash, or something like that, and had consequently gotten beaten up very badly, as in broken jaws, black eyes, and even once, in the case of a guy we all knew as "Slim," two fingers cut off. This was exactly the kind of guy my parents were afraid I would run into at the Fair.

The Ferris wheel began to turn. It groaned and creaked. I think I must have gasped.

The Satan's Choice guy turned his face to me and my heart stopped.

"You scared?"

He had an accent, a French-Canadian accent like Michele. I made a sound, something like a nervous giggle.

"Heh heh, no."

"I think you're scared."

I couldn't tell if he was joking or not, so I changed the subject.

"Are you from Québec?"

"Ha ha. How did you guess?"

"Your accent. My friend Michele, she has an accent like that. She's from Québec. Chicoutimi."

"Me, I grew up in Baie-Saint-Paul. Prettiest town in Canada."

"Any place is prettier than Kingston," I said, although I secretly found Kingston mostly quite beautiful.

"So, es tu effrayé?"

"Not really." I was proud that I understood what he was saying. Sometimes I remembered some vocabulaire, but other times nothing. I remembered this one. I liked my French teacher, Madame Bernier, because she had long, dyed-blond, messy hair and she laughed a lot and she didn't flinch when she looked at me, like most of the other teachers.

"You should be."

"Why?"

"Because this thing is ready to fall a-fucking-part, pardon my other French."

"Ha ha. Other French, I get it. But how do you know it is ready to fall apart?"

"My friend Toby, he runs this monster. It's his baby and he tells me she's just about to go. To fall to the ground in pieces, like a Lego set. Just like my poor old great aunt Lou. Toby dared me to go for this ride. He owes me twenty bucks now!"

"Oh."

My sense of right and wrong soon overcame my fear of him. Besides, there was something in his easy manner and his caramel voice that made me trust him, despite everything I had been told.

"Well, they should not sell tickets if it's dangerous."

"Ha. That's funny. You're funny. Didn't you know? Every ride at a fairground is dangerous. You know why? They got no money for repairs. Or they do, and the bosses pocket it. They are just livin' on a prayer, these carnies. People do get hurt, every year. Every year, someone dies on one of these things. That's the truth they don't want you to know."

"I would like to get off, actually."

"Too late now, copine."

"Shit."

"Hey, I don't like to hear that language coming from a young lady."

"Sorry."

"I don't want to hear that again."

I felt a kind of flush of warmth when he said that. I guess I liked being bossed by a possibly dangerous guy? What was wrong with me? Was I some kind of freak?

"By the way, I'm Matt. My real name is Matthieu, but nobody here can get their tongue around that, so I just go by Matt." His voice was like Superman's voice, not Patty pretending she was Superman. A voice that wrapped around your whole body and then found its way inside.

"I can say 'Matthieu.' I'm pretty good in French. Always get above eighty. I'm Ana."

"Oh. Okay. You don't look like an Ana."

"No?"

"No way. You look more like an Ange. French for Angel."

I did not know what to say.

"Did I embarrass you?"

"No! I mean, maybe. Sort of ..."

"Je suis desolé! I did not mean to embarrass you, chèrie!"

"Ana."

We were now at the tippy top. The city was below us. I gasped.

"You like it up here?"

I looked down at grand old St. Mary's Cathedral, where I said my confessions every Saturday to cross-eyed Father O'Malley, and old City Hall by the lake, and the market. I turn the other way and there it is. Like looking at evil. Regi. I could see the football field clearly, and the spire of the chapel, the part of the back lawn where I almost died of the seizure.

"Yeah. I do."

"I don't think she's gonna break down today."

"No?" I liked the way he called the Ferris wheel "she."

"Not today. Maybe next week, when the Fair is in Calabogie."

"We should warn them."

"You are a girl with a conscience! Maybe I'll drive down on my Harley and warn everyone! 'Don't go to the shitty little touring fair! The rides are for shit! Your kids could die! They might even die from the cotton candy!'"

"Really?"

"Oh yeah. I seen mouse turds in the cotton candy."

I was aghast. I thought about the mouse turds I might have eaten in the past but also about how furious Miss Prior always was when she heard Graham Morton say "seen" that way.

"You haven't seen 'em? You kidding me? Mice love anything sweet, oui? Cotton candy, that is mouse paradise."

The Ferris wheel started up again, taking us for another full spin around. A full spin around with no stops!

Matthieu took my hand. It was as if he lit a sparkler inside my hand, which shot through my whole body. I didn't dare move at all. So different from even the good feeling with the creep, because that feeling was always tinged with disgust, and this was pure goodness. His hand was big, so much bigger than mine, and I could feel his roughness. I liked that.

"Do you believe in magic, Ana?"

I didn't really know what to say, because if miracles are magic, I believed in magic. The dry earth where Bernadette dug with her bare hands became a running stream of holy water in Lourdes that has cured thousands of people of their ailments. Jesus turning water into wine. Jesus rising from the dead was a miracle. Me surviving the last seizure, which I sometimes felt was sent to kill me, that was a miracle. My thoughts tumbled. He squeezed my hand with force and my first orgasm happened. I had no idea what it was at the time, even though I had heard the word here and there. I certainly never thought it was something that happened from holding hands.

I just knew that that sparkling in my belly and below, it intensified more and more till it was too much to bear and then it exploded, like fireworks. It exploded in every colour and shape through my whole body right through to the tips of my fingers and tongue and toes.

"Are you all right?"

"Oh. Yeah. Just a bit of heartburn. From this hot dog I had before."

"You had a hot dog from the Fair? Didn't anyone ever tell you? Those things are poison!" He looked right into my eyes as if he was looking past the eyeballs and right into the part of me I keep hidden from everyone, even myself.

"Do you believe in magic?"

His eyes were a dark blue, almost purple, and I felt they were like those X-rays in shoe stores that show you the bones of your feet.

"Maybe."

"What do you mean by maybe?"

Nobody had ever questioned me like this before. Nobody, except maybe Paulie, ever really wanted to know what I thought.

"Well, some magic is just tricks, but other magic, you can't explain."

"Like what?"

"Like when you are thinking of somebody and they call you."

"Yeah."

"Like God."

"Oh. You believe in God?"

"Yes."

"That's really sweet."

"It's not sweet, it's —"

"What?"

"It's just true. There is a God. And God sometimes makes magic happen. For children. Moments that we call a miracle but are not technically miracles, so they are magic."

"Oh, Mon Dieu, elle croit en toi!"

"Anyway, it's not sweet."

"What is it, beautiful girl?"

I could feel myself turning a deep, furious red. Beautiful? With fifty acne cysts? Either he was taunting me, which I was used to, or he was trying to get sex from me. Like that filthy creep who picked me up on the Bath Road.

"Why would you say that?"

"What?"

"I'm not beautiful. Not with ..." I pointed vaguely to my face.

"Oh that."

He pointed out a few pockmarks on his own rugged but Prince Charming–level handsome face.

"You'll grow out of that. I see what's underneath. Those eyes, oh hosti, those eyes could shatter a windowpane. And your mouth? One look at those lips ..."

Nobody had ever talked to me like this. My lips? What about my lips? We were at the top again. I was desperate to change the subject.

"See down there? That's my school."

"Oh. Yeah?"

"Regi."

"The Catholic school?"

"Yeah."

"Do you like it there?"

"Where, Regi?"

"Your school."

"Not really."

"That's too bad. Those can be long years if you aren't having a good time."

"Very long."

"What's going on?" He looked me right in the eyes again.

Should I tell him? If I told him the truth, he might see me the way they all saw me. An ugly loser.

"Oh nothing, just some of the boys are ... It doesn't matter ..."

"They can be assholes."

"Yeah." I felt that he understood everything I had been through.

"They are just fuckin' losers. You know that, eh?"

I didn't answer because I was trying not to cry. There was something about sympathy that allowed all that repressed self-pity to flow. I looked away so he wouldn't see my watery eyes.

"Sorry for the language. It just makes me so furious."

"That's okay."

"No, no, it's not. A gentleman should never use that language in front of a young lady."

I breathed slowly and deeply to ward off a sob. It worked.

He started stroking my arm. The little white hairs stood on end.

"Heh. Electricity. I guess there is electricity between us, eh?"

I turned red again, fast as a streetlight. I couldn't answer that one. I looked at my feet. I had lovely feet — creamy and high arched with perfect toes. The one perfect thing about my body. We were down at the bottom. I hadn't even noticed.

Toby was unlocking the carriages and people were getting out, almost delirious with excitement — or maybe relief from fear — laughing too loud and talking too fast. When he got to us, he looked right into Matthieu's eyes, and Matthieu winked at him.

"First date?"

"Oh, no, no, we just ..." I croaked out.

"First date," said Matthieu assertively, squeezing my hand again.

I couldn't believe it. What did it mean? Was that a joke? I never knew when people were joking. As Matthieu rose out of the carriage and stood up I saw him, really saw him for the first time. He was handsome. Outrageously, fiendishly handsome, as my mum sometimes would say. He had broad shoulders and those tanned arms, man arms with muscles. He had a tattoo of a butterfly on his biceps. A tattoo meant a person was in a motorcycle gang, or they had been in the navy or in prison. Regular people did not have tattoos.

He really did have a beautiful face, just like the guy he had waved to when the Ferris wheel started. And those purplish eyes were actually violet in different light.

"So, Ana, what now?"

"I don't know." Why was I such a dumb bunny?

"You don't know? Well, I'll tell you what. We are going to go for a ride on my Harley."

"What? Oh, no, I mean, I would like to, but ..."

"You have a problem with that?"

"No, but ..." I showed him my unused tickets. I had my mother's frugality. I had bought tickets; I had to use them.

"Oh, you paid for those?"

"Yes."

"Let's do it, then! Let me win you a prize. We'll go for a ride after."

I felt a sharp pang of danger, a warning, but the pleasurable flush though my body when he looked right into my eyes won.

"Okay," I said with a little quarter-smile.

"Let's go win you a giant teddy, girl!"

This was the most exciting thing that had ever happened to me. I longed to be seen with a handsome tough guy carrying a teddy bear for me. I would rise in everyone's esteem. The hyenas would be way too intimidated to bother me again.

We went to the shooting range and Matthieu won me a giant, chemical-pink rabbit.

I hugged the rabbit to me. She was not soft, but she was still huggable. "You're still kind of a kid, aren't ya?"

"I was just feeling how he hugs for my little cousin, Lacy," I lied.

"You're givin' him to your cousin?"

"It would make her so happy. She's kind of a sad kid." I didn't have a cousin Lacy. This lying was new to me. It felt kind of great, like when Frances stole a can of frosting.

We were in front of the Haunted House, my favourite thing at the Fair. He noticed my excitement.

"You like to be scared? Me too. Come on, let's go!"

We crammed into the shabby carriage that took us through the Haunted House. His rough jeans felt good against my bare legs. I jumped when the carnies, dressed as ghouls and monsters, flew out at us making terrible growling and grunting noises.

"They aren't real, you know."

"I know."

"You are a funny kid."

"That's what they tell me."

The next ghoul that jumped out wasn't a carnie in a wild costume. It was Patty! Was I losing my mind because of the orgasm? Was I hallucinating? I looked right into her eyes, and I felt a gigantic wave of goodness and love and I knew for sure that even if I had hallucinated her, this was a miracle. She disappeared, and an ordinary old carnie with white makeup and fake blood and ripped clothes appeared in her place. I was so startled, I screamed.

Matthieu held me tightly. "Oh, mon chouchou, it's okay."

"I know, I know."

"Then why'd you scream?"

"I don't know."

"I'll remember that."

"What?"

"That scream! Nearly shattered my ear, little girl!"

"Sorry. I startle easily. My mum is like that too."

"Hah. That's okay. A girl needs a good scream, right?"

"Yeah, I guess."

"That scream could save your life."

Another zombie jumped out, howling, white hair flying, red-rimmed eyes flashing, grey hands with long black fingernails flailing. I didn't scream this time because nothing could frighten or startle me after having seen Patty. I turned to Matthieu, and he was already staring at me.

He held my face with both his rough hands, pulled me towards him, and kissed me.

This was not like the creep's kiss.

This was a real French kiss, the kind I had watched in the movies, but when I watched the kisses in the movies I hadn't realized about the thunderbolts going through the kissers' bodies. I hadn't realised that this would happen, but it did, and we kept kissing and kissing and I felt like we were a planet unto ourselves, spinning in space, and suddenly we are out of the Haunted House and it's too bright as it's July and it's only eight thirty at night and the carnie is letting us out of the carriage and kind of smirking at Matthieu, and it is as if the kiss didn't happen at all, and I feel the sharp blade of shame.

"Hey, is something wrong?"

"No."

"Hah. You are a shy one. But that's the way I like my girls. Come on. I'm gonna take you for a ride on a Harley. A ride you ain't never gonna forget."

I couldn't believe he said "ain't." The only other person I knew who had said "ain't" was Patty's father. When he was showing me their vegetable garden.

I looked at Matthieu and suddenly I had too much saliva in my mouth. I swallowed a couple of times.

"I don't know if I can. I told my parents I would be home by nine."

"Well then, I'm gonna take you home. Right to your door."

That was out of the question, but if he let me off a couple of blocks away, no one would know. I figured I would tell him where to stop when we came to the right spot.

"Come on then, beautiful."

He grabbed my hand and led me through the Fair to where his Harley was parked. I was brimming over with genuine pride, something I had never experienced before, to have a tough, scary, movie-star-handsome man leading me through the Fair.

NEXT THING I knew I'm holding on "for dear life," as my mum would say, to Matthieu's waist as we speed up Princess Street and onto Division and over towards Skeleton Park, where Emilie and Michele and I used to hang out, hoping to catch the attention of the cute guys from KCVI who used to go there to smoke hash or drop acid. It was rumoured that there were over three thousand bodies from olden days buried under the park, three and four stacked on top of one another. A teacher told us that when they began to exhume so they could build a park, they were horrified to find that most of the bodies were only partially decomposed — something to do with the water in the soil. Many of them had died of smallpox, so there was that concern as well. They ended up just putting them back in the ground and built the park overtop. Skeleton Park. Sometimes, when we were hanging out, we would find what looked like a human bone. I was thinking about those bones when we pulled in alongside the park. He cut the engine and turned around to look at me.

"Do you want to stay out here, or come in while I do business?"

Business? Was he buying drugs? Or selling them? I kinda liked that idea even though I didn't.

"I'll stay out here, thanks."

"Be cool, ma blonde."

Why was he calling me "ma blonde" when I wasn't blond? I didn't dare ask. He almost sounded like a real hippie when he said, "Be cool," but I knew he wasn't. Not at all. Bikers were not hippies. He then disappeared inside the leaning, dirty, white house with peeling paint. Why did he call me "little girl"? I wasn't sure I liked that, but strangely, I did like it coming from him.

My brain was in a tangle again. It was similar to, but not exactly like, the aura before a seizure. When I had that aura, I always had a seizure. Dr. Stalker told me that that was because once I had the aura, the seizure had really started. He had leaned in towards me, with a very serious expression on his face. "Imagine a forest. Do you see that forest? Okay, now imagine a little patch of long grass. Do you see it?" he asked, irritatingly, with his face a little too close to my face for comfort.

"Yes."

"Now imagine someone throwing a lit match into that patch of grass."

I nodded.

"Do you see the little fire?"

"Yes."

"That, Miss Burns, is your aura. Soon enough, the whole field will be on fire, and then the trees surrounding that field, and then the houses near the trees. That is what we call a wildfire." He looked at me expectantly, so I nodded again.

"That is what is happening in your head when you have a grand mal seizure."

While Matthieu was gone, I tried to untie the tangle.

I could just leave now and walk home. It wasn't that far, maybe an hour's walk. I would never have to see him again. On the other hand, this could be an adventure. He was so cute, and seemed like a nice guy, a little old for me, and kinda rough but so cute. And this was a real date, the first one I had ever been on. Something to tell Emilie and Michele. But this feeling of something not right, this glimpse of an alluring but scary world, was making me uncomfortable. But his handsomeness and sweetness, along with his dangerousness, won. He walked out of the drug house, smiling.

"You ready, little girl?"

"Sure. It's eight thirty, so I do have to get home."

"I'll tell you what. I'll take you home right now, you can introduce me, and we can hang out and have a beer with your dad. What do you think?"

"No." That was not even a remote possibility. I was not going to tell him that my mum and dad would not be home till midnight.

He laughed, a honking laugh.

"You don't think they'd like me?"

"It's not that."

"Their sweet baby daughter with a biker??"

"It's just my dad, he follows the news, and he is very paranoid. For instance, he might think that you are a member of the Satan's Choice."

I could not believe what had come out of my mouth. He looked right through me this time. I shrugged, feeling really stupid.

He turned around to show me the logo on the back of his vest.

"What does it look like?"

"It looks like you are."

"And what does that mean to you?"

"I don't know."

"You don't know?"

"Not exactly."

"You know what it means? It means I am a member of a motorcycle club, just the way your dad might be a member of the golf club. He likes to play golf, and I like to ride my Harley."

"But I heard about drugs and violence."

"All bullshit. We don't do more drugs than any group at your school. We don't fight any more than any other group of guys. We are a motorcycle club. End of the story."

"Oh. Okay. That's good." I did not believe him, but I said that I did. It didn't diminish my crush on him. It made it a more piercing, throbbing crush.

"Come on. Get on. Careful of your leg on the exhaust there. That'll burn a hole right into your pretty, freckled calf."

He thought my calf was pretty. Nobody had ever said that.

"Before I take you home, we are just gonna pay one more visit."

I was wary, but I did not know how to assert myself.

As we rode away from downtown Kingston, I thought, *What if I have a seizure?* If I had a seizure, that would be it. I would let go of him and then I would be like a smushed squirrel on the road. The wind made it seem much colder. My hair whipped back. After a terrifying twenty-minute ride, he pulled into a typical split-level, fake-white-brick house in the outer suburbs of Kingston, a place called Reddendale. I could hear the lake waves crashing into the rocks, though I couldn't see the lake.

"I think you should come in this time."

I followed him towards the house. The door opened and there was the beautiful man he had waved to from the Ferris wheel. He was wearing a suede fringed jacket and jeans, and his glossy black hair curled around his shoulders. He smiled.

"Matthieu, sale chien. How old is this one?"

"This is my brother, Bear. He's an idiot. And she's eighteen, by the way."

Bear laughed, a high-pitched, sarcastic laugh. "Yeah, and I'm sixty!" He turned to me with a sweet smile.

"Hey, kid, this guy is trouble. I'll call you a cab."

I was thinking about the kissing we might do later. "That's okay."

"You hear her, Bear? She said it's okay. I am being a perfect gentleman, right Ana?"

"Yup." Bear's boots were pointy at the end, like a cowboy.

"If he gives you any trouble, tell me and I'll call a cab."

Bear had dimples when he smiled and I felt like I could trust him.

"Come on, let me introduce you to everybody while Matthieu does whatever he does."

Matthieu gave him a sly look and bounded up the stairs.

Bear took my hand. I couldn't figure out why he was called Bear, when he was really quite feminine. He had a feminine voice, and Crayola violet eyes and that shimmery black hair and the dimples and he swayed just like Patty had, when he walked.

"Don't worry, Matthieu's business shouldn't take too long."

I knew that *business* must mean something to do with drugs, but that didn't scare me. Everyone at my high school was doing drugs, or selling them, or buying them. Even though I was only fifteen, I smoked hash whenever it was offered, and I always had what we called "a nickel" of hash in my purse because it made me feel like maybe I was cool. I would stick a little crumble of it on the end of my cigarette and sort of inhale. I never felt anything, so maybe it wasn't the real thing.

We were in a sunken living room, with dirty beige wall-to-wall shag carpet. There were about twelve people lying on the floor, beside each other, all stroking each other, and a couple of ginger cats walking over them. I thought I smelled cat spray — the worst smell ever.

Bear took my arm. "So, do you think you can remember everyone's name?"

"I don't know. I could try. I have a pretty good memory," I bragged.

"Okay, everybody this is ..." His voice faded out because I saw her. The Mother of Jesus, the Virgin Mary. Did this mean I was going to have a seizure? Was this an aura? She was looking right at me, and she had a sort of golden halo, or was that just the setting sun coming in through the curtains? I was hallucinating again. Maybe Matthieu had put something in the Orange Crush he bought me at the Fair. No, it really was her, in her sky-blue dress with the folds, her white mantilla, and her creamy bare feet. My heart was pounding. I lost my balance for a moment, so I held on to the wall.

Bear laughed. "Did Matthieu get you stoned? What an asshole."

"No, actually, I just ... I never ..."

"Don't worry, they are just meditating! You've heard of meditation, right?"

I didn't answer, because there was no point. I gaped at the Virgin Mary and the others. Who were the others? They all had their eyes closed except the Virgin Mary, who was staring straight at me. She was looking right at me. She had answered my prayers! She wasn't mad at me anymore! Bear looked down at them with that dimply grin.

"You guys finished your ohhhhmmms?"

No answer.

He took my hand. "We'll just wait till they finish doing their thing. Wanna smoke?"

He pulled out a tin of tobacco. Then rolling papers. And rolled two perfect cigarettes.

"So, you and Matthieu?" His eyes were dancing, implying that we were a couple. This made me really uncomfortable.

"Oh, no. No, we just met. He's taking me home and stopped here on the way."

"Be careful, eh?"

Silence.

"Why?"

"Matthieu has a girlfriend."

I couldn't even reply. Was he joking?

"Did you hear me?"

I nodded. I was finding it hard to get my breath.

"Donna finds out about you, she will rip your pretty face off."

"Jeez! There is nothing to find out about. He is just being a gentleman, driving me home from the Fair."

"A gentleman?" He hooted with derisive laughter. "That is a good one, chèrie."

I started to feel pretty scared. What if Donna found out about the kissing? Would I find her waiting outside Regi one day after school, with long nails like knives?

"Just givin' you fair warning. She might even show up here."

He laughed through his nose. "You want me to call you a cab? I'll call Amey's for you."

"I don't know." I wasn't sure if he was telling the truth. He did have a weird twinkle in his eyes as he told me.

"Although, you might have fun hangin' out with us. A very groovy bunch of people. And nobody will be taking advantage of you."

"Matthieu didn't take advantage of me."

"Girl? You have no idea. So, you gonna hang with us?"

I looked down at the figures lying on the carpet. They did look like real hippies, though they were in costumes that made them look like they were from the Bible.

"Maybe for a little. Why are they dressed like that?"

"Hah! You'll find out when they want you to find out." Then he whispered in my ear. "Don't tell Matthieu I told you, eh? About him being spoken for."

"I won't," I lied.

The Virgin Mary sat up and spotted us. I could now see that she had acne just like me and she was kind of fat. That somehow made me feel better about everything, even though her face wasn't nearly as bad as mine. She gave Bear a wide smile.

"Who's the new chick?"

"I'm Ana," I said, my face turning crimson.

"Cool! And what brings you here?"

"Matthieu brought her!"

"You wanna watch Matthieu, kid. He's a heartbreaker."

I smiled.

"You are a kid, aren't you?" demanded the Virgin.

"Not at all."

She interrupted me with a tone of outrage. "You couldn't be older than fourteen."

"I'm sixteen."

Bear put his arm around my shoulders, in a friendly, but not sexual way. "I was gonna call her a cab but then I thought it might be nice for her to meet youse all."

I noticed that he said "youse" instead of "you," reminding me of Graham Morton and some of the other Portsmouth kids. Miss Prior would have had a fit.

"I guess you wonder what we are doing on the carpet?" The others giggled, like they were actors pretending to be little kids.

"No," I lied.

She looked at Bear. "Does she know about the show?"

"I didn't tell her."

"We are the cast of a musical about Jesus's resurrection. It's really cool. Pastor Jim wrote it! You should come see it."

"Sure, where is it gonna be?"

"Down at the Princess Street United Church. Starting on the fourteenth, seven p.m. every night but Monday. You have to come! We have a great youth group down there. Led by the most amazing pastor, Jim. Primo writer, groovy musician, and best pastor ever. He is third from the left. Isn't he handsome?"

I looked down at the hippies lying on the floor, side by side.

"Say hi, Pastor Jim!"

The pastor sat up and smiled. He was the only one not in Bible costume. "Hello, young seeker."

"I'm Catholic, actually."

"That's groovy! We welcome everybody. Even devout Catholics!" Everybody snickered, as if on cue.

"I'm not really devout about it. Sometimes I'm not even sure if I believe."

"That's what I thought, a seeker! Hey, you look thirsty to me. You want a pink lemonade? We have some in the fridge."

"Um, sure. Why not?" The mention of pink lemonade made me feel safer, and later I realized that that was the point.

The pastor leaped up as if he were a dancer and with a wide, toothy grin bounded to the kitchen to get me that lemonade.

These people seemed so nice. They nodded and grinned at me.

"Come on, friend, sit down on a beanbag," offered the pastor, handing me a tall glass of cold, sweet pink lemonade. Bear smiled, reassuring me.

"Go on, we're not gonna bite you." Jim, the pastor, laughed.

I sat down on the beanbag, careful not to spill the lemonade. The rest of the group began to rouse. The guy dressed as the Good Thief addressed me.

"Well, hello there! Who are you, sacred young lady?"

Bear responded for me.

"Matthieu's latest conquest. She's waiting for him to finish a deal."

I started to object to the word *conquest*, but I was overcome by shyness.

"The acid?"

"Yeah, the Windowpane from San Francisco. He's gonna sell down in A Bay."

"A Bay" was Alexandria Bay, the small American town just over the border. The football players and the cheerleaders would drive down there to party after the games.

"Hey, girl, don't let Matthieu persuade you to drop Windowpane. Hit me like a hurricane last time," said one of them, I couldn't really tell which one. Another one pointed at me. "Messed me up for weeks. It's still messin' me up."

"Yeah, this fool tried to jump off the roof of the Lucerne Hotel," said a young guy, who couldn't have been older than grade nine.

"He was saying, 'I'm Peter Pan and I am flying to Neverland, come with me, come with me.' We were trying to convince him 'You're not Peter Pan and you are not going anywhere' but he jumped, broke both legs, and hadda get his spleen removed."

The jumper answered in a voice that sounded like crying, or a child whining, "I didn't even grok what you were saying, man it was just a jumble of words. I was totally sure I was Pan."

Grok. I recognized that word. Oh yeah. It was from that book, *Stranger in a Strange Land.*

"Is that from *Stranger in a Strange Land*?" I loved it when people had read the books I had read.

"Girl's got good taste."

I loved that book. I had read it three times, because I myself always felt like the stranger in a strange land. I wondered, sometimes, if I was actually an alien, like that character, only I didn't know it.

"You are a reader then?" asked the pastor, putting a dad-like hand on my shoulder.

"Sometimes."

The lemonade looked delicious with the glass all frosty, but I was too nervous to drink. I wanted to go home. I scanned the group. There were about nine of them. Bear, walking on his tiptoes, his black ringlets falling past his shoulders, touched the heads of three young guys who weren't much older than me.

"Time for introductions! These idiots are Petey, Mack, and Richard. Aren't they just so cute in their costumes? They go to KCVI, don'tcha, boys? Although Richard, you just dropped out, you naughty delinquent, you!" KC was one of the other high schools in the city, known for its drama program. Petey had a pointed, pale face, and curly hair and glasses. Mack was tall and olive skinned and scary thin, and Richard was blandly handsome, with a good tan and a kind of feminine quality. They were giggling and poking each other.

I felt very uncomfortable. The pastor looked like he was getting ready to leave, gathering his things. I could ask him for a ride, I was thinking, *just ask him for a ride*. But I didn't have the courage. He had a leather jacket on despite the heat, and his car keys in his hand.

"Goodbye, lovely people! We will see you for rehearsal tomorrow first thing!"

"Bye, Pastor! Bye! Sweet dreams!"

The one person I felt safe with was gone. Where was Matthieu?

Bear continued, grabbing the hand of one of the girls.

"This hippie chick is Miss Haley Cecile! Say hi, Haley!"

Haley smiled at me and stuck out her tongue. I wasn't sure what that meant. She was a dumpy girl with frizzy red hair and freckles. Now Bear was grinding against a very short and pointy-faced girl from behind. "May I introduce you to Miss Primmy, the tiny prostitute!" I gasped.

"Don't look so surprised!"

"I'm playing Mary Magdalene."

"She is gonna be the best Mary Magdalene you have ever seen! She's the real thing!"

I had heard of prostitutes but not really. Bear then pinched the handsome boy's cheek.

"Oh Judas, you are so gullible and nice. How could you be a traitor?"

The guy playing Judas protested, "Man, I am no traitor, I am just playing the part."

Bear winked at the boy and kept talking and pointing and pinching. There was something about this scene that was really creeping me out. I really wanted to get out of here.

"Ana is uncomfortable because Primmy is a prostitute. What, you don't like being in the same room as a prostitute?"

"No, it's fine, I'm fine."

"I am a prostitute too." He laughed a long, high-pitched laugh of delight. "What, little girl, you didn't know boys could be prostitutes?"

I had never heard of a male prostitute.

"You are so green and so very sweet. Honey, it gets very busy down in Portsmouth Village on a Friday night for a handsome devil like me."

The group clapped and blew him kisses.

"My johns are all married men. But I figure, I make 'em happy, then they go home to their wives and children, a better husband, better father."

I looked away. Was he talking about the married men having sex with him? I could hardly believe that. I was sure he was lying.

"Does that scare ya, Ana? Oh, you are so green. Don't be scared. It's all beautiful. It's all love! Love is beautiful!"

Crabapples in my throat again. "I'm not scared."

But I was.

A short, thick man with curly blond hair and a bushy blond beard and piercing ice-blue eyes, dressed like pictures of Jesus, walked in. I knew he was revered by the group as some kind of a holy figure because they all stood up and straightened their costumes nervously. He stared daggers at me and then walked ceremoniously towards the group, who had gathered themselves in a line, as if for inspection. The members of the group, including the Virgin Mary, all smiled in a goofy way that made me think they were all high on drugs. Or was this a cult? I felt like I was going to throw up. I began to tremble, quite violently.

I looked out the front window at the deserted suburban street. It was already dark. I had to get home. The streetlights had turned on. I was sure I could probably find my way home if I left before Matthieu came out from wherever he was. I might be lost for a while, but we were still within the Kingston city limits. I could call my parents from a pay phone. I had change in my purse, and they would be home around midnight.

The bearded man stood in front of the Virgin Mary, staring into her eyes. She began to sway, back and forth, and tears ran down her face. He slapped her, hard, leaving a red mark on her cheek, but a grateful smile on her face. He then moved onto the next would-be hippie, the curly headed Petey, with the wire-rimmed glasses. Him, he kissed. I could tell it was French kissing because their mouths were open, and it went on for a long time. The Jesus guy turned around to face me and then beckoned with long fingernails.

I looked to Bear, who was leaning on the railing watching.

"It's okay. He is actually a very nice person, Ana. After all, he's Jesus!"

I trusted Bear until I saw him looking conspiratorially over at Jesus, as if to say, "Don't worry, she trusts me." A voice in my head whispered, "Leave. Leave this place now. Now."

But I still did not know how to say no. Nothing had changed since I was nine years old. I was still the moth. Once a moth, always a moth. Frances was right. She was right about everything.

I stood in front of the Jesus guy. He moved towards me, and he began to kiss me, thrusting his tongue in my mouth. I felt it was a knife. I jumped back. Jesus and Bear laughed. Jesus snickered in a high-pitched, sneering way, and Bear laughed. My heart pounded against my chest. I had to get out of here. I looked out the living room window again, and this time I saw Patty, outside the window looking in. Like a large, human bird, she was hovering, about ten feet from the ground. Beckoning me. She was in her blue dress, with the white cardigan around her shoulders.

I ran to the window but the closer I got the more she seemed to fade away, like she was drawn from invisible ink.

Jesus looked at me, still daggers in his eyes.

"Look at me, girl. Look. At. Me."

I looked at him.

"Now come here."

I hesitated, but then walked over slowly, until I was directly in front of him again. He put a hand on my breast. I froze.

"Just as I thought. You are uptight and frozen." He addressed his followers. "Needs a good fucking."

Everyone laughed.

A GLIMMER OF light. Patty's hand, reaching. Her hand is warm; her eyes are kind. I woke up, prickles bouncing in my head. Ping ping ping. I was on my back on the shag carpet. I looked up and saw a circle of freaked out faces. I must have had another seizure. *Shit. I just hope that Matthieu didn't see me jerking around.*

Fat Freda was on the floor with me.

"Give her space, guys!" Nobody moved.

"I turned you on your side. That was a long one, though. If it went on any longer, I was gonna call the operator," she whispered.

"Oh, thanks." I trembled with cold. The room was still swirling.

"Have a sip of your lemonade, girl. You probably have low blood sugar."

I realised that I hadn't had any dinner, and I had only had a sip of the lemonade. My blood sugar would have been low, and that was a trigger for me. I drank up the lemonade, spilling quite a bit on my front.

They all looked at me with zero expression on their faces, except for Jesus, who looked over at me with a combination of lust and disgust.

"Sexual frustration. Like I said. Girl needs to get fucked."

The others nodded vigorously in agreement. I realized then they were assholes, and I had to get out of there.

Bear looked right at me as he was going out the door and rolled his eyes.

"Scene's not cool, gotta go," said Bear, with force in his voice.

"I really need to go home."

"To your parents, little girl?" I didn't notice who said that.

"Don't call me that," I muttered. "I need to go home."

"Don't bother her, guys," said Fat Freda, squeezing my shoulder. "Those can be really serious. My brother's friend, Andrea, she died of one. In the bath! Also, did you know that after having one, they can have more? Give her some freaking space!"

My eyes filled with tears. It was so rare to have a person who knew about epilepsy and didn't think it meant I was weird. Even though I was grateful to Freda, I still really needed to get out of there.

"Matthieu?" I call weakly.

"Matthieu will be a while yet," somebody said.

I felt like I was in prison. I looked out the picture window to get some relief. Patty was still there, waving to me. Suddenly my voice had some colour. "Um, hey, I see this friend of mine from school!"

"Groovy!" Freda was so encouraging! The trembling was calming down.

"Yeah, I'm just gonna go out and ..."

Jesus turned to me, and with his mosquito-whine voice said, "You're not going anywhere. You just stay on the couch, and you are going to have a moment of enlightenment." The group giggled, high-pitched, stupid giggles.

"I'm, I really don't think ..."

"Freda? Help the robot girl back down to the carpet. We are going to introduce her to transcendence. We are going to bring you to life, and cure you of your fits, which, as you know, are possession by the devil."

Robot girl? Nobody had ever called me that before. What did he mean?

"Um, I really don't think ..."

"Stop beeping, robot. Beeping blocks enlightenment." This was getting scary. This was reminding me of school, and those boys going after me. I was not feeling well at all. I just wanted to be home. Fat Freda took me by the hand and squeezed. Her hands were clammy.

"Don't worry, hon', he is so kind. He's only trying to help you. Believe me, this is gonna change your life."

I did not know what the hell she was talking about, but I did not like the sound of any of it. I decided just to walk out of the house. *I will follow Patty. She will lead me to safety.*

I TRY TO get up off the couch, but my body is made of mud. Like those dreams when you try to run but it's like running through thick mud. *Maybe this is a dream? Maybe it's not real?*

Fat Freda starts to sing, quite beautifully. I still can't move. Did they put something in my drink? Jesus moved towards me, like a crocodile.

"She needs a good fucking, that is what she needs."

Freda jumped between us.

"Me, please, me first, Jesus?" Then she whispers something to him.

"You are so horny, fat girl!" He snickers. "Okay, so this little bitch can watch how it's done."

I really do not like being called "little bitch," but I still cannot move.

"WHAT THE FUCK is going on here?"

They all looked up, a little fear on their faces.

"Hi Matthieu!" they said cheerily, overlapping each other.

"It's a love-in," said the Virgin Mary.

"Fuck that. My friend here is underage. Ana, what are you doing on the floor? Did you assholes —? Hold on a minute ... How do you feel, Ana?"

"Like I am made of cement."

"You fucking assholes. I could report you."

Jesus grinned and laughed in a tinkly kind of way. "You go ahead, Matthieu Lemieux. You go right to the police and report us. They'll be right over when they hear your name, won't they?"

Matthieu gave Jesus a look of hatred.

"Let's go, Ana."

I pushed through the cement feeling and sat up. The group looked to Jesus to tell them how to respond. He grinned at them and said, "Let's run some songs, kids. Gotta be ready for rehearsal tonight!"

They clapped their hands like children and cheered.

Matthieu extended his hand to me. I took it. His hand was so large and warm, it felt safe. As we walked to the door, I could hear them singing one of the folksy songs from their musical. I felt like I had escaped a pit of writhing, talking snakes.

I saw the end of Patty, disappearing into the leaves of a huge maple tree, along with two quarrelling sparrows. I wondered if she was just a play of brilliant light, tricking me, in my post-seizure state. I stopped and stared at the tree, hoping to spot her somewhere in there, but all I saw was her blue hair band and then nothing. I let out a cry. Matthieu turned me around and held me in his arms.

"I'm sorry, little girl. I am sorry you had to sit with those creepy hippies. I didn't realize the pastor would be leaving."

"It's okay," I lied, almost weeping with relief that he recognized what I had just been through.

"Did they touch you?"

I told him how the creepy Jesus was about to do more than touch me, when Fat Freda intervened because she felt sorry for me. Matthieu explained that the Jesus guy was actually just this nasty low-life who had done time for interfering with juvenile boys, and when he got out, he joined these Christian youth groups at various churches, trolling for adolescent boys. Matthieu said how he had this special power over people, even though he was such a loser, how he would look them right in the eye and they would think he was really seeing their souls, but really, he was just checking for what he could get from them. He'd learned that in jail, where he had become a bit of a cult leader amongst the sex offenders. At the church youth groups, he would target girls because they were far easier marks, and once they were his followers, they would attract the young guys, and then he could go for the guys.

"Araignée."

I remembered from grade ten French that that meant *spider*.

Matthieu held me closer and took my face in both hands and kissed me. This time, his tongue was in my mouth, and I felt like he had lit birthday sparklers all through my body again. I knew I should ask him whether he really had a girlfriend named Donna, but I didn't want to ruin the moment. As he stroked my face, he promised he would never ever take me there again.

Long silence. I was having trouble catching my breath. He held me closer, so tight I could hardly breathe. It just felt so good. I could feel that he cared about me, and I trusted him more than I had ever trusted anyone except Paulie and my mum and my dad and my cat.

He kissed my neck, which caused ripples all through my head. Then he backed up and looked into my eyes. I needed to tell him.

"I think I had a seizure."

"What?"

"Epileptic."

He nodded, as if it wasn't such a big deal.

"I mean, it's mostly under control. With the Dilantin and phenobarb. Sometimes, if I am really under stress, or I forget to eat."

"If those assholes put something in your drink, I'm gonna fucking kill them. And I'm gonna take you home, kid. You need home right now."

I was trembling, from the excitement of his kiss but also the aftermath of the seizure. My doctor had told me the trembling would happen because during a seizure the blood rushes to all the major organs, like the liver, the heart, the kidneys, basically to save your life, and so that's why you get cold, because there isn't any blood warming your skin.

I have to admit, trembling or not, I was pretty blissed out, on the Harley motorcycle, my arms around his waist, holding him tightly. I loved the way the rough denim felt in my hands and knowing his warm body was so close filled me with that delicious warmth. We were driving so fast, making crazy noise, passing car after car, weaving in and out. I was scared but exhilarated.

We got to the corner of Johnson and Cataraqui Hills Crescent. "You can let me off here," I shouted as loudly as I could. "I can walk down the hill, it's better."

If anyone saw me on a motorcycle with a Satan's Choice member, my name would be tarnished forever. My parents would be disgraced. If my parents saw me, I would be grounded.

"Huh? No way. I'm taking you right up to your front door."

I jumped off as quickly as I could, explaining in an overly apologetic way that if my parents saw me arriving on a motorcycle with an older guy I would get in a lot of trouble. Matthieu laughed and shook his head and then grabbed my hand and told me how beautiful I was, and that he was sorry he got me mixed up with those dirty hippies.

"Bye, thanks for the ..." I didn't want to say date, and adventure sounded stupid. I had left the chemical-pink rabbit at the hippie house. I didn't thank him for that.

"Bye bye, chèrie."

I watched him tear down Johnson Street, weaving in and out of the cars. He didn't look back. I figured I'd never see him again. I was a little sad, but also relieved. It was just too much. I was only fifteen, and young for fifteen at that.

Our house looked so safe and good. I opened the front door. It was never locked.

"Mum? Dad?"

I could see them in the kitchen moving back and forth. They were home early. From the rising, tense sound of their voices, I knew a fight was going to happen. It was good to be home anyway.

"John, you must stop making a mockery of me."

"Oh, Joanna, for God's sake, can't you take a joke?"

"John, you know it was not a joke. You had the whole party laughing at me."

"I give up."

I heard footsteps, which meant he was going to lock himself in his study.

"Hi Mum."

"Oh hello, darling." She sounded out of breath, as if she was trying not to cry in front of me. "Did you have a good time?"

"Yeah. It was so fun."

"Did you have cotton candy?" she asked as she poured herself a beer. I loved the way the froth looked. Her fingernails were perfect, long and red and perfectly shaped.

"I hate cotton candy. There's mouse poo in it."

"I see. I'm not surprised. Now hop off to bed." She was still telling me to hop off like I was a child even though just hours ago I had been making out with a Satan's Choice member.

"Do I look like a rabbit?"

Mum forced a grin and turned away, pretending to straighten her knick-knacks on the shelf above the sink. My mother usually stayed up well past midnight, often till two or three in the morning, pacing, and talking to herself. Paulie said she was practicing for what she was going to say. My dad would go to bed early, always tired. Always exhausted. Never rested.

It was so good to be home.

I'M SEEING A fairy castle. With red spires, and bright green fields of corn surrounding it, sunburned men working in the fields, picking, digging. Cars whizzing by on the Bath Road. A dirt-caked dark blue Honda pulls into the parking lot. Inside the Honda are Marnie, a popular local drama teacher and director, married to a geology professor at Queen's, and me, Ana, sixteen, in grade eleven now at a different school, less than half the acne, almost all covered up with Maybelline foundation, curled eyelashes, wearing GWG jeans and body-hugging tops in various shades of blue. Now actually fairly popular, with a small but formidable group of bookish friends, friends who know about exotic foods, like halvah and goat cheese. Friends who read Dostoevsky and Margaret Laurence and Sylvia Plath, friends who make sculptures out of metal in welding class and who are buddies with the art teacher, and who take in baby squirrels that have fallen to the ground and feed them with droppers.

The other girl with me is Diane, a magazine-cover-level beauty who has just arrived from Calgary to study nursing at St. Lawrence College. Both of us girls have light brown hair down to our hips, but Diane's has been lightened liberally with Sun In, which comes in a spray bottle with the directions *Just sit in the sun and spray in your hair and the lightening will begin!!* My hair is quite wavy, and Diane's is straight.

WE ARE GOING to be part of Marnie's all-convict production of *One Flew Over the Cuckoo's Nest.* It is actually going to be performed at the Grand Theatre in downtown Kingston, which has over seven hundred seats. I am trepidatious, but also very curious. I have imagined the inside of that prison every time we drive past on the Bath Road. I imagine the hundreds of criminal men all packed together — an intensity of badness, rudeness, and crudeness that was repellent and fascinating. I imagine them plotting train robberies, bank holdups. I imagine them like the cowboys I saw in American movies. But at a certain point my imagination just stopped. I need to see what they are really like. And that is why I agreed over my parent's objections. It is part of growing up.

The three of us walk towards the enormous front door of the prison. Marnie looks like the youngest of us, even though she is actually thirty-five. She is just five-foot with a young, bright face, a snub nose, twinkly brown eyes, and the body of a twelve-year-old, but she speaks with a deep and authoritative voice, the kind of voice that makes people listen. People like the rich Kingstonians she needs money from to run her programs. I like Marnie. I am pretty excited at this point, feeling a kind of shivery thrill, because I have never been in a prison before.

Marnie presses a button, there is a loud buzzing, and a guard opens the door. Marnie explains why we are there and he checks his sheet, never smiling. He has an enormous stomach. With a grunt, he lets us in. Suddenly, I don't want to be in, I want to be out. I come very close to making some excuse and getting the hell out of there.

Clang. Big metal door shuts and is locked. I feel like I am going to pass out. Peeling paint, stale, weird smell like the boys' locker room, windows high, high up. Not like what you would expect from the outside at all. A real disappointment. All the walls are a kind of faded hospital green.

We are led down several long hallways. I have a distinct feeling that I will be locked in a cell because of all of my sins. I know I won't be, but I still have the feeling that I will be. Finally, we are in the rehearsal room, which is a big, sad-looking room with fluorescent lights in the ceiling and a kind of dirty-looking floor.

I don't know what the room has been used for before. Maybe a classroom? After about ten minutes, the prisoners file in. All men. All prisoners, all in the same blue shirt and grey pants. They sit in the classroom kind of chairs, which have been arranged in a circle. We introduce ourselves. Diane speaks in a whisper, but I speak almost too loudly, I think, to hide how afraid I am. I suddenly feel angry at my parents for letting me be part of this. Any of these guys could suddenly attack us, or hold us hostage, and only return us safe in exchange for their freedom.

But that never happened. They were actually really nice. They were protective, funny, tough, and very smart. Way smarter than I had ever imagined they would be. They were interested in me and my life. Some of them were good conversationalists. My favourites were Rocky Thibeault and Frank Camerello. They were a lot like the Cowardly Lion (if he wasn't cowardly) and the Scarecrow, if he wasn't floppy. Rocky was short and stocky, going grey, with a raspy voice. Everything he said sounded like he was laughing, so I thought of him as the Cowardly Lion, crossed with a grandad. Frank was taller, skinny like the Scarecrow, and had wild, thick, black hair that was so shiny I asked him about his shampoo. He laughed. "It's my Italian heritage, kid," he said. He really looked out for me. Frank started calling me "apple face," on account of my face would go bright red whenever I felt any emotion at all. Then Rocky joined in, and soon all the guys were calling me "apple face." If it had been in my high school, I would have been humiliated, but in this setting, I liked it.

One day in a rehearsal break I asked Frank why he was doing time in prison when he seemed like such a nice guy. He paused and said, "You know you don't ever ask a con what he's in for. Right, apple face?"

"Oh," I said, turning deep red.

"What do you think I'm in for, apple face?"

"Stealing a canoe from Canadian Tire?"

Frank laughed for so long that it got awkward. The other conversations stopped. Everybody looked our way. He then stopped laughing abruptly and looked me in the eye. I felt a thrill of fear.

"No apple, none of those things. I had a business. I sold marijuana. Also ... I had some ladies working for me."

"Oh." I wasn't sure, but I thought he might mean that he was a sort of manager of prostitutes.

"Like your part in the play! You and Diane."

We were playing the prostitutes that McMurphy hires for Billy.

"I took care of them. Made sure nobody hurt 'em. Like a big brother."

"I believe you."

"Now, no more questions."

I did not ask anyone else what they were in for, no matter how curious I was. And I was curious. I was staggeringly naive. I was excited by their presence. All those men. Paying attention to me. All that maleness. I loved how they rolled their own cigarettes, taking the tobacco from the green Export "A" can with their yellowed fingers. They rolled them so fast, with such dexterous finger skill, that I wanted to learn to do it myself. When I did it, it took me ten minutes and all the tobacco would fall out. They thought that was hilarious, and more often than not would roll the cigarettes for me. Though they burned my throat and smelled terrible, I loved them. They made me feel edgy in a way I had never felt before.

Diane and I only had tiny parts in the play as Frank mentioned. We were the whores that were brought in by McMurphy to liven things up, and to introduce shy Billy to the joys of sex. We climbed in the window, and we each had about four lines. I realised later that the reason we were at every rehearsal — when we really only needed to be at one or two — was as a lure for the guys. If they knew two pretty girls were going to be there, they would turn up. I didn't have a problem with that; in fact, I really looked forward to Friday nights. I was comfortable with them, they became my community, my friends. Almost every one of them begged to write me letters, so being a naive idiot, I handed out my home address to any prisoner who asked for it. I gave them our address because I trusted them, despite what the neighbours had warned us about. I trusted my instincts about them. My instincts had never failed me, and they told me that these men would never hurt me or my parents or Paulie; they would never break into our house.

I found out later that the only reason that our house was not broken into was because Rocky and Frank threatened those who were considering it. I guess Frank and Rocky had connections with some kind of powerful gang back in Montréal, so they actually threatened the others.

After that, our home mailbox was packed with letters from the penitentiary. I got letters from all of them, but especially Joe Dio, a small-boned Portuguese Canadian with slicked-back hair and an innocent face. When I met him, Joe was incredulous that I had never tried a toasted Western.

Another guy, Wayne, talked incessantly about Dodie, the love of his life. He wanted me to meet Dodie. Dodie with the long red hair and the whisky voice. Dodie, who was a goddess to Wayne. He gave me her telephone number. I called her once, but she did not seem interested.

I found out later that he was in prison for almost beating her to death. When he got out, a few months after we did the play, he did beat her to death. Frank and Rocky told me all about the most famous inmate, Steven Truscott, who had been fourteen when he was wrongfully convicted, on zero evidence, for supposedly murdering a twelve-year-old girl near the Clinton air base. He had originally been sentenced to hang, but thousands of people signed petitions and wrote to the prime minister. He was finally given parole in 1969, even though the government still considered him guilty. Frank and Rocky told me that Steven Truscott was definitely innocent. He had been pushed into confessing, thinking it would get him parole, and it did. Franco said that everyone knew that the person who did it was this freak in the area who had been in and out of prison for years for attacking young girls. The story made me think of me and Birdie escaping those guys on the golf course that time.

I loved getting letters from all those prisoners, opening them with my mother's shiny golden letter opener, and reading pages and pages dense with religion and protestations of love for me and of their innocence.

WE PERFORMED THE play at the Grand Theatre downtown, for about two hundred people, mainly from the social work sector, who cheered and clapped all the way through. The guys were amazing in their roles, especially Rocky as McMurphy. He could have played the part in a Hollywood movie; he was that good. Diane and I had fun doing our parts at a real theatre. In one dinner break I went out and got a bottle of whisky for a few of the guys, even though it was strictly forbidden. It was exciting smuggling it past the guard. I cried saying goodbye to all of the guys and told my parents that they were the best people I had ever met.

My feelings changed months later when I was at a Christmas party at Marnie's house. We were drinking Mateus and Marnie and I were on her grey velvet couch near the end of the evening, around one a.m. The seven-foot Christmas tree was sparkling in front of us. I felt happy. We were both quite drunk, especially Marnie. She hugged me hard, then broke down and told me what each of the guys had done to get themselves into prison.

Frank, the one who called me apple face? Who really had my back? He worked with the Montréal Mafia, and the drugs he sold were a lot stronger than marijuana. Rocky had got into a bar fight and killed a guy. They had all committed crimes worse than what I imagined.

But the worst, the worst, which I have never told anyone, is something Marnie did not tell me when we were sitting on her grey velvet couch. Rocky Thibeault told me in a ten-page letter about a year later, written in surprisingly fancy handwriting with lots of flourishes. He had been taking a penmanship course in prison.

This time, Marnie had been doing a children's play with the same group of guys. She had asked me if I wanted to be part of it, but I was busy preparing for an art show at school. My friends and I were often in the school till two or three a.m. getting things ready. It was one of the best times of our lives. Apparently, the prisoners and the kids were playing moose, and owls, and barnyard animals. Marnie brought a few children from her kids' drama group, which usually met Saturday morning. Rocky said they played the kids who were saving the animals from the brutal farmer.

One of the prisoners whom I had trusted was a man named Kip. He had had a small part in *Cuckoo's Nest*. Kind eyes and a kind voice, like Dr. Stalker, always calm and measured. Very clean and shiny dark hair. We would talk quite a bit. I once said to him, "You would be a really good therapist. Have you ever thought of studying psychology?" He laughed. He really looked at me, really saw me when he talked to me. He once said, "If anything is bothering you, you know you can talk to me anytime." I was really touched by that. His crimes, as related by Rocky, were so unthinkable, so evil, I have never said them out loud, not to anybody. I did not even allow myself to imagine them. To think I had talked with him. That I had accepted a rolled cigarette from him. That I had trusted him. That he sort of reminded me of my dad. With the black Irish looks. Blue eyes, and thick, shiny black hair.

What prompted Rocky's letter was a near tragedy, which meant that the facts of Kip's previous crime would be all over the news. Kip had been playing Owl and his character was a special friend of Chipmunk, played by a six-year-old boy. At the lunch break, Kip told the boy he was going to take him to see a real owl and real chipmunks in the magic forest nearby, but he could not tell his mum, who was waiting for him in the green room with sandwiches and a drink. Kip called a cab, and the security was so lax at this downtown theatre that the two of them slipped away out the stage door without anyone noticing. Police found them in a motel just a few miles down the Bath Road about two hours later. Incredibly, the boy was still alive.

Like a bolt of lightning, I realized my intuition was shit. "Perfect intuition?" It was just something I had made up about myself. So, from then on, no matter how strong it was, I ignored it.

MY STRANGE EVENING with Matthieu a couple of years before had become my screamingly funny story at parties in grade twelve. I was invited to a lot of parties. People would gather around me, every one of them drunk and stoned, and hoot with laughter about the tacky fair and then the creepy hippies in the sunken living room and the friendly male prostitute, Bear. I didn't include the part about seeing Patty, or the seizure I had, because that would have been a downer. KCVI was a completely different world than Regiopolis-Notre Dame. The kids were cool looking and curious and smarter. There was a drama club, and the teacher adapted plays from novels. In November of my grade twelve year she adapted Marie-Claire Blais's *Mad Shadows*, and it was brilliant. Everyone said so, they all said it was as good as any professional theatre. I was on the design team — we had an amazing time creating the interior life of the characters on stage.

Other than telling that funny story, I rarely thought about Matthieu. I imagined that he was long gone, living in Québec somewhere. I had had several boyfriends since then, and some sexual experience. I always kept the vow I made with Emilie to only have sex with a guy if I really loved him, even though we didn't see a lot of each other, because she was still at Regi, and also, we were drifting apart. My boyfriend was a cute, older guy, Nelson, a self-proclaimed Buddhist who wore a Boston Red Sox baseball cap and worked loading the *Whig-Standard* newspaper onto trucks. He was saving up money to spend a year in the

Himalayas, so he never paid for my drinks or food, like other guys did, but I didn't mind. It made no sense for guys to always pay when we went out. All it meant was that they were investing in the possibility of sex. Nelson introduced me to Kahlil Gibran and books like *Zen and the Art of Motorcycle Maintenance* and Brautigan's *Trout Fishing in America.* He played guitar and sang in a haunting falsetto. He would sing "Wild Horses," by the Rolling Stones, looking right into my eyes the whole time. He had interesting friends, including a reedy fellow named Roland who was doing his M.A. in philosophy at Queen's and who, when stoned, would rant about Heidegger for hours. I was fascinated and even bought a second-hand copy of *Being and Time.* I read at least twenty pages of it — just enough to quote a line or two to annoy my friends.

Nelson would tell me he loved me while we were making out on the grass in Coronation Park. He would whisper it to me while trying to undo my jeans so he could finger me. I would laugh and say, "Yeah, right."

"I mean it!" he would protest. I was so bored with him relentlessly trying to finger me. He whined constantly about how he desperately craved sex, how all the cool girls were doing it, how every girl from BC does it.

"Really? Every girl from BC? How do you know that?"

Then one day, we were walking by the water, feeding the ducks, when I told him I was ready.

"Today."

"Really? Today?"

"Yup. Today. Or never."

The reason I agreed to sex was because I could feel him pulling away. He said that when he came back from the Himalayas, he was going to move to BC, and he would only be back once a year to visit his folks. I could feel that he was already gone. I wanted him to ask me to go to the Himalayas with him, I wanted him to say he couldn't live without me. I thought having sex with him might make him say those things.

He lived in the basement of his parents' house, so he led me down there by the hand while his large, blond sister, Jennifer, practiced piano and his mum hummed while peeling potatoes in the kitchen. When I looked at her, she briefly glanced up at me. I was sure that both she and his sister knew exactly what was going to happen. His room was dark, with Buddhist sayings on the walls and a poster of the Rolling Stones and one of Bob Dylan. I was trying to read one of the Buddhist wisdoms when he gently pushed me onto his bed. I felt like I was in the doctor's office, totally passive. He pulled off my GWG jeans and my cute lacy underwear. Nothing happened. I really didn't feel anything. Did I black out? Did he drug me? Afterwards he said, "Now you are a woman." I was thinking *now that what?* I hadn't felt a thing. I knew that the first time was supposed to hurt a lot, but I didn't feel anything. When Nelson was called up for dinner I went straight to Emilie's house because even though we had drifted apart, we had promised each other that we would be the first to know when one of us had done it. I showed up at her house on Casterton Avenue and rang the doorbell. She was in the middle of dyeing her hair auburn, but she was friendly. When I told her, she whinnied like a horse, and asked me if she could tell Brigitte, who had been helping her with her hair. When I told them how I didn't actually feel anything, Brigitte told me that some guys have what they call a "micro-penis." She said it wasn't their fault at all; they were just born that way, and it's very embarrassing for them. Sometimes they never have a girlfriend because of the embarrassment. Brigitte and Emilie decided that that must have been the case with Nelson. I shrugged and we tried to look serious but then we all burst out laughing. We were doubled over, holding each other, laughing so hard that Brigitte cried and I squirted pee, and Emilie couldn't catch her breath. For the next hour we lay on the floor of Emilie's parents' dark den and laughed. We would stop for a while, and someone would say, "We really shouldn't laugh," and then we would all hoot with laughter again. Afterwards, walking home, I really felt like a mean girl, laughing that way about Nelson, who was a pretty nice guy. I broke up with him the next time he called me.

Then one day a few weeks ago, I was in Cooke's Fine Foods buying one Rogers' orange cream chocolate, which I have had a yearning for these last few months, when I saw Matthieu again. I couldn't believe it. My heart began to race, and my mouth dried out instantly. I really did not expect to ever see him again. Two years was an eternity; I was a totally different person now. Neither I nor any of my friends would ever consider dating a member of the Satan's Choice. I was a lot smarter about those things now. But when he looked me in the eye and said, "Beautiful Ana," it was as if every bone in my body disintegrated. Later he called it a "coup de foudre," which means "struck by lightning," but is a French expression for falling in love at first sight. It was so powerful it scared me again, so I was polite, but distant. He grinned.

"Has your phone number changed?"

"Nope."

"Okay." He smiled and squeezed my shoulder. The room spun. I watched him walking away, laughing with a friend. He didn't look back.

It was all I thought about for the next few days. Would I go out with him if he called? I was already seeing another guy, Toby, who was tall and thin with shiny dark hair down to his waist, and was reputed to be the best guitarist in Frontenac County. Everybody said he was going to be famous. At this point, we hadn't gone all the way but basically had done everything but. We would mess around and then he would play his guitar for hours. I got bored after twenty minutes or so and would make an excuse to leave.

After more than a week had passed, I was sure Matthieu would not ever call. I had been stupid to think I was significant in his life the way he was in mine, even if I had never admitted it to myself. I was a young girl he drove around for one evening almost three years ago. Someone he knew for a second. And he had a girlfriend, although I was hoping they were no longer together. I went on with my summer. It was the summer before grade thirteen, and I was determined to enjoy every minute. I wore cute cut-off jean shorts and sundresses, with elaborate leather sandals made by one of my new buddies. I had been teaching art to kids, in a city day camp, going to barbeques just about every night, and there were open invitations to friends' cottages. I even loved just hanging out in our backyard and reading. Sometimes Paulie would hang with me on the Canadian Tire lawn chairs. Mum would bring us tall glasses of iced tea or lemonade, and it was just really nice.

Then, just three days ago, on Saturday morning as I was rushing out the door to teach the kids at Skeleton Park, the phone rang. I figured it was Toby.

"Don't get it, I'll get it. Do not get it!!" I screamed, because Toby was very awkward with parents. My father watched me rush to the phone, shaking his head.

It was Matthieu. I was floored. Why would he call me at all? It did not make any sense. We didn't have anything in common. What would we even talk about? But somehow by the end of the call, I had agreed to go with him to a picnic outside of town, on Monday, in the countryside somewhere.

"It's a groovy spot to make a fire, eat something good, have a few beer, smoke some pot or drop some acid. You are gonna love it. Besides, I miss you, kid. Ever since I seen you in the cheese shop, you gave me a pang in my heart."

"Cool. Is it just us, or is someone else coming?"

"Just a couple of friends."

"Okay, cool."

"See you at seven."

"At the top of the hill."

"At the top of the hill."

Over the next two days I felt like I was walking on air. I kept breaking glasses. They would just slip out of my hands. My mother would shriek, "How could you be so clumsy, that was a wedding present!"

Lying in bed for the next two nights, thinking about the date, I was scared. I was scared because no other guy since had given me that feeling Matthieu had given me — that sparklers-exploding-shooting-star feeling that he could make happen inside me. I knew that it would weaken my will to not have sex with him.

He was a man. Not a guy. A man. I was still a girl, despite what Nelson said about me being a woman now.

As the sun was going down yesterday, I lay in the backyard under the maple tree, the dappled light skittering across my hands and my legs and I felt a kind of ecstasy.

It didn't matter that Matthieu was a man, I thought. *I'm almost eighteen. I will see him tomorrow. I will kiss him tomorrow.*

We will have fun, just a really fun time. A picnic in the country, with trees and flowers. We'll listen to Crosby, Stills, Nash and Young and Led Zeppelin in the car and smoke Matthieu's grass with his mystery friends. Maybe even drop some acid and finally understand eternity.

I wondered if I should bring a fruit salad. I had taught myself how to make an impressive one with blueberries, strawberries, cherries, raspberries, and apples. With lemon sprinkled on top to keep it all fresh. After pondering it for some time, I decided against it. It would seem too eager to please. And that was deadly with guys.

What I was imagining pretty much day and night was his kiss. I decided I would just have to have one more kiss with Matthieu. I remembered vividly the way he held my face in his hands, and I wanted to feel that again. No other guy had done that, not exactly. I would allow the kiss to go on for a long time. And if he wanted to caress my breasts, sure. That was something I really liked, and it was not dangerous. But when his hands started to move downwards — I knew now, how to say no. How to say yes. And how to say no.

"Nope, no way buddy. You are a man, and I am a teen."

Still, I was excited about my date. Excited about saying yes and then saying no and just being myself.

I walked up to the top of Cataraqui Hills Crescent and stood in front of Dr. Broadbent's red brick and yellow wood two-story house. He was the bachelor dermatologist who had tried to hang himself in that house, according to neighbourhood gossip.

There was no sign of Dr. Broadbent on that day. I often wondered if he had ever noticed how severe my acne was when my mum and I sauntered around the block on gentle spring evenings, looking at people's gardens. I wondered if he would have had a better solution than Dr. Stalker did.

Suddenly a dark purple Honda pulls up, and Matthieu gets out of the driver's seat. I didn't know he had a normal car. He is looking so handsome it takes my breath away for a moment. I feel my face turn bright red.

He opens the passenger door for me without a word. Which is very strange. What is up?

I look at him, and I am about to ask him how come he isn't driving the Harley, but he seems agitated, so I stay quiet. He doesn't look me in the eye. I have a bad feeling. He is just not himself. Part of me wants to make up a lie about having cramps and just go home, but the other part of me is curious. What is happening with him? Would I be able to cheer him up?

After a few minutes of this weird silence, I think *what the hell* and I speak up.

"What's wrong?"

"Nothing. Mind your own business."

"Hey, that's rude. You seem different and I want to know why."

"Ana, Ana. Sweet Ana, you are right. I am different. It's nothing to do with you, it's just — business. Listen, I don't want to ruin your evening with my mood, so why don't we make it another day?"

"Really?"

"Yeah, another day, soon."

I have a strong feeling that if I agree to another day, that other day will never happen. This is my last chance to see him again, and to work out my feelings about him.

"You know what, I'm really busy these days with teaching art camp to little kids in the park, and doing gymnastics in the evenings, and going to friends' cottages on the weekends. So, let's just stay with tonight."

His face breaks out into a flirtatious smile.

"Okay, Ana. I promise to stop thinking about business as of now. I'm with my girl! My lovely little girl who screams in haunted houses." He grins and musses my hair with his free hand. At this moment, I want to belong to him.

We drive down Princess Street, oddly slowly, past the old drinking motels like the Beachcomber Room, and the Manor, both notorious for different reasons. When we pass the Dairy Queen, there is the usual crowd gathered in the parking lot, sharing tokes, flirting, buying and selling acid or speed, and just hanging out. I slide down in my seat when I see a few of the girls from Regi.

"See somebody you know?"

"Just some girls I don't want to see. Girls from the past."

"Stupid bitches, don't pay them no mind."

I have to hold my breath to stop myself from correcting his grammar. We continue down Princess, past the infamous Lino's pizza, which everyone knows is a hangout for the Montréal Mafia. We pull up in front of a United church on Princess near Division. My mum always says that United's services are way longer, but that they aren't so strict. She says that to be United you don't even have to believe in God. I can't imagine not believing in God.

"Why are we stopping here?"

"Just picking up some friends."

Even though he had mentioned friends coming, I freeze. I had forgotten. Anyway, I didn't expect we would be picking them up on the street, whoever they were. I am deeply disappointed and relieved at the same time. Disappointed because what about our passion for each other, and relieved because now, with him actually sitting beside me, I know that if we were alone in the woods, I might have had a very hard time saying no to anything once he kissed me.

Matthieu gets out of the car and heads towards the front steps of the church. He does not look happy. He looks like he is doing a job he doesn't want to do.

There are two tween girls sitting on the front steps with their schoolbooks.

I suppose they must have been at summer school. When they see Matthieu they giggle and get up, straightening their hair and pulling down their short tops as they walk towards the car.

This is odd. Who are these teenyboppers? He leans in my open window and introduces me to Barbara and Bernice. One of them asks him if I am his girlfriend and he smiles his wicked, adorable smile. They trundle into the back seat, shifting this way and that on the hot, sticky seats.

"We're just old friends," I offer, craning my neck to look at them in the back seat.

Matthieu laughs a big dad kind of laugh.

I turn back to Barbara and Bernice. "Don't know why he's laughing, it's true."

They giggle and look only at each other. Matthieu puts one arm around me and drives with the other. I loved how that felt.

"So now we pick up the big cheeses, girls!"

He had told me that we would be picking up the girls' uncles, who were also members of Satan's Choice, but higher up in the club than he was. Apparently, the girls' mothers, who were the uncles' sisters, had asked the uncles to take them on a picnic because their houses were being fumigated. We turn down a dead-end street and pull up in front of a house with the bricks all painted black. Even the windows had black blinds.

Two scary-looking guys in full Satan's Choice colours came down the steps, carrying a two-four of beer and a couple of bottles of whisky. The fat one has a long beard, and the other is skinny with messy light brown hair down to his waist. Looks to me like they are high, maybe on speed, which is everywhere in Kingston. They squeeze in the back with the girls, breathless.

"Hey little sweeties," says the fat one.

The girls giggle.

"Hi Uncle Joe. Hi Uncle Layne," they said in voices tinged with vinegar.

I turn around.

"What grade are you guys in?"

"Seven."

They both say it, almost in unison, in very childish voices. No vinegar.

"By the way, my name is Ana."

"Hi Ana."

The smaller one leans forward.

"Excuse me? Ana?"

"Yes?" I answer brightly.

"Do you have chicken pox on that side of your face?" she asks, pointing to the left side of my face, where there is still a sprinkling of acne, nothing at all like what it was before. I have even applied foundation before leaving the house, but nothing can be hidden under the bright light of a late summer afternoon.

"Just pimples."

"Don't you ever wash your face?"

I look at Matthieu, but he clearly hasn't heard. He is concentrating on driving. I feel that familiar knot in my throat.

The skinny uncle, who has a pockmarked face, tells them sharply to stop asking stupid questions. They look a little scared of him. Matthieu is driving fast, well over the speed limit, which is quite exciting. We drive over the bridge past RMC, up the hill past Fort Henry, past the barracks, and past the abandoned motels from the forties along the underused highway. Then Matthieu makes a sharp right turn onto a country road. There is a hand-painted sign that reads *Flower Road*, but whoever made it didn't plan well, so they had to cram in the last two letters. I've never heard of a road named Flower. I am hoping there will be a field full of flowers where we are going. I'm thinking how nice it would be to have a picnic in a field of flowers, maybe six-foot sunflowers surrounding us. After another few minutes of driving, we pull into an overgrown, abandoned-looking field. No sunflowers, but there are sprinklings of sweet little yellow flowers here and there.

Matthieu drives right into the middle of the field.

"Look, you're scaring the rabbits!" I scream when I see two rabbits hopping away as fast as they can.

"Fuck the rabbits."

I did not like it when he said that. I shook my head and whispered, "Asshole."

"What? Did you say something?"

"No."

"Okay. Because I thought you said something."

"Nope." I lied, scared of him for the first time.

He grins and nods and turns Led Zeppelin up as loud as it will go.

The little girls drum on their thighs and nod along with the beat, pretending they are grooving to the song. The uncles laugh, too loud, as they open their beers, and pull the girls out of the car and onto the grass. I can't decide whether they are on speed or LSD. Most young people in Kingston, especially the hippies, drop lots of LSD. Many stories of kids trying to fly off roofs or diving naked into the Quarry in the middle of January. But bikers, I've heard, mostly do speed or MDA plus a lot of booze.

There are no houses in sight. There is a forest at the end of the field. Thick, bright woods with resplendent maples and towering evergreens and birches in full leaf. I've always loved birches, with the white bark. When I was little, in Connecticut, we used to drink birchbark beer. I loved that taste and have not experienced anything like it since we came to Canada. In thinking about it I can actually taste birchbark in my mouth, just the way when you think about eating a lemon your mouth fills with saliva. Matthieu turns the music off.

"A perfect place for a picnic," I croon. "Look at all the yellow flowers!"

The girls laugh and tease their uncles who tickle them and tease them back. The fat one picks Bernice up and swings her around in circles, which she seems to love. Barbara begs for him to swing her too. "Come on, Uncle Layne, me too!"

"No way, this little firecracker here has tired me out. I'm smokin' too much." Matthieu snickers and whispers in my ear, "He's just fat."

Another Satan's Choice person emerges from nowhere, as if he is the rabbit a magician pulled from a hat. He looks young, about eighteen, with huge muscular arms and a moustache, and a very deferential air about him. He almost bows, like a servant in an old movie. Matthieu introduces him as Scraper. He doesn't say much, but he shows us a big cooler with hamburgers and hot dogs and Coke for me and the nieces. I'm quite hungry. The uncles didn't bring anything except the beer and whisky and their Export "A" cigarettes. I can't figure out how to place them in my mind. They are unpredictable in their movements — a bit off. I am not sure what it means, but it is making me uneasy. They don't really talk to me, just their nieces, who they keep roughhousing with.

"When you were little, I used to throw you up in the air, kid," says one of the uncles to one of the girls, a little too loudly, like he wanted me and Matthieu to hear. The girls both laugh, also a little too loudly. Matthieu shakes his head. The girls are dressed almost exactly alike, in short jean shorts and tube tops and sandals. They both wear the same pink lipstick and way too much mascara.

Bernice's hair is the most beautiful natural auburn, similar to my mother's — glossy and wild. Barbara's hair is dishwater brown and fine. They both have perfectly clear skin, which makes me jealous.

Will I never have clear skin?

The two uncles lead the way to our picnic spot, right at the edge of the forest. It is a sunny with cloudy periods kind of day. Cool for August. I can hear the weather lady on CKLC, the Kingston station that I listen to constantly at home, saying, "Sunny, with cloudy periods, friends. Cooler than normal for this time of year, so get out your light cardies." I've brought a jean jacket along in case of mosquitos. I put it on, but then it feels too hot, so I take it right off, but then change my mind and put it right back on when I catch one of the uncles looking at my chest.

"Hey, pretty girl, your jacket is inside out." Matthieu is shaking his head at my bizarre behaviour.

"What?"

"Your jacket. See the tag? You're such a kid."

"Oh. How embarrassing."

"Don't be embarrassed. You never have to be embarrassed in front of Matthieu. You know that, right?"

"I guess so."

"No guessing about it. You know so. Right?" He leans in so his face is really close. I am quite sure he is going to kiss me and feel the flush shoot through my body.

But he doesn't.

"Right."

It is true. I am not embarrassed by my face when I am with him. The only other people in the world who I'm not sick with shame about my face with are my family. And sometimes Emilie and Michele.

With Matthieu, I am just myself. Partly because I want to repel him, and partly because I know that he likes me just the way I am.

Scraper gets everything set up for our picnic. Nobody helps him. When I look at Matthieu with a *what the hell?* expression, as I was brought up to always help out in this kind of situation, Matthieu whispers to me that Scraper is what they called an Associate, which means someone they are considering making a Prospect, which is what Matthieu apparently is. The uncles, he tells me, are higher members, or what Matthieu calls "full patch." The uncles seem to relish bossing Scraper around, even cuffing him upside the head. I look at Matthieu and he puts his finger to his mouth. Scraper doesn't seem to mind, so I don't say anything more.

The hamburgers smell so good. I haven't eaten at all today. I am ravenous, so I devour my hamburger in about twenty seconds. The girls hardly touch theirs. The uncles have two each and finish what the girls didn't touch. Scraper doesn't eat, he just cleans up our mess and then he seems to disappear.

Matthieu takes his time, chewing carefully. He eats one and a half hamburgers. It reminds me of my grandma in Ottawa, who always chewed her food fifty times before swallowing, doctor's orders. I wonder if he was afraid of choking too.

When we are all finished and wiping our ketchupy hands and faces with the cheap napkins, the uncles get to their feet.

"Come on, girls, let's go for a walk. Your mum's asked us to bring back some wild mushrooms."

One of the girls searches around in her purse.

The uncles look impatient. "What are you doing?"

"Just lookin' for my smokes. Hold your horses."

"Does my sister let you smoke?"

"No."

"Heh. She is a strict mother. It's not a problem, kiddo." He throws her a cigarette. "Just don't tell my sister I let you smoke!"

The girls look at each other and laugh, again, too loudly. "We won't," they say, practically in unison. It is spooky how they do that. They aren't even twins.

And then the four of them head off into the woods. The fat Satan's Choice puts one of the girls on his shoulders, and she laughs and laughs, delighted. The skinny one takes the other girl's hand — maybe she told him she was scared of the forest, and so he was making her feel safe. The girls look so small, from behind, even more childish than they did from the front.

Matthieu takes my hand in his warm and calloused hand. That feels so right and so good. We watch the four disappear into the woods. I feel like I am in a movie. But suddenly I can almost hear the movie music start to change tone, to something less merry.

"Where are they going?"

"Like they said. For a walk in the woods."

"How come they didn't invite us?"

"I told them I wanted to be alone with my girl."

My body suddenly fills with hot golden liquid.

"You are looking so beautiful tonight."

"No way."

"Yes way, Ana. I cannot resist you, my girl. Thought about you for two years."

"You liar."

"It's the truth, girl."

He begins to stroke my hair. Small fire in my belly.

"I would like to make love to you here, Ana, among these yellow flowers." He kisses me hard on the mouth, his tongue all over my teeth. I almost faint. I am having trouble breathing again. *What is wrong with me?*

He puts his hand on my breast. He has never done that before. Full flame. My whole being disappears into his hand.

"Ummm." I remove his hand. Fire's out.

"Ce qui se passe, mon petit?"

I know that means "What is happening?" but I can't speak at this moment.

"I know you like it."

Why is it so hard to speak? I move away from him. I am feeling more myself. More and more myself. He puts a hand gently on my shoulder and asks me what is wrong.

"Listen. I'm only seventeen."

"Ahhh, but you are an old soul."

"And you are a lot older."

"How old do you think I am?"

"Maybe twenty-four?"

A silence, which I realize means that he is older than that. Maybe a lot older. Maybe thirty.

My mouth fills with saliva. I swallow and swallow.

"When we went to that house, two years ago, your brother said" — and the next part came out like a croak — "you had a girlfriend. Do you still have a girlfriend?"

"Bearie said that?" His voice goes strangely high.

"Is it true?"

He licks his lips and tells me that he would never lie to me. I know what that means.

"Does she know you're with me?"

The crickets are early. It isn't dark yet. He admits that she does not know he is with me. I ask him her name, and he says in a very soft voice that it is Genevieve. I say what a pretty name that is, and I ask if he loves her and he says that he does, sometimes.

I understand everything now. I push him away from me and ask him why he was trying to make out with me, a young girl, not yet eighteen. I cut him off when he begins to speak because I know what he is going to say. I speak as if I am an actor in a movie.

"I am not your sweet little girl."

I feel like a car that has just been filled with gas after running on near-empty. I feel strong, I feel good.

"You have been very nice to me. You have even ... awakened something in me I have never felt before, to be honest. In different circumstances, maybe we could have been boyfriend and girlfriend. But not now. Not possible now, not at all. I would like to go home."

"I can't take you till the boys are back."

"What about Scraper? Can't he ...?"

"No."

I am surprised by this, and a little panicky. I decide on my next move. Then I surprise myself.

"Okay. I am going to walk home."

"Hah." He turns that hah into a long, ridiculously long laugh. "You can't walk home."

"Why not?"

"It's ten miles. Maybe twenty."

"I'll hitchhike."

"Oh no, I'm not letting any girl of mine do that. Haven't you read about the girls that have gone missing after they were last seen hitchhiking?" It is true. There have been several girls in the news lately, seen on the side of the road with their thumbs out and then never seen again.

"First off, like I said, I am not a girl of yours. Second off ..." My voice starts to waver. I am not sure what to do, but I know I need to get out of there.

He turns away.

"Je suis desolé, Anastasia."

He plucks a violet and hands it to me. I take it, but I do not know what to do with it. I crush it between my thumb and forefinger.

"I want to go home."

"Oui, oui, chèrie. As soon as they come back."

"What are they doing out there, anyway?"

"They told us, chèrie, going for a walk. Picking mushrooms for their mamans."

Then Matthieu opens his can of tobacco and rolls a cigarette and hands it to me. I think about the prisoners, and wonder if that is where he learned to roll so adroitly. I take the cigarette and savour the bits of loose tobacco in my mouth, because it is as if those little bits of tobacco are some part of Matthieu. He lights the cigarette, and then rolls his own, expertly. He looks so sexy doing that that I am losing my resolve. I want him to take me in his arms again.

A long, very long loud scream pierces the air. Matthieu holds my face in his hands. "May I kiss you one last time?"

I want this so badly, with every cell in my body. But what is that scream? I listen carefully. Another scream.

"Are you crazy? Did you not hear that?"

Another scream. Several. But now they are short, agonized screams, one after the other.

"What is that?"

Scraper appears out of nowhere and stands statue still, looking at the ground.

I am scared now. Scared for those stupid girls.

"What is going on?"

"Who knows? Girls scream. They just scream over everything. Tripping on a root, maybe a garter snake."

"That was a different kind of scream."

"Listen, there are snakes everywhere around here. The woods are crawling with them. It is the snakes for sure. The uncles are probably being idiots, throwing them at their nieces."

Something feels very wrong.

"Are they really their uncles?"

"Like I said. I do not lie."

"They aren't."

He shakes his head.

"Why the lie?"

He shrugs.

"That is what they wanted."

A wail this time. A fractured sob. And then a howl.

"There is something terrible going on. I am going to stop it."

"Okay, Superman. Do you really think you could take those guys?"

"What? What are you saying?"

"I am saying that you are going to stay right here."

"What? Why?"

"You do not interfere with other people's business. Especially when those other people are dangerous."

"What? What do you mean?"

"I mean, that if you mess with them, there might be very serious consequences."

"But what about the girls? Something is happening to them right now. I think those guys are attacking them. Do you deny that it sounds like that?"

He does not answer that question.

I begin to walk towards the woods.

"Are you coming? We have to stop whatever it is that is happening."

"What do you think is happening, girl?"

"I think they are being raped."

"I really don't think so. If true, it's too late now."

I can't believe it. I can't believe this is the same Matthieu, the man of courage I thought I knew. He doesn't seem to care what happens to the little girls. It's as if the girls are insignificant, like pigeons.

"No. No. It's not too late, Matthieu! This could go on for hours. I have read about these kinds of attacks; they can go on all night. These girls are only twelve and thirteen. For God's sake, help me."

"Oh, no. You play policeman, you are on your own."

"What? You don't care?"

"I mind my business."

"You approve of what is happening? You think it's okay to rape a twelve-year-old?"

"I didn't say that."

"Please, please pleeeeeease," we hear from the woods.

"I'm going in. We have to save them."

"Do. Not."

"What? Why?"

"Because they will do the same to you. Maybe worse." His voice sounds different, more serious than he has ever been, and somehow defeated.

"But I'm with you, doesn't that ...?"

"I am lower down in rank. In the club. I can't do fuck all. What is mine is theirs, if you know what I mean."

I was outraged.

"Are you saying that you wouldn't be willing to go against whatever the Satan's Choice rules are? Are you really saying that?"

"My first loyalty is to the Choice. I'm sorry, little girl."

"Well, fuck that. I have lost all respect for you, Matthieu. Fuck that." My voice is as strong as my dad's. "Fuck that. I'm going in."

Matthieu shakes his head.

"I can't let you do that." He grabs me by the waist.

"Just try to stop me."

I run. I run with a speed and a strength I did not know I had.

He runs after me, but I am faster. I have a kind of speed I never had before. Matthieu is a young and powerful man, so he almost catches up to me, but shockingly, he trips.

Ahead, I see Patty floating in the air above me, same blue dress, same blue eyes, same dark blond hair in a flip. She is laughing, indicating that she caused him to trip. She beckons me. She fills me with speed and strength. Matthieu, pathetic man that he is, stands up.

"Ana!"

"You can't stop me!"

"Please. I am begging you. Come back."

"No. I'm going to do the right thing. You should help me."

"There is nothing you can do. I promise you." I hear him accept that he cannot change my mind. "You are on your own, girl."

I hear him turn and walk to the car.

I am in the woods, and I can't see a thing. It is so dark. So dark. I'm listening for the girls. I think I hear them.

"Please, just let us go. We won't tell anyone."

"Promise."

"Just wanna have more fun, first. Don't you girls wanna have more fun?"

"I have to get home for nine or my mother will worry. She'll call the cops."

"Did you say cops?"

"She will. She's like that."

"Ha. We have them on our payroll."

"Please. I'll do anything."

"We can do this every week, for sure, for sure," says the other girl. "You can pick us up at the church every Friday, honest to God," she says in a shaking voice.

I walk into a clearing and there they are. The girls tied up, naked, blood coming from their mouths, as if they have been punched.

The guys, the uncles, swilling beer.

"Ooooh, hello babe, you come to play? Did Matthieu send you as an offering?"

"You aren't their uncles."

"Ho ho ho, you must be a detective, are you a detective?"

"Like Columbo?"

"That was a lie. About being their uncles."

The girls' eyes are so wide, their faces so pale. I hate that they are naked, I want to cover them. I want to free them.

"I'm taking these girls home."

The guys look at each other, and hoot, each in their own ugly way. They remind me of Miles and Bernie, who I haven't thought of since we left Connecticut.

I walk over to the girls and begin to untie Bernice. She trembles from head to toe.

"I'm so cold. So cold."

"We'll find a blanket for you in the car." I look around for their clothes. The guys aren't saying anything. They're sharing a joint.

"Me too. Please."

I untie Barbara, who is shaking in jolts.

I think she might have asthma, because she's having trouble breathing.

"Where are their clothes?" My feet are shaking. I don't like the way the men are staring at me, inhaling the weed. Saving the little girls is all that matters here.

The guys look at each other and laugh.

"Hey, Dudley Do-Right, you are gonna get a gold star when you get back to the station."

"Where are their clothes?"

It's astonishing. I have no fear.

"They're around."

"Treasure hunt!! You three go looking for the clothes. If a chipmunk hasn't eaten them!!"

They roar with laughter. The thinner one laughs so hard he falls against a tree. They are totally sloshed.

The guys laugh and smoke and watch me. I can't believe they're letting me take the girls and gather their clothes. It seems too good to be true. I figure they have mothers and sisters, and maybe they have consciences too. They don't seem upset. They clearly got what they wanted and probably hadn't planned on anymore.

I take both the girls' hands. They're crying now. Their mascara runs down their pale faces.

"Come on. It's fine. We'll find your clothes." I speak very softly, as if I am a nurse. I am not afraid. I look back at the guys.

"And you two? You ought to be ashamed of what you have done. You are both going to hell for sure."

"Ha. Well, we are Satan's Choice, little rat!"

The guys lean on a tree, smoking, taking swills of a bottle of whisky. They nod to each other. *Assholes*, is all I can think. I wonder where Patty is now. I can't see her. I imagine she is watching me, though. She'll be proud of me.

The three of us set about finding the clothes. There's a pair of pink underwear hanging from a tree branch. Short shorts under pine needles. A little bright yellow top quite high in a birch tree.

We find everything. The girls get dressed, shaking violently as they do.

"Can we go home now?"

"Yes. Matthieu will drive us. Come on, we will just walk back to the firepit. He's waiting. He and Scraper are waiting."

We don't find their sandals. But the floor of the forest is soft and forgiving. We walk slowly but surely towards the field. It's dusk, and we are walking west, and through the trees we see a beautiful sunset.

I am doing something right. For the first time in my life. I have the strength. It's all me. It really is all me. The girls and I are holding hands. Their hands tremble.

We reach the edge of the woods. The field is covered in daffodils and bluebells. They hadn't been there before. *How could they have bloomed in that short time I was in the woods saving the girls?* They are spring flowers, so it isn't possible. Maybe the danger of the situation has me hallucinating. Or maybe Matthieu slipped acid into my drink. The girls' hands are still cold, but they've stopped shaking. It is going to be fine; they are going to be fine. We are walking into the setting sun, which has made streaks of fire through the sky. Me and the girls, we step with our bare feet out of the woods and onto the mustard field. "Run," I whisper, and I feel happy seeing the girls run barefoot across the field and down the dirt road towards the highway and the abandoned motels. They are safe now. Someone will see them and take them to safety. I scan the field for Matthieu. He stands by the car. There is no sign of Scraper. He is not looking at me.

I hear a voice behind me. "Hey, Dudley! Dudley Do-Right!"

I turn around and the uncles are moving towards me. They are not smiling. The fat one is holding a knife. The other reaches for something in his pocket. Their eyes are like stone.

I scan the field for Patty. And there she is, a shimmering, just beyond the birches.

She is my witness.

I do not run because I know there is no point. This is the risk I took, and I am ready.

YOU DECIDE TO get off your bike. The sun has set but there is still some light in the sky. I hear you lean the bike against the tree again, and I wait. You spot the shabby green car blanket, still here, in the far corner of the field, right at the border of the woods. I can sense you gathering your courage. You take off your shoes, so you can feel the grass and the mustard flowers under your feet. You stride towards me, full of resolve, fearless. You are close, you are hovering over me. I can hear your breathing. You bend down slowly, as you have knee pain, and you gingerly lift the green blanket. You gasp. I can't really see you because everything is blurry, but I do see your light, and it is so bright it is dazzling me. Blinding me, but in a good way. You hold me in your arms for the longest time, muttering "I'm so sorry, I'm so sorry, I'm so sorry." I don't know what you should be sorry for. I don't regret what I did, not for a minute. It was the only thing I ever did worth mentioning.

ACKNOWLEDGEMENTS

Huge thanks to Marc Côté for your brilliant insights, to Sarah Cooper for your faith and your support, to Barry Jowett and Matthew Poulakakis, and to Katherine Zheng, Fei Dong, and Marijke Friesen, all superstars.

Thanks to my brother Bill for being the first outside of Cormorant to read the book, to Dionne Brand and Tessa McWatt for commissioning and including my short piece in *Luminous Ink*: the story in that piece became the seed of this book.

Thanks to Jeannine Prevost (R.I.P.), Gabrielle Jonas, and Sheena Macdonald, and, always, to Gregor.

We acknowledge the sacred land on which Cormorant Books operates. It has been a site of human activity for 15,000 years. This land is the territory of the Huron-Wendat and Petun First Nations, the Seneca, and most recently, the Mississaugas of the Credit River. The territory was the subject of the Dish With One Spoon Wampum Belt Covenant, an agreement between the Iroquois Confederacy and Confederacy of the Ojibway and allied nations to peaceably share and steward the resources around the Great Lakes. Today, the meeting place of Toronto is still home to many Indigenous people from across Turtle Island. We are grateful to have the opportunity to work in the community, on this territory.

We are also mindful of broken covenants and the need to strive to make right with all our relations.